"Do you think it'll be a c

"I hope not." Mark focused his gaze on her. "I'd like to spend my time doing more interesting things."

Britt licked her lips, a move he didn't miss. "Such as?"

"Getting to know a Nordic princess who ran away from me last night."

Britt frowned. "I'm not a princess. And I didn't run away."

"You didn't stay, either." He tilted his head.

What could she say? "You're right. I had a business to run."

He nodded slowly. "And I should have had the courage to approach you, but I had work to do.

"However, destiny seems to be in our favor." Detective Hawthorne reached into his shirt pocket and pulled out a business card. "This is in case you think of anything else you'd like to tell me." He pulled a pen from the same pocket, turned the card over and scribbled something. "And this is in case you'd like to talk about anything other than work."

Dear Reader,

Have you ever met someone who knocked you off your feet? I met a famous actor during a film festival in Toronto, and I was stunned—as in, I couldn't speak. He was much more handsome in person and lovely to talk to once I found my voice! But for several seconds, everything and everyone disappeared around me until all I saw was him. My pulse raced, I started sweating (which was embarrassing!) and I was literally shaking with excitement.

For Detective Mark Hawthorne and bakery owner Britt Gronlund, the same amazing thing happens to them. However, Mark is in the middle of a police investigation, and he loses his opportunity to talk to Britt as she disappears into the Friday night crowd. They both regret not making the first move.

Fate gives them a second chance. As Mark canvasses the area for witnesses, he meets Britt again at her bakery and no way is he going to mess this up. Britt doesn't believe her luck when the man who stole her breath away reappears, and as they get to know each other, she senses how they are connected in so many ways.

But as Mark digs deeper into his case, he discovers that Britt is a possible suspect. Oh boy...

I hope you enjoy the story as Mark and Britt conquer their obstacles to get to their happily-ever-after!

Charlene Parris

DEFENDER AFTER DARK

CHARLENE PARRIS

HARLEQUIN
ROMANTIC
SUSPENSE

HARLEQUIN®
ROMANTIC SUSPENSE™

Recycling programs
for this product may
not exist in your area.

ISBN-13: 978-1-335-59405-1

Defender After Dark

Harlequin Enterprises ULC
22 Adelaide St. West, 41st Floor
Toronto, Ontario M5H 4E3, Canada
www.Harlequin.com

Printed in Lithuania

MIX
Paper | Supporting
responsible forestry
FSC® C021394

Charlene Parris has been reading books for as long as she can remember and romance stories since high school, after discovering her mother's cache of romance books. She loves smart, sharp-witted, independent heroines; strong heroes who respect them; and of course, happy endings. Charlene writes for the Romantic Suspense line because she loves adding twists and turns to her stories. When she's not writing, Charlene is working her full-time job. And for fun, she reads, walks and is learning yoga.

Books by Charlene Parris

Harlequin Romantic Suspense

The Night Guardians

Watchers of the Night
Defender After Dark

Visit the Author Profile page
at Harlequin.com.

To my family, and especially my cousins, Rochelle and Kim, who have cheered me on and demand when the next book is coming out. Gotta love the enthusiasm!

To my darling friend Britt, who is the inspiration for the heroine. Love you! <3

Chapter 1

When Detective Mark Hawthorne stepped out of his vehicle, he looked around in confusion and frustration. "What the hell?"

The crime scene was across the street, within the dark bowels of a construction site. Unfortunately, the area in front of it was filling up with curious onlookers, their cell phones held high and lights flashing as if they'd spotted a celebrity.

"Damn it." He looked at both ends of the narrow two-lane street. The intersections were blocked off with police vehicles and bright yellow caution tape. However, the officers were having a difficult time removing pedestrians who had already wandered over to see what was going on. An ambulance was parked a few feet away.

He jogged to the closest officer, who was yelling into his walkie-talkie. "Detective Hawthorne," he shouted, showing his badge. "Are there more officers coming?"

He waited while the officer finished providing instructions. "They're on the way now. Seriously, I don't know how these people found out about this. I got here five minutes after the call."

Mark swore—social media these days was a pain in the ass for stuff like this. "I'm the lead on this case." He spotted a bright light and the silhouette of a crime scene bar-rier. *Good, Walsh is here already.* "As soon as your backup arrives, get these people out of here."

He'd been notified of a murder while at the precinct, and despite the gruesomeness of the investigation, Mark was itching to get started. Weeks of working on burglaries, car thefts and other minor cases had started to get on his nerves. He wanted what Detectives Timmins and Solberg routinely got—the meatier investigations, ones that made them really think through the clues until they solved them.

And now he was finally going to get his chance.

He observed his surroundings. The building consisted only of stone pillars, some wooden walls and a roof. A chain-link fence encompassed the site, and its front gate stood slightly open. Barely visible within the semidarkness of the building, he could just make out piles of cut lumber, neatly stacked. "Where's the witness who called it in?" Mark asked the officer.

"Over there, just inside the fence with two of my guys. She's pretty shaken up."

"Okay, let me check in with Forensics, see who the murder victim is first."

"Well, that's the odd thing," the officer said, rubbing his forehead. "There's a victim for sure, but he's not dead."

Mark frowned. "Come again?"

He pointed. "He's in the ambulance getting medical attention. The witness who found him panicked and called it in as a homicide. By the time we got here, the guy had regained consciousness, but he's beat up pretty bad."

Mark pursed his lips, annoyed and relieved at the same time. No one was dead, but bringing in police forces across the region... "Thanks."

As Mark headed in the direction of the witness, he noticed that she couldn't be more than twenty-five. She had taken off her hard hat, a hint that she worked here. She was quite pretty, with light brown hair tied up in a bun and blue eyes. He saw the worry and fear etched in her face. "Hey," he called out. When she turned around, he showed his badge. "Detective Hawthorne. Can you tell me what happened?"

"I'm not in trouble, am I?" she asked. The woman was visibly upset.

He gave her a smile. "Why would you think that?"

"Because I thought I saw a dead body—my God, it scared the crap out of me. I managed to call 911 without screaming into the phone and waited outside." She made the sign of the cross on her chest. "When the ambulance and police arrived, the body got up and started walking toward us. I swear, I thought it was a ghost."

"But he's not, thanks to you." Mark looked around again. Construction sites followed strict rules regarding safety. "How do you think he got in there?"

"Oh, he was inspecting the site and chatting with the supervisor about an hour ago."

Weirder and weirder. "Who is he?"

"Mr. Edward Ferguson."

She said the name like he was supposed to recognize it—he didn't, and shrugged.

She raised her brows. "He's the guy who owns the Mighty Big Bakery chain."

Ah, now he was getting somewhere. Edward Ferguson was a conglomerate powerhouse who owned one of the biggest baked goods store chains in southern Ontario.

"I must have really panicked. Maybe he just tripped

and hit his head on something," the woman said, twisting her construction hat between nervous fingers.

"I'll see how he's doing. You don't have to hang around, but I would like you to come to York Regional Police 4 District tomorrow morning to provide a witness statement." He brought out his business card.

"Of course." As she took the card from him, she smiled, which transformed her face. "You don't seem like a cop."

"I try to display the friendlier side of the force. We're not all monsters."

"No...you're not." She stuck his card into her back pocket. "Maybe when this is over, you can continue showing me your nice side."

Mark knew his eyebrow went up. Did she just ask him out on a date? She didn't seem in any hurry now to leave, but he had to get back to work. "How about you get a good night's rest and I'll talk to you at the precinct at nine tomorrow morning?"

"Works for me. Oh, and in case you missed it, the name's Jenny." She sauntered off.

Definitely an invitation.

He turned his attention to the ambulance, where Mr. Ferguson was reclined on a stretcher. However, as he got closer, Mark noticed that Mr. Ferguson was arguing with the paramedics.

"Listen to me, I told you I'm fine. Now will you let me go?"

Mark watched him, surprised at Mr. Ferguson's attitude. He had been beaten pretty badly, his face covered in bruises and a split lip, but now the man was fighting the people trying to help him.

"Sir, you might have a concussion," a female medic

told him. "At the very least, we need to take you to the hospital for observation…"

"I'm not going to a damn hospital! I need to get back to my office!"

Mark watched the struggle a bit more, then stepped in. "I suggest you do as the medic advises," he said, keeping his voice neutral.

The man glared at him. "Who the hell are you? And do you know who the hell I am?"

"You're Edward Ferguson."

That shut him up for a hot minute.

"And I'm Detective Mark Hawthorne." He held up his badge. "While you have every right to refuse medical attention, I'm afraid you still have to go to the hospital. The police will need the doctor's help in collecting criminal evidence from you." Mark smiled—he couldn't help himself. "After you're done, I'll interrogate you at the hospital for information. Which means you'll need to stay there until I arrive."

Mr. Ferguson mumbled something under his breath.

"I don't know what you're complaining about. York Region's finest is providing you the fast, courteous assistance I'm sure you'd expect," Mark added.

"Fine, I get it." Mr. Ferguson lay back on the stretcher as the medics strapped him in.

Mark rubbed his face with one hand. It had been a long day, and it was going to be a longer evening. But it wasn't an excuse to talk to Mr. Ferguson like that, even if the man had it coming. He'd probably get an earful from the captain first thing Monday morning.

"The sarcasm is strong with you tonight," an amused voice said. Myrna Walsh, the new forensics investigator with his precinct, was a fiery redhead with a personality to match. "For a second there, I thought you were going to describe how the medical staff would poke and prod him. You managed to restrain yourself."

He sighed. "I'm sure Ferguson will give Captain Fraust an earful, followed by her doing the same to me."

"Cross that bridge when you get to it." She glanced over her shoulder. "Looks like we finally have the place to ourselves. Come on, we've got a crime to solve."

"Yeah, let's go."

The construction site was bordered with an eight-foot chain-link fence. A section of it was slightly ajar. Normally there would be a chain and padlock securing the gate after-hours. Both were nowhere around.

Mark pulled on a pair of thin plastic gloves and pulled the fence wide enough for him and Myrna to pass through. She handed him a flashlight, and when they passed beneath the unfinished concrete pillars, he turned it on.

They stood in a wide rectangular area about twenty feet across, while the rest faded into blackness. "The witness said she saw Mr. Ferguson lying where I've set up the screen." Myrna pointed. "How did she even see him?"

"She must have come this way when her shift was over and spotted his body." Mark followed her to the crime site, lit up by the harsh brightness of a portable lamp. Dark stains smudged the concrete flooring, and several unknown items lay scattered around it. "Are you finished?"

"No, I've got a few more things to look over."

"I'll let you get to it. I'm going to walk the perimeter."

"Here, put these on." She handed him a pair of booties.

After slipping on the plastic coverings, Mark moved farther into the building, scanning the ground with his light. This case was his first significant one as lead investigator, but he wondered if he would have even received it if Timmins and Solberg weren't already involved in other projects.

No, he needed to shut that down—it wouldn't do to let his insecurities get in the way. Besides, Timmins told him he could handle this with no problem and had offered his support if Mark needed a sounding board. Still, that little twitch of nagging doubt persisted…

He stopped. Just within his flashlight's field, he spied the chain and padlock. He knelt down and placed a yellow marker by them, then scanned the area with his light. He could just make out several footprints. "Myrna, I found the security chain and padlock," he called out. "Might have something on them. I also see footprints, probably belonging to the construction workers, but no harm in checking them out, either." He pulled out his phone and snapped some pictures, then marked the prints with several of the small yellow cones.

"Okay, I'll get over there as soon as I can." Her voice echoed across the space.

Mark continued his observations, spying more footprints. He placed his markers as he completed his sweep. "What did you find?" he asked as he approached her.

She sat back on her heels. "Well, I'm sure the blood is Mr. Ferguson's, but I took samples from a number of areas just in case we're lucky and some of it belongs to the suspect." She pointed to a piece of wood in a large plastic evidence bag. "That was used to beat him. I found more blood and hair samples, and I'll see if there are any fingerprints I can lift."

Myrna then gestured behind her. "The suspect tried to sweep away his footprints, but he—or she—didn't get it all. I took photos of a distinctive sole pattern. You said you found footprints, too?"

"Near the chain and padlock back there. Might be fin-gerprints on those as well."

"I'll bag them." She stood. "Other than that, I haven't found anything else, but I'd like to keep the area roped off for another day, just in case."

"You got it." Mark looked down at the footprints Myrna had found. Streaks of dust and debris surrounded the spot where Mr. Ferguson had been discovered, but on the edge of the disturbed space was a very clear shoe print. He hun-kered down to take a closer look at it, until he spied a dis-tinctive logo. He whistled. "This should prove interesting."

"What is it?" Myrna asked.

"See the logo? We can narrow down our search based on this."

She frowned. "Really? How? This running shoe is more than just famous, you know. I've seen babies wearing these!"

Mark pointed. "The tread pattern. Shoe size. And be-cause I know this brand makes limited quantities of exclu-sive editions every year. This footprint is one of them." He pulled out his phone again and took a few close-up shots.

"Are they the same footprints as by the chain and pad-lock?"

He stood. "Don't know. Finish up what you're doing, then let's check the rest of the perimeter. I also want to talk to the site supervisor."

The supervisor, a man in his late forties, had nothing to offer. "I gave Mr. Ferguson a tour of the premises and provided updates. That took about an hour. He said he was going back to his office, and the last time I saw him, he was heading for the exit."

"You didn't hear anything odd?" Mark asked.

"No, sir, I didn't. So damn noisy around here."

It was late evening now, and dark within the half-constructed building. "Can you take us around the outside of the construction site?" Mark asked. "I'd like to see if there's anything else that's helpful."

"Yeah, sure. Both of you need to wear these." The supervisor gave them hard hats. "Let me turn on the portable light towers first, and I've got a large flashlight. I'll bring that, especially as you both need to watch your footing."

The powerful beam cut through the pools of darkness the light towers didn't reach as they slowly walked along a narrow dirt pathway. "Is Mr. Ferguson okay?" the supervisor asked.

"He's got cuts and bruises. I told him to go to the hospital in case anything's broken." Mark didn't want to say too much.

"I keep telling him he needs to wear the hard hat and work boots when he's here. Sometimes he'll wear them, but those other times…" The supervisor let out a loud sigh. "The man can be stubborn."

"Do you work with him frequently?"

"This is my first job as supervisor with him. He's very smart, but his common sense needs a bit of work, in my opinion."

As they came around a corner, the supervisor stopped. "What the hell is that?"

Mark looked at the red container, its shape immediately recognizable. "You weren't expecting to see a fuel canister?"

"At a construction site? Hell no." The supervisor made a move to reach for it.

"Hang on." Mark looked at Myrna. "Can you see if you can get any prints off that?"

"You betcha." She crouched in front of the fuel can as the supervisor held his flashlight steady. "You think the suspect might have wanted to start a fire in here?" she asked. "Maybe Mr. Ferguson caught him in the act and got beaten up?"

"What?" The supervisor wiped his brow. "Hey, this is getting to be too much."

Mark had to agree. A plan to burn down a building with staff inside had just raised the stakes of this investigation. "We'll take it with us," he said, waiting until Myrna finished her analysis. He grabbed the container with a gloved hand. "We'll check if there are any more, then head back."

Thankfully, there were no more fuel cans, but Mark's sixth sense was acting up. "Mr. Smith, I think it best you give your staff the day off tomorrow. I'd like to check the construction site one more time to make sure there aren't any more of these." He held up the fuel canister. "Or any other viable clues."

Mr. Smith shook his head. "Mr. Ferguson won't like it."

"I'll talk to him. In the meantime, don't let anyone come into work tomorrow. But we'll need you here to escort us through the rest of the building."

"Sure, sure."

Mark handed him his card. "Is tomorrow morning around eleven thirty okay with you?"

"Yeah, I'll be here." They had reached the front gate, and Mr. Smith switched off his flashlight. "I hope you catch the son of a bitch who did this."

"That's the plan. I'll be talking to one of your construction workers tomorrow morning as well at the police station. You and I will do a thorough search of the premises. And see if you have another way to secure the site. The last thing we need is some jerk taking videos of himself at the crime scene."

He paused beside the chain-link fence, uncertainty creeping through his skin, gnawing at his gut. This case had taken an odd twist. A homicide was one thing—catch the killer, throw him in jail, give closure to the family. That might be a bit oversimplified, but that was how it seemed to progress when the other detectives worked the investigations.

But this… Someone had tried to kill one of the biggest store owners in Ontario, and if that gasoline had been spread around and lit, several construction workers might have lost their lives as well. Everyone knew Mighty Big Bakery, and the spotlight would be on Mark, glaring at everything he did until he solved the case. To say that he felt the pressure was an understatement.

"Hey, you okay?" Myrna asked.

"Not really. This investigation is going to be…" He didn't finish.

"Don't sweat it. We'll get it done." She took the fuel canister from him. "I'll do an initial analysis when I get back, see if I can come up with some more answers for you."

He smiled, thinking of a memory. "You sound like Cynthia."

Myrna laughed. "What can I say? Ms. Cornwall is one of the best. She sort of rubs off on you."

Mark talked to the officer in charge about security while watching the few remaining curious bystanders, including a pair of young teenagers. "We can open up the street to traffic," he told him, "but I'd like a rotating shift for tonight. I'm coming back to finish looking around tomorrow." Across the street, he noticed the familiar markings of a television van and groaned. "When the hell did they show up?"

"About ten minutes ago. The interviewer is over there."

The officer frowned. "May as well get it over and done with."

With Myrna gone, Mark felt vulnerable, like a team member had taken a hit and he was left holding the ball. But he refused to let that show. His interview was brief and vague, despite the demands for answers—answers he didn't have and wouldn't provide if he knew. Captain Fraust should be okay with that.

He walked to his car, exhaustion making him drag his feet. It was nighttime now, and the street had been re-opened to traffic. Car lights and incessant honking grated on his nerves until he thought he'd yell with frustration. He would need some serious downtime when this case was over. He hadn't been under the impression that he'd pushed himself too hard, but his brain and body were giving him other ideas.

And yet, a tremor of exhilaration coursed through him. This was his first major case as lead investigator. How could he not be excited about that?

He would have a load of stuff to do tomorrow, but for now, a hot shower and his bed were calling him.

He pulled out his key fob and clicked it, hearing the familiar chirp as his car door unlocked. Halfway across the street, Mark let his gaze scan across the pedestrians as they traveled to whatever entertainment awaited them on a Friday night, until he noticed a woman.

She stood on the sidewalk just ahead of his car, so that he had a full, unobstructed, amazing view.

The first thing that caught his attention was her long blond hair, tied back into a ponytail, although some strands had escaped to frame her face. The color was so striking, it looked like a halo around a pale, serene expression. She was tall—about five feet nine inches—and wearing a pair of slim denim jeans and a white T-shirt that couldn't hide the toned body hidden beneath them.

He couldn't see the color of her eyes, but he felt sure they would either be an icy blue or as green as the British Columbia forests that surrounded his old home. A classic Norwegian princess who literally took his breath away. Mark noticed nothing else—only her.

She remained still, watching him, her arms wrapped around a tote bag, one eyebrow raised. He noticed that she was studying him just as intently but hadn't moved. His feet chose to answer for him, drawing him closer, step by agonizing step. That clichéd phrase of moths being drawn to flame ran through his mind. This beautiful vision, only mere feet away, was a flame that lit up emotions Mark had buried so that he could concentrate on his job and claim back the life his father had taken away.

She made a move as if to turn away, and he stopped, holding his breath. *Please*, he thought. *Just three more seconds...*

The sudden squeal of tires, followed by the loud, blaring sound of a car horn, made him jump, his heart pounding in his chest. He turned to look at the white SUV and the irate driver waving her fist at him. "Get off the street!" she screamed. "What the hell are you doing?"

"Sorry," he called out, and got out of the way. But when he turned back to his dream come true, she was gone.

Britt Gronlund closed the door behind her, then leaned against it, clutching her purse so tight to her chest she was afraid she might have ripped holes in it with her nails.

The front window of her bakery shop was a wide pane of glass, and unable to help herself, she turned toward it, wondering if the gorgeous stranger had possibly followed her. But after a few minutes, she realized it wasn't the case.

She sighed, trying to decide if she'd made the right choice. When she'd noticed him crossing the street, she believed the Fates had something to do with it. Britt had been late getting to the bank, and the long lineup had tested her patience. It also didn't help that the police had closed down her street to do an investigation. When the area finally opened up, she'd quickened her pace, thinking about the things she needed to finish before closing up for the evening.

But when she'd seen him, thoughts of work had flown out of her mind. Britt had no way to describe what she felt when he came toward her. He'd seemed distracted, yet his confident stride and aura made her stand at attention. This was a man few could ignore, including her.

She had stopped and stood at the curb, watching as he dug out a set of keys and automatically unlocked his door. As she frantically debated whether to call out a greeting, he looked up, and their gazes locked on each other.

The intensity in his eyes sent shivers through every part of her, and she'd held her breath. Britt had never believed in love at first sight, but the stranger's continued look woke some part of her that she'd believed dead and gone...

The sudden noise of a car horn had propelled her out of her fantasy. Damn it, why was this happening now when she still had her life to get in order? Any kind of intimate relationship would only stall her goals, and Britt had promised herself that she would come first.

So, with one regretful backward glance, she had blended into the Friday-night crowd, memorizing what little she'd seen of the handsome stranger.

Life must still go on.

Blowing out a frustrated breath, she frowned as she stared at the half-constructed building almost across from her, wondering why the police had felt it necessary to shut down the street. She'd seen the barrier and police officers on duty keeping away the curious. Bright lighting illuminated the starkness of the construction site.

That building belonged to Edward Ferguson.

Pursing her lips, Britt carefully wove between waiting customers to get to her office. Betty and Kevin moved around each other like two dancers as they fulfilled orders for those in line, while other customers sat at a few of the half dozen tables throughout the room. One corner held a dedicated free library, where customers could pick a book and read while enjoying a drink and their favorite pastry.

The pace was steady, and her staff were handling it with their usual efficiency and upbeat friendliness. Britt headed toward the back, passing the door to the large well-stocked kitchen and Jacques, her head baker. He waved at her. "Britt! Did you hear?"

Britt hesitated at the entrance. "About what?"

"The assault across the street." Jacques was an older man in his late forties, and had worked with her for almost three years, helping her build the business from the ground up to where it stood now.

"Assault?" She walked into the kitchen, now curious. "Was that what all the commotion was about?"

"Yeah." He was folding dough. "It was Edward Ferguson."

"No way." The CEO had been trying to buy out her store, and she'd told him, using colorful language, where he could shove it. It seemed like karma had paid him a visit. She allowed herself a tiny moment of petty elation before asking, "Do you know if he's okay?"

Jacques gave her a disgusted look. "Should we care? He wanted to shut us down, *chérie*. He's bought a lot of the small bakeries in Toronto already."

"I know. It's just…well, there are other ways to handle a man like Mr. Ferguson."

"I suppose." He portioned out the dough, placed it on a metal pan and covered it with plastic before sliding it into the huge fridge. "However, you and I know that Ferguson is not the diplomatic type. He's a bully."

"Can't disagree on that."

In her office, Britt turned on her computer and checked her email. They had received orders through the week, but there was always someone who would frantically put in a last-minute request for the weekend. This time, there were two—a small order for tomorrow in the early afternoon, and another larger order for the day after, Sunday morning. Thank God they weren't catering events, or she'd have to decline them.

Britt was proud of the work she'd put into Konditori, her bakery and life's dream. The sudden change in direction had been scary, but in the end, well worth it.

She sent the replies, drew up invoices and made notes. She would need to advise Jacques, of course, and have him bring in Thomas, his assistant. She'd leave messages for Jasmine and Oliver coming in for the weekend shift, and she'd be here, overseeing everything.

It's not as if she had a date or weekend plans, right?

Chapter 2

Mark stood in the hospital room that night, tapping his foot impatiently as Mr. Ferguson continued talking on his cell. Ten minutes had already lapsed, and as the man's voice started rising in irritation, he suspected it could go on much longer.

He moved to stand in front of the CEO. "I need to talk to you," he said loudly. "This is a criminal investigation, remember?"

Ferguson gave him a look, but Mark didn't back down. Finally with a sigh, he nodded. "Look, let me call you back. I don't have a choice—there's a police officer standing in front of me." He clicked off the phone.

Mark chewed his lip in frustration but didn't bother correcting his job title—the effort would have been wasted, and he needed to pick his battles with someone as influential as the man lying in the hospital bed before him. "Thank you," he said, trying not to grit his teeth. "So, give me a rundown of what happened." Myrna had arrived earlier to collect the forensic samples taken by the hospital staff.

Ferguson drank from a glass of water, then lay back down. "I have no idea why this kind of shit would happen to me."

I have a few ideas, Mark said to himself. "It can happen to anyone."

"Not to me."

Mark let that one slide and pulled out his work phone. "I just need to record our conversation so that you don't have to come to the precinct later." He placed the instrument on a small table beside the bed and sat down. "What happened?" he repeated.

Mr. Ferguson rubbed his arm, which was bandaged. "I don't know. I had a meeting with the site supervisor at four this afternoon. I was running late and called him to say I'd be there in another fifteen minutes.

"When I got to the site office, he insisted I put on the hard hat and boots. I took off my shoes, and I remember struggling with the boots. I got ticked off and said let's get on with it."

"Do you remember putting on the hard hat?" Mark asked.

"Nah, hate the damn things. I wasn't going to be there long anyway. We went in and did the inspection. That was it."

Mark leaned forward in his chair. "You didn't see anyone suspicious?"

"I wasn't looking for anyone suspicious," he retorted. "As far as I'm concerned, I'm just there to make sure everything's on schedule."

That sounded like him. "Then what?"

"I went back to the office, put on my shoes and got ready to leave. Said I was happy with the progress, and the supervisor confirmed the store would be ready to open by the end of the year."

Mark nodded, more to himself. It sounded like an ordinary day to the bakery owner. And yet… "How did you get lured back?"

Mr. Ferguson turned his head to look at him directly.

"I was in a hurry and didn't wait for the supervisor. I got to the front gate and saw someone walking to the back with a gasoline container. He wasn't dressed like a construction worker, either, only had on the safety vest and hard hat, and nothing else. I've been in enough sites to know. And the gate hadn't been locked, so I was sure it was a trespasser.

"I ran after him and started shouting. I actually got my phone out to call the supervisor. I could see the guy was scared, but when my phone started ringing—I had it on speaker—he must have panicked. Little prick ran at me and pushed me over, knocked the phone out of my hand. Next thing I know, I'm getting hit with something hard. I started kicking and yelling, and pretty sure I scored a couple of hits."

Mark was impressed—Mr. Ferguson was an observant man. "Did you see his face?"

He nodded. "For about three seconds. I don't think I can identify him. But you managed to find some clues, right?"

"We have some evidence, yes." Mark decided to keep the discovery of the fuel container to himself, along with shutting down the site tomorrow. He had a suspicion the CEO would throw a tantrum, and he wanted to avoid that.

"Good, I want that asshole arrested, you got that?"

Mark got up and retrieved his phone. He had a theory and decided to confirm it. "Do you think you were attacked because of your…business ethics?"

Mr. Ferguson laughed. "People need to understand it's a dog-eat-dog world, son. If you can't keep up, you'll be run over. Anyone who tells you different is lying."

Mark pursed his lips. Of course, he held a different view, but what was the point in arguing it? "The doctor told me you should be able to go home tomorrow. I'll keep you up to date on my progress, but if I have any more questions, I'll let you know."

He walked out of the hospital feeling gross. There was just something about Ferguson that rubbed him in all the wrong ways. It was one thing to say you wanted to beat your competition, and another when you'd do anything it took to climb on top.

It was one of the reasons he had decided on law enforcement. He believed in defending people who didn't stand a chance against men like Ferguson. Bullying and intimidation didn't sit well in Mark's view.

So it was ironic that he had to defend a bully. "Will wonders never cease?" he muttered as he got into his car.

Mark woke and stretched his arms over his head. He heard birds chirping outside his window, and when he glanced at his clock, saw that it was just past seven in the morning.

He grabbed his work phone and checked the timing on the two interviews he had scheduled. Jenny, the construction worker, was at nine, while Mr. Smith, the site supervisor, was at eleven thirty. Myrna had texted him as well, letting him know she had stayed at the precinct until late last night, and would arrive midmorning.

After a shower and shave, he felt human again. But when he opened his fridge door, he swore. He'd forgotten to pick up some groceries last night after being distracted by the Nordic princess.

Damn it, he wished he'd been more on the ball. Mark had been awestruck by the woman's beauty and hadn't gotten his act together in time to approach and maybe say a few complimentary words to her. Bad luck on his part, and the chances of seeing her or having the same spell-bound reaction to another woman again was close to nil.

He slapped the fridge in frustration. He knew that had been a once-in-a-long-time encounter. Maybe, if the stars aligned themselves, he might see her again, but he wouldn't get his hopes up.

An hour later, Mark sat at his desk after grabbing a breakfast sandwich and a large cup of decent coffee from the local takeout store close to the precinct. He read through his notes, though the case was still fresh in his mind. He had an idea of the questions he would ask Jenny, the construction worker, and Mr. Smith, the site supervisor. While he believed Smith would be straightforward, he wondered how Jenny would behave during the interview. It may be a bad habit in his profession, but thinking the worst of witnesses and suspects before they proved their innocence did get him around obstacles. If he fell for her flirting, where would that end up, especially if she was guilty of something?

A phone call from the officer at the front desk confirmed her arrival. Timmins wasn't in the office yet—he had texted, saying he'd be there in ten minutes. Mark grabbed his notepad and headed to the reception area to pick her up. "Good morning," he said. "Thanks for coming in."

"Hey, no problem." She stood, and he immediately noticed that she had put care into her appearance. Jenny wore makeup, had styled her hair in waves that framed her face, and her clothing was more suited for an evening out than a weekend police interrogation. It wasn't hard to put two and two together that she was making an effort to continue flirting with him.

"Come on, we're going to an interrogation room to get a formal statement."

The ride on the elevator was silent. He caught Jenny watching him out of the corner of his eye, but he remained quiet while he led her down the fluorescent-lit hallway and into a barely furnished room. "Have a seat."

She looked around, rubbing her arms. "This looks like a jail cell."

Mark dropped his notepad and phone on the bolted table. "You know what the inside of a jail cell looks like?" he asked. That was an odd statement from her.

"Only from the television shows." She sat down, continuing to take in her surroundings.

"Did you want anything? Coffee?"

"No, I'm good."

He looked at his watch. "Detective Walter Timmins should be here in a few minutes."

She frowned.

"We always need two officers during an interview. Protocol."

"Oh." She sounded disappointed.

That will keep her from trying anything funny.

A couple of minutes later, Timmins walked in. "Sorry I'm late," he apologized, and took the seat at the other end of the small room.

"No problem." Mark lifted his hand toward the camera in the wall to signal he was ready. After introducing himself and Timmins formally and describing the purpose of the interview, he got started. "Can you give me a full rundown of your day up to when you discovered Mr. Edward Ferguson?"

"Yeah, sure." She glanced back at Timmins, then took a breath. "All of us knew Mr. Ferguson was coming by yesterday afternoon at four o'clock. Smith, our site supervisor, runs a tight ship—really organized. Everyone knows what they're supposed to be working on each day. But he wanted me and one other coworker to walk the area and clean up any loose debris, check that everything was in its place, that sort of thing."

"What time did this start?" Mark asked.

"I got to work at my usual time, eight in the morning. I think maybe an hour later?"

He wrote some notes. "And when you finished?"

"The coworker and I started our shift. I was helping with the steel girders on the second floor, but I don't know what my coworker's job was."

"Did you work on that during your whole shift?"

"For the morning, yes, until twelve thirty, then I had lunch."

"Do all the workers take their lunch at the same time?" Timmins asked.

Jenny half turned in her chair. "No, lunchtime is split into two shifts."

"So Mr. Ferguson arrived when all of you finished lunch."

"Well, it's not like he needs us with him while he's inspecting," Jenny retorted. "Mr. Smith was there, and I think he took two of his junior assistants with him."

Mark jotted down the assistants' names—he'd verify that with Smith later. "And after lunch?"

"Got back to work. We were starting the electrical, so I was on hand for that until my shift was over, around six that evening."

"Did you see Mr. Ferguson and your boss at all during the afternoon?"

Jenny shook her head. "Nope. Just kept my head down. We were on a schedule."

"And after work?"

She shrugged. "I headed to the front gate and saw something weird on the ground within the site. That's how I found him."

"It's pretty hard to see that distance when it's dark under there," Timmins stated.

"It wasn't that dark where Mr. Ferguson was."

Mark paused in taking notes. "But it would have been difficult to spot him immediately."

She shrugged. "We're trained to spot inconsistencies. I don't know what else to tell you."

The rest of Jenny's story was almost verbatim to what she'd told him last night.

"Thanks for your help," Mark said, getting up. "If you think of anything else, you have my business card."

"Sooo, I'm not getting arrested for anything?" she said innocently, holding her wrists together.

He almost rolled his eyes, then caught Timmins hiding his face with a hand. His cough sounded suspiciously like a laugh. "No." He opened the door to let her out.

In their office, Timmins mimicked Jenny's failed flirtation attempt. "Are you sure you don't want to arrest me, officer?" Timmins asked, imitating Jenny's voice and doing a bad job of it.

"Knock it off."

"Jeez, you're moody this morning. And I thought your witness might have been your type."

"She's not."

"Yeah, maybe she's too kinky for you."

"You know what? That's kinda unpleasant, coming from you."

Timmins leaned back in his chair. "How's your investigation going so far?"

Thank God Timmins changed the subject. "I have to talk to Myrna to find out what she's discovered, but I'm interrogating the site supervisor at eleven thirty if you want to back me up again."

At the appointed time in the interrogation room, Mark wasn't much further ahead. Mr. Smith verified his assistants were with him when they escorted Mr. Ferguson around the premises. "Did anything seem out of place?" Mark asked him.

Mr. Smith shook his head. "Everyone had been doing a fantastic job, and all on time, too. I gotta say, I'm grateful for this team."

"What time did Mr. Ferguson leave?"

The supervisor pursed his lips. "Between five and five thirty."

So in between the time Mr. Ferguson left and saw the intruder, and Jenny discovering Mr. Ferguson's unconscious body, the gate would have been open. There was about an hour in that time frame where a suspect could have done some serious damage with the fuel canister. Mark wondered if the suspect even knew Mr. Ferguson was on the premises. What if beating up the bakery owner was better than burning down the building?

He jotted down his thoughts. "If you don't mind, Mr. Smith, let me do one more sweep of the building with you before you bring your employees back."

"Yeah, sure."

More than an hour later, Mark was satisfied there was nothing hidden around the construction site that could blow up. The supervisor had given his employees the day off as Mark had suggested. The police tape was still up, and one officer was on duty. After thanking Mr. Smith and watching him head to his car, Mark approached his colleague. "Hey," he called out, and showed his badge. "How's everything?"

"Quiet, which is how I like it. There were some kids hanging around when I came on duty, but they took off."

"I'm pretty sure we've collected all the evidence we need." Mark looked around, thinking he'd need to reconfirm that with Myrna.

"I heard it was some big shot that got beat up. The guy who owns those big-box bakery stores."

Mark nodded.

"Probably had it coming to him."

He frowned. "Why are you thinking that?"

The officer's eyes widened, and his face flushed red. "Sorry, sir, that was out of line."

"Not from what I've heard." No one had anything good to say about Edward Ferguson, and Mark now wondered if there was more to this beating than the CEO was letting on. "Tell me why you said that."

The officer shrugged. "My cousin worked for a well-known chain in the Italian community out in the west end. This guy bought the business and promised my cousin and the other workers they'd have jobs when the changeover was finished." He turned and spat onto the ground. "Lied through his teeth."

That seemed to be a consistent trait of the conglomerate. "I'm sorry about your cousin," Mark told him.

"It's okay. She found a job she really loves now." The officer glanced up at the building. "I guess he's gonna try and force out the couple of little businesses along this street. What a douche."

Mark eyed the stores opposite him—a bank on the corner, a variety store, a small grocer's and, at the far end, a bakery painted bright pink with the word *Konditori* spelled out in dark blue letters above the large window. Several customers waited outside to get in.

He decided to skip the bank and started with the variety store, since it and the other stores faced the construction site. An older gentleman sitting beside the front counter barely spoke English, but after Mark pulled out his badge, the man yelled something, and a young woman appeared from the back of the store. A few questions came up empty.

He moved on to the grocer's, where several employees kept busy stocking produce. This time, he got some interesting information from another older gentleman, who spoke perfect English. "That Ferguson man, he tried to buy the stores on this side of the street," he said, his accent thick but understandable. "We all told him no and to get out."

Mark wrote that down. "He wasn't nice?"

"He has plenty of stores. Why does he want more? I told him to leave us alone and don't come back."

Mark pointed out the door. "But he bought property from someone across the street?"

The old man nodded. "Nice people. Butcher shop, fruit and vegetable grocery, and clothing store that also sold flowers. The grocery and butcher owners sold with no argument. But the lady who sold the clothes and flowers refused. Always busy. But I heard bad things happened to her."

He frowned. "What bad things?"

The man leaned forward, and his voice dropped. "Bad people destroyed her store, tore up the merchandise. Broke windows and painted awful words on the building. I'm sure it was Mr. Ferguson who did this. After two weeks, we found out the owner sold her store. That was late last year. She moved back home to Europe." He frowned. "Now all we see is Mighty Big Bakery. No one is happy."

Mark wandered down the street, thinking on what he'd heard. Ferguson had given the impression he'd do whatever it took to get what he wanted, yet somehow, he didn't get the stores on this side of the street first. He jotted that down, intending to question the CEO about it.

The last store, called Konditori, was a quirky-looking bakery. Inside, the space was well lit and bright. Pale gray walls were the perfect background for the colorful wall art. Tables and chairs made of thick white oak were set up neatly to one side, while a tall bookcase covered half a wall at the opposite end.

Two employees—a man and a woman—were behind the long counter, taking orders and moving around each other with a practiced ease born of experience.

"Welcome to Konditori," the man greeted him with a wide smile. "How can I help you today?"

Mark couldn't resist—the smell of fresh-baked goods surrounded him, making his mouth water. He selected a pastry and a large coffee. "I wanted to ask if the owner was here," he said as he paid for his meal.

"Sure is. She's in the back office."

"Could you let her know that Detective Mark Hawthorne is here? Just wanted to ask if she knows anything about what happened across the street last night."

"You bet. Give me a couple of minutes."

"Thanks." He took his snack to a table nearest the front window. The day was turning out cloudy and gray, and as he watched, the sidewalk glistened from a light sprinkle of rain that sprang up out of nowhere.

From his seat, he had a clear view of the half-constructed Mighty Big Bakery. At this angle, he noticed how large the building was, about a half block in length. When it was completed, it would overshadow the stores on this side. Hopefully, the store owners had a plan for that.

Mark heard a gasp behind him, and when he turned around in his seat…

Oh my God, it's her.

Her golden presence slammed hard into his chest—he was glad he was sitting down. Her thick blond hair was braided today and hung over her shoulder. Instead of the casual look from last night, today she wore wide-legged pants and a loose blouse. But he only noticed these things because he was trained for that.

What held him in his chair was her eyes, so green he imagined that he was swimming in them. The ocean off the British Columbia coast had nothing on this woman's gaze. Sparkling, bright, its depths a tantalizing mystery.

Her eyes were wide with surprise, and while he didn't dare to guess, Mark hoped her thoughts were in sync with his.

The temptation to just sit and look at her was overwhelming. But he finally remembered to get his bearings and scrambled out of his seat. "Hello," he managed to say in a normal voice, although there was nothing normal about seeing her again—someone was smiling down on him today.

She blinked several times, as if refocusing. "Good afternoon."

Her voice only enhanced her beauty. Smooth and low-pitched, it had a European accent that gave her voice a musical lilt. Although it could also be her luscious full lips that made her voice sound so delectable.

Crap, don't stand here staring at her like a drooling twit. Inhaling a deep breath, he held out his hand. "Detective Mark Hawthorne. Thank you for seeing me."

Her handshake was firm and warm. "Britt Gronlund."

He pulled out a chair for her. "Please join me."

As she sat down, her hair brushed against his hand. It was silky soft, almost a caress, and his body tingled with heightened awareness. He took another deep breath to calm himself before sitting down across from her.

But looking at Ms. Gronlund this close increased his urge to talk to her about everything else except work. *One day.* Mark paused, surprised at the unexpected thought.

"I suspect you're here to talk to me about Edward Ferguson?" she asked.

"Yes, that's right." He pulled out his work phone, hit Record and placed it on the table between them. "This saves a trip to the police station," he explained when she glanced down at it.

"Makes sense."

Mark deliberately sipped his coffee, allowing him a few moments to figure out how to start. Her comments had been short and to the point, which wasn't a problem. However, to own a bright, cheery bakery like Konditori, with friendly staff and customers who seemed to know each other, Ms. Gronlund's mannerisms seemed off-balance. Maybe she was nervous.

He held up his cup. "This coffee is amazing. I think I'm wired for the rest of the day."

She smiled, but it didn't quite reach her eyes. "Thank you. It's a special coffee roast I get from my supplier in Ethiopia."

"And the Danish? Was it made fresh this morning?"

Her eyes widened in shock. "How did you know?"

"My family had friends who owned a bakery in British Columbia, and I could guess when they had freshly baked goods ready." He pointed to the store name located above the cashier. "What does Konditori mean?"

She glanced over her shoulder. "It's Norwegian for cake shop."

"I like that. It feels authentic."

She was starting to look more relaxed. "It reminds me of home."

He nodded, then looked around the bakery. There was still a lineup, although he knew at least a dozen people had come and gone. "Is it always this busy?" he asked. "It's what, about two o'clock now? I've never been to a bakery that had so many people in it."

This time, her smile lit up her face. "It's always busy, but especially on the weekends. Customers like to pick up dessert for their weekend events. It makes the days go by faster."

Mark wasn't sure how to take her comment. Did she want her days to fly by because she had nothing else to do? "Sounds like my schedule, sometimes."

She raised an eyebrow at that.

"Speaking of schedules, I don't want to take up too much of your time, Ms. Gronlund. Can you give me a rundown of what you did on Friday?"

Mark loved listening to her voice. She was methodical and precise, describing everything until she reached the evening.

"After I left the bank, the police had stopped pedestrians from entering the street. They mentioned there was a police investigation. A lot of people took alternate routes, but I decided to wait. It gave me a chance to catch up on work emails."

He watched her face, wondering what she would say next. "And when the street reopened?"

"I hurried back to the store, as we were closing in thirty minutes. I'm very strict on that. My employees' well-being comes first, and I wanted them to enjoy their Friday night."

Ms. Gronlund lowered her gaze, as if thinking. But then she slowly propped her elbows on the table, linked her fingers together and rested her chin on her hands. When she looked up, her eyes had darkened. "Then I saw you."

There were no words to describe the strange vibrating pulse that coursed through her body when she saw him.

Britt half suspected that the police would pay a visit to see if she knew anything about what happened Friday night. When Oliver had told her a Detective Hawthorne was here to talk to her, she'd been ready.

She'd stepped out of her office, then slowed to a complete stop. The detective was half turned while looking out the window, and she had a clear view of his profile. A strong square jaw, straight nose and a muscular neck swept up from the collar of his shirt. His hands and manicured fingers were agile as he fiddled with the mug. And despite the looser cut of the shirt, Britt caught glimpses of well-defined muscle beneath the material as he moved.

Her hand came up to her chest, and she released a sigh that was louder than intended. He turned around, no doubt hearing her, then held still.

And Britt experienced the same damn uncontrollable emotions that hit her last night.

When he stood, she almost had to take a step back. There was something about him that demanded respect, but it wasn't threatening, a trait that made her want to know more about him. In retrospect, Britt thought it was his eyes. They were a warm brown with flecks of gold, and she wondered if they changed color depending on his mood. And his voice…deep with a hint of roughness. She could spend all day listening to him recite a damn dictionary.

That in itself excited and scared her at the same time.

Detective Hawthorne had asked for a summary of her Friday activities, which didn't take long to discuss. However, she was more interested in talking about another topic. "Were you at the crime scene last night?" she asked.

"I was." He turned off his phone and stuck it into his pants pocket.

"Do you think it'll be a complicated case?" Britt knew where she was going with her questioning but wasn't sure if the detective would catch on.

"I hope not." He focused his gaze on her. "I'd rather spend my time doing more interesting things."

She licked her lips, a move he didn't miss. "Such as?"

"Getting to know a Nordic princess who ran away from me last night."

Britt frowned. "I'm not a princess. And I didn't run away."

"You didn't stay, either." He tilted his head.

What could she say? "You're right. I had a business to run."

He nodded slowly. "And I should have had the courage to approach you, but I had work to do."

They sat in silence for a few moments, and Britt thought hard about how to ask if he'd like to…oh, she didn't know, go on a date? It had been a long time since she'd been out with a man, and feeling rusty was an understatement.

"However, destiny seems to be in our favor." Detective

Hawthorne reached into his shirt pocket and pulled out a business card. "This is in case you think of anything else you'd like to tell me." He pulled a pen from the same pocket, turned the card over and scribbled something. "And this is in case you'd like to talk about anything other than work."

Britt took the card between two fingers, suddenly realizing that while he was flirting with her, the detective had left the ball in her court. She was liking him more already.

Chapter 3

It was past three in the afternoon, and Mark sat at his desk. His notes, photos and statements were strewn in front of him like so many puzzle pieces. Myrna had arrived at the precinct while he'd been out, and he was waiting for her to give him an update on her findings.

He mulled over Mr. Ferguson's attack and the small amount of evidence gleaned from the man. No doubt the CEO would gnash his teeth in frustration when he learned his newest store was in limbo until tomorrow. Curious, he looked up Ferguson via the internet on his phone and frowned at the information he found.

It seemed like Edward Ferguson took his dog-eat-dog motto to heart. He bought smaller bakeries, independent family businesses, then fired all the original staff and re-modeled the purchases into his design. There had been a couple of lawsuits against him, but with his money and elite law teams, no one stood a chance against the conglomerate.

The CEO knew nothing of compassion.

This case smelled of revenge. To deliberately bring a gas container with the intention of arson was one thing. Mr. Ferguson's beating was another level. He wondered how many people hated the CEO enough to risk being caught and shuddered at the possibilities.

He started to organize his information, moving the pieces around until they resembled a timeline. Mr. Ferguson's and Ms. Gronlund's statements were still on his work phone, and Mark tapped the necessary buttons to transfer them to his computer.

"Hey there." Myrna walked through the open door, her arms laden with several folders and her laptop.

"Hi." He watched as she dumped her stuff on the small meeting table. "How late were you here last night?"

"Oh, until about two in the morning."

"Myrna, you didn't have to do that."

"I know, but I wanted to because I knew it would be quiet. Besides," she added as she opened her laptop, "this case is a big one. You and I need to get a decent report together to present to Captain Fraust first thing Monday morning."

Mark groaned. "I'm surprised she hasn't called me yet."

"Be careful what you wish for, Hawthorne."

He sat opposite her. "We can cross-reference with my evidence," he told her, pointing to his desk. "But I want to find out what you've got first."

She tapped a few keys. "So the blood and hair in the area all belonged to Mr. Ferguson, along with the footprints that led from the site's entrance to that particular spot. I managed to lift the suspect's fingerprints from the fuel canister and the piece of wood used as the weapon. But when I ran the prints through the database, I didn't get any hits. The canister is a common brand sold at Canadian Tire stores—it'll be hard to track down the location that sold it."

"Guess I can't be surprised at that." Mark leaned forward. "What about the sneaker prints?"

"Ah yes, you hit the bell on those. The majority of this

brand's shoes have the recognizable circular pattern on their sole, with the logo located in the middle. This one, however, is different." Myrna turned her laptop so that he could look at the screen. "The distinctive logo is at the top of the sole this time. There's another symbol under the heel of the shoe."

"Yeah, I know this edition. There was a stink a few years ago about that symbol. It resembled an Arabic word."

"And as a result, the company had to stop selling that particular shoe, but not before the initial 225 pairs were sold in Toronto."

Mark knew his brow went up in disbelief.

Myrna nodded. "That's it. We can get a list of buyers."

"That's it? Myrna, that's a lot of customers to get through." Mark envisioned the amount of time and manpower involved in that task. "What if the suspect sold off his shoes?"

"Do you really think that? Those shoes are worth a lot of money, especially after that debacle. I don't think he'd sell them."

"So you know they're men's shoes. Good work."

"Not only that, but we won't have to go through the full customer list." She tapped a couple of keys. "Take a look at that."

He stared at a photo with two different-sized prints. "We're looking for two suspects?" he asked.

"No. These were the only prints in the immediate area."

He thought hard, wondering what the investigator was trying to show him. He pursed his lips and shook his head. "You've lost me."

Myrna grinned. "Our suspect's feet are two different sizes."

The stroke of luck that Myrna provided him had Mark

feeling they would be close to nailing the bastard. "What size are we looking for?"

"That's even better. According to my measurements, he's wearing a size 14 on his right foot, and a size 12 on his left. Average height would range from five foot ten inches to six foot three inches."

So a man wearing two different-sized shoes of a limited edition. How much luckier could they get? "Myrna, I could kiss you."

"Now, now. No office hanky-panky, please." Her grin was contagious.

He parked his car at a lot within the Queen and Yonge Street area, then waited for a westbound streetcar. Checking his searches on his phone, he found most of the hip sneaker stores were in the west end, within a five-mile radius. He could easily walk to about half of them.

The first store was the top hit on his list. A three-story black building, it had a mural consisting of several Toronto Raptors players.

Inside, the white shelves and walls were a perfect backdrop for the sneakers that came in every color. The floor was an ingenious idea—skateboards were displayed beneath a thick plexiglass cover. *Look, but don't touch.*

In the middle of the space were floating glass displays of rare sneakers, caps and T-shirts from some of the most famous brands out there. A security guard stood at the front door, carefully watching everyone.

Mark headed toward the back, where a cashier was ringing through a purchase. As he waited, he checked out the prices on a couple of interesting pairs. "Holy hell," he whispered, and glanced at some of the others. The average price was five hundred dollars and up. It wasn't that he couldn't afford a pair, but he didn't think he'd wear them outside.

When the cashier had finished, he approached her. "Good afternoon," he said, then showed her his badge. "Detective Mark Hawthorne with York Regional Police 4 District in Vaughan."

The woman, in her twenties, with thick black hair tied up in a bun and bright brown eyes, frowned. "I was told the theft from a couple of weeks ago had been resolved."

"No, this isn't about that." He pulled out the picture of the footprints from the crime scene. "Someone was assaulted, and I recognized these prints from a limited edition that got backlash because the symbol resembled a holy Arabic word."

"Yeah, I heard about that. It was before I started working here." She leaned forward. "You're looking for a guy who owns these?"

"Yes, and in particular, the person who bought a size 14 right foot and size 12 left."

"Wow, different foot sizes. I've heard of that, too, but it's rare. Give me a second."

He waited as she typed, but in a few minutes, she shook her head. "We don't have a sale like that in our records," she told him. "I'm not too surprised, either."

"Why is that?" Mark noticed a waiting customer out of the corner of his eye.

"With limited editions, we want to sell the matching pair, especially as they're collectible items." She tugged on her earlobe. "There are other stores in the area. Do you want me to find out anything for you?"

"No, thank you. I'm going to visit each one until I find my answer. Thanks for your help."

"Good luck."

Well, that was a strike. He crossed the store off his list. But the cashier made an interesting comment. Selling matched pairs of sneakers made sense if a collector hoped to eventually sell them to another interested buyer. What if there were *two* customers with different-sized feet? Was it possible one store might have sold a set to the suspect, knowing the second set would be bought by someone else? It was one hell of a long shot.

The next three stores on his list were within a two-block radius, and didn't give him any results. When Mark walked into the fifth one, however, he was impressed. It was larger, with more stock, and emitted a cozier, warmer atmosphere. He could see why this store was in his top five results when he had searched for cool sneaker shops. There were two security guards this time—one each at the front and back of the store—and it was even busier.

The young man behind the cash register was on the phone, and as Mark waited, he noticed something that offered promise—this particular store had four locations, and the pictures displayed behind the cashier were famous basketball, football and baseball players.

"Hey," the young man greeted him after he hung up the phone. "How can I help you today?"

Mark showed him his badge. "I'm looking for a customer who bought a pair of limited-edition sneakers from a few years ago, featuring a symbol that was offensive to a religious group." He mentioned the brand.

"Yeah, we had those." The cashier hit some keys on his computer. "I've got the list pulled up. There were only about fifteen sneaker stores that got these, all in the downtown core. Each store got fifteen pairs."

"The customer I'm looking for had different-sized feet. Right foot is a 14, the left a 12."

The man's gaze traveled down the computer screen. "Oh yeah, I know the dude. The only reason we offered to sell them that way is because we have a customer in Abu Dhabi who bought the other set."

Mark couldn't believe his luck. "Can you provide me his name, address and phone number?"

"Sure, let me print that out for you."

Several minutes later, he stood outside, looking at the sheet of paper. Henry Toussaint. His address wasn't far from Britt's bakery and Mr. Ferguson's building site.

The streetcar ride back to the parking lot took longer because of traffic and road construction, and he chafed at the delay. He finally got to his car and drove to Toussaint's address. Mark wanted to check out the house and neighborhood first before charging in with a team. He knew he had struck pay dirt finding the shoe owner so quickly, and he couldn't afford to mess it up by going in half-cocked.

About thirty minutes later, Mark cruised along Sierra Court. The houses were two-storied, with wide, deep lots and mature trees. Every house had at least two cars parked in the driveway. Nearby was a school and day care center, and as he continued driving, he noticed that the houses got bigger. The street ended in a cul-de-sac, and he turned around, continuing to mentally record the area while wondering how the hell he was going to arrest Toussaint without causing too much of a scene.

It made sense the suspect could afford those sneakers. This neighborhood was upper middle class, if not higher.

Henry Toussaint's house sat just south of Lomond Avenue, and Mark slowed his car down to get a good look.

Deep driveway—it could easily hold eight cars. Large two-story home, big front yard, several trees and a nice landscaped area filled with flowers. He could just see the security cameras, one over the front door and another covering the double garage. He was sure the backyard would be even bigger.

Mark decided to drive around the neighborhood, as he'd never been up here before. It was large, with Cunningham Pond and a park and play area beside it. Traveling north, he discovered another park, a huge spot with an off-leash area, with dogs barking and running in all directions. Behind it, a kiddie splash pad and a large stage made up the center of the park. It was certainly family friendly. Maybe he'd bring Mom up here once she was out of the hospital, to give her a new place to check out.

At the precinct, Mark turned to the computer to see what information he could dig up on Toussaint. There wasn't much—former soccer player for the Toronto team but had to retire due to an injury. There was some noise about offering him an assistant coach position, but as Mark read through the sport articles, he couldn't find anything else. He added these findings to his ever-growing folder and sat back in his chair, thinking. If he could get his hands on Toussaint tomorrow, he felt sure he could wrap things up by Monday night. However, there was something about Mr. Ferguson that nagged at him. He just wasn't sure what it was. Maybe paying the CEO an unannounced visit tomorrow morning would catch him off guard.

Mark liked that idea. He scheduled the two items into his work phone, alongside a visit to his mom in the hospital.

Suddenly, his personal phone pinged with a text. When

he retrieved it and read the message, he smiled—his Saturday night just got a whole lot better.

Hello, Mr. Detective, I wondered if you'd like to solve the case of finding a good meal? It has to be within a five-block radius of Konditori, fast and most important, tasty. Are you up for the challenge?-The Nordic Princess

P.S. I close up shop in forty minutes, just to give you added incentive.

Britt sat in her office, sipping a cup of tea as she reviewed emails. Today's order for an afternoon party had been a hit with the guests, judging by the three very happy messages from her repeat customer. Jacques and Thomas had Sunday's order well underway, with Betty, her full-time weekday employee, coming in to help them. Jacques had mentioned Betty possessed the instincts of a natural baker and wanted to foster that, to which Britt agreed. She wanted her employees to be happy, with ambitions to do what she and Jacques had accomplished. Nurturing dreams had become a mantra for her.

Her cell phone pinged. When she glanced at the message, a little thrill of excitement zipped through her.

Evening, *vakker*, mystery solved. I'll report to you in fifteen minutes.-Mr. Detective

Wait a minute. Britt read the message again, focusing on one particular word. *Vakker?* That was the Norwegian word for *beautiful*. Did he really just call her that?

Oh, Detective Hawthorne was really stepping up his game.

She shut down her laptop, stuffed it into her tote and headed into the store. "I'm going to start closing up," she announced to a few remaining customers who stood in line, and her weekend staff, Jasmine and Oliver. "Oliver, can you stand at the front door to let the customers out? I'm going to get the lights." Britt had learned the hard way that leaving the lights on was like a beacon. It was fantastic being so popular, but it had its annoying moments, too.

With the last customer finally gone, she and her staff cleaned up, pulled down the blinds at the front window and got everything ready for tomorrow. "Thanks, you two," Britt told them. "I'll see you tomorrow at ten."

In the kitchen, Jacques and his team were working steadily. "Are you sure there's nothing I can help you with?" she asked, looking around. It seemed chaotic, but her head baker had a method to his madness.

"Don't worry, *chérie*, we'll be fine. Another hour, ninety minutes tops."

"All right." Jacques knew she worried about her staff. "I'm heading out the front door tonight. I'm meeting someone. I'll see you all tomorrow. And don't forget to set the security alarm."

Betty picked up a large piece of dough and moved as if to throw it at her. "Would you get going already?" she demanded, laughing.

As Britt walked back to her office, she noticed a figure standing at the door and went to see who it was. Detective Hawthorne was waiting. She unlocked the door. "Hours are ten to five on the weekends," she quipped.

He kept a serious expression. "I was told there was a damsel in distress at this address. Said she would die from starvation if I didn't save her."

Britt's laugh turned into an undignified snort. "Oh my

God, look at what you made me do!" She hadn't laughed that hard in months.

His grin was wide. "Are you ready to go?"

"Let me get my purse." She let him inside, then ran back to the office to collect her stuff.

"Soo, what is tonight's mystery, detective?" she asked as she bolted the door behind her.

"About two blocks west and one street south. And the name's Mark. Only my mom loves calling me detective every chance she gets." He rolled his eyes.

"How sweet! I go by Britt, but I don't mind being called Nordic princess if the mood hits you." Man, that was a bold statement, even for her.

His smile looked sweet, almost shy. "Would you like to walk? If not, I brought my car…"

"No, walking's fine. It's nice to get outside."

They strolled toward the stoplight. "How was your day?" he asked.

Britt sighed. "Busy, as always."

"That's a good thing, right?"

"It is. I can't complain. And I have great staff, too. I wouldn't have gotten this far without them."

At the red light, Mark turned toward her. "It's rare to hear an owner compliment their staff like that. You have a kind heart."

This close, Britt noticed the dark stubble on his face and fought the urge to touch it. "Thank you."

People had started to cross when the light changed, but he held her gaze for a moment longer before following the crowd. She kept pace, her mind a whirlwind of untapped feelings.

The Korean restaurant Mark had chosen was small and brightly lit, with wide open doors letting in the evening's cool air. Several voices chattered loudly as Mark stepped aside to let her in first.

"Welcome!" a young man called out. "Please have a seat."

Britt stopped for a minute to look around. She'd never eaten Korean food before, but the smells were delicious.

He stood beside her and touched her back. "Let's sit near a window," he said into her ear.

She eased into a bright red wooden chair and plopped her tote on the table to one side. "I have no idea what to eat," she told him. "You've taken this mystery to a whole new level."

He inclined his head. "I aim to please."

That comment could be taken in so many ways, and she chided herself for going down a dirty-minded route. Although, looking at Mark, could she blame herself?

A waitress came over and handed them menus. Britt looked at the pictures and brief descriptions for each meal, unsure.

"Most of the food I've tried so far has a bit of a spicy kick to it." Mark leaned in close and pointed at a couple of items. "Since you haven't had Korean food before, let's stick with something less intense. Bibimbap is rice, mixed veggies, beef and an egg on top. They add chili paste for seasoning, but it's on the side. I like the *japchae*, that's glass noodles, vegetables and pork sautéed in soy sauce."

"That sounds great."

He placed the order, and she listened in wonder as he spoke a few words in Korean. "Do you know the language?"

He laughed. "No, just some words and a few simple phrases."

She was still impressed. "But you made an effort to learn, which says a lot." She wondered what else he could surprise her with. "How was your day at work?" Britt asked.

"Tiring… A lot of footwork today."

"Are you still trying to figure out what happened to Mr. Ferguson?" She bit her lip, nervous. "Sorry, I wasn't sure if that was classified…"

"It is, in a way. I can't discuss active investigations."

She nodded. "Gotcha. The mystery thickens."

He smiled at that. Britt noticed the dimple in his left cheek, which made his handsome face even more so.

Before she managed to say something embarrassing, their dinner arrived, along with a teapot and two small bowls. Britt admired her meal while Mark poured the tea. "This looks delicious," she murmured, then looked at his. "Those are noodles?" she asked, staring at them. "How are they so translucent?"

"I just know they're made from starch, like potatoes or beans."

"Oh, I see." Her cooking hat came on. "And probably mixed with water, then shaped into the noodles."

They ate in silence. Britt had used chopsticks when eating Japanese food, so she had no problem. Mark showed her how to mix the egg into the meal before taking her first bite. "Oh my God, this is so good," she exclaimed, talking around a mouthful of food. "How did you find this place?"

"During one of my investigations. There was an assault in the neighborhood. A respected elder got beaten up by a pair of teenagers who stole his money. Found them hiding in here, holding the owner as a hostage."

"Holy crap, they were armed?" This sounded like a thriller novel.

"No, but every kitchen utensil known to man was back there. I couldn't take a chance they'd use a knife."

"What did you do?"

He scooped some *japchae* into his mouth and chewed for a moment. "Basically, I told them don't make it worse. I had a neighbor translate my commands until they finally came out." He frowned. "The old man needed to go to the hospital for treatment. He didn't want to press charges, but I told him if you expect them to learn their lesson, they needed to go through the procedures." Mark's expression was sinister. "I had them locked up overnight and told them every possible thing that could happen. Next day, they were very apologetic. Last I heard from the waitress here, they were doing volunteer work for seniors and the homeless."

"So you had a positive influence on them. I like that."

All too soon, dinner was over, but Britt knew it would be another long, busy day tomorrow. "Thank you for dinner," she said as they made their way back.

"Thank you for inviting me. I loved your text."

She giggled. "Your mission, if you choose to accept it," she replied in a robotic voice, which had Mark laughing out loud.

He had parked his car close to Mighty Big Bakery. "Could I give you a ride home?" he asked quietly.

"Thank you." When she slipped into the passenger seat, Britt glanced up at the construction site, a stark building against the bright security lights. "Mark, I need to tell you something." Listening to him tonight, she knew she had to let him know about her first encounter with Mr. Ferguson.

He turned the car light on. "What is it?"

She felt foolish for not saying something during her

interview, but her mind had been on Mark. "Mr. Ferguson tried to buy my bakery."

He nodded. "I'm not surprised. When I talked to the other store owners on your street, they said the same thing." He frowned. "Did he threaten you?"

The question stirred up ugly memories she'd rather forget. "My neighbors and I got a peace bond against him. He wasn't allowed to come within one hundred feet of our stores."

His expression hadn't changed. Britt felt sure Mark picked up on what she didn't say, but didn't push it. "Seriously? That's some accomplishment." He got the car started. "Where to?"

She gave him the address, then eased back into her seat, watching the city lights pass by in their multitude of colors. Tonight had been the first night in a long time that she'd gone on a date, but it felt different with Mark. They had immediately clicked, like two pieces of a puzzle that fit, and she bit the inside of her cheek, pondering that thought.

The drive was short, surrounded by a comfortable silence until he reached her condo. "I had a really good time tonight," he told her as they walked to the front door.

"So did I. Are you up for doing it again?"

"Definitely." His voice had grown deeper. "Just say the word."

Britt suddenly remembered. "I need to know something. In your text, you called me *vakker*. Do you know what that means?"

"Yes." He stepped close, and she could smell the cologne she hadn't noticed at all until now. "And it's so goddamn true."

His eyes reflected her own emotions—how a chance

meeting evolved into the possibility of something they'd both been looking for.

He caressed her chin with a finger, and on a sigh, Britt touched her lips to his, tasting their texture and warmth.

Mark muttered under his breath, and she gasped as his arms wrapped around her. He tasted of hopes and promises, of a future that didn't feel so lonely anymore.

Chapter 4

Mark parked the car in front of Mackenzie Richmond Hill Hospital the next morning, knowing his mom was expecting him. He loved spending time with her, just not under these circumstances.

On the eighth floor, he turned left, then right, walking down a long hallway. He heard two voices laughing before reaching the nurses station.

"Mark!" Evelyn was a slim and fit woman in her forties. She'd been a nurse for close to twenty years. "How are you? How's your weekend been so far?"

He shrugged. "I'm on weekend shift and I have a case."

"Well, damn." She propped her hands on her hips. "I hope you get that solved soon. Come on, your mom just finished breakfast."

Evelyn sang a tune under her breath as she led the way, her voice enriched with a Barbados accent. Mark had immediately connected with her when they first met, and he was glad Evelyn had made herself the primary caregiver for his mother.

She swung open the door. "Ms. Hawthorne, I have a visitor for you."

Mom turned away from the television tuned to a talk show. "Mark! Sweetie, I'm so glad to see you."

"That makes two of us." He thanked Evelyn and grabbed

a chair to sit beside his mother's bed. "How are you doing today?"

"A lot better. The doctor said I could go home in about a week."

Mark grasped her hand and squeezed it. "That's great. You've always been a strong woman. It's one of the things I admire about you."

She smiled. "I've got you to thank for that. I had to keep you out of trouble."

He laughed. "You know I wouldn't risk my ass by hanging out with the wrong crowd. I was more scared of you."

"Got that right." She smoothed her hand over the bedsheet. "I'm glad you came by," she said quietly. "I'd love to see you more often, but I know you have your own life to live. And the detective work must keep you on your toes."

"It does, actually." He sighed.

"Are you working on a case?"

Mom was a puzzle-solver. She loved mysteries and putting the pieces together. Occasionally, he'd tell her about one of his investigations—leaving out names and certain information—and she would give him ideas that he never would have thought of. Some of her suggestions had panned out in the five years he'd worked at the precinct. "A man got beaten up pretty badly on a construction site this past Friday."

"Edward Ferguson? It was on the news." She made a face. "Asshole."

"Mom?" He sat back, surprised. "Do you know him?"

"I know of him. Owns Mighty Big Bakery. Odd name for a business." She snickered. "Maybe it's big to compensate for his small…ahem. You know what I mean."

Mark sat in shock for all of two seconds before he lost

it in a fit of laughter. "Did you just say that?" he asked between gasps.

She shrugged. "It's an ego thing, isn't it? He's a bully, too, from what I've heard."

"A lot of people are saying that." It seemed to be the CEO's reputation.

"Do you remember that little pastry shop we used to go to on Sundays?" Mom asked. "The French one where you liked the owner's daughter, but she ran away every time she saw you?"

He shook his head. Mom remembered the weirdest things. "They made the best chocolate croissants."

"That store was in the family for generations. Suzie, the girl you liked? She took over and ran it for several years."

He frowned, suspecting where this was leading. "Mr. Ferguson bought her out?"

"Mr. Ferguson threatened her—I was there when he showed up." She shuddered. "It was awful. I found out from Suzie he had bought the two properties next door to her and wanted her building, too. She told him where to stick it, and in French, too.

"Next thing I knew, I heard on the news that her store had been broken into several times that month. They trashed her equipment, broke things, spray-painted awful words…" Mom stopped to compose herself. "Suzie had no choice but to sell. She and I always suspected Mr. Ferguson had set up the vandalism, but we couldn't prove it."

Mark nodded. He wouldn't put it past Ferguson to do something like that. "I hope Suzie got a lot of money out of it."

"She definitely did. Enough to decide to move back to France and take her parents with her. They're living in a lovely village called Amiens."

Mom also had a knack for getting along with people. *When you're nice to them, they're nice to you* was her motto, and it worked every single time. "I'm glad to hear she's well," he stated. He squeezed her hand again. "Speaking of chocolate croissants, do you want me to sneak one in for you?"

Her brown eyes widened in surprise. "Have you found a bakery that would pass even my scrutiny?"

"I have. An amazing little place called Konditori. It's a Norwegian bakery. Best Danish and coffee I've ever had."

"That's amazing. Will you bring me something tomorrow?" Mom paused. "Only if you have the time."

"I'll make it work, don't worry."

"Wonderful!" She clapped her hands. "Let's hope that Ferguson man never discovers this bakery."

It was too late for that, but Mark didn't want to spoil the visit by telling her.

He chatted with Mom for about another hour and let himself be smothered with her hugs and kisses before heading out. At the nurses station, he waited until Evelyn finished her phone call. "Has Mom had visitors?" he asked.

She shook her head. "The nurses know to call me as soon as someone asks about your mom. Your father's photo is front and center on the bulletin board over there." She pointed at a large corkboard, and he sucked in a breath, staring at Dad's scowling expression. "Everyone knows they're supposed to call Security. One of my nurses knows self-defense. I've seen her in action at one of her competitions and I would not want to meet her in a well-lit alley. I also suspect a couple of the ladies have something in their bags, but…" She stopped.

"Let's just hope it doesn't come to that. Thank you for looking after her."

As he drove home, he thought about how his mom had ended up in the hospital—a freak accident, she said. She'd fallen down the stairs at home, broken her right leg and fractured her hip. She had managed to drag herself to the phone and call him, and he had summoned every emergency vehicle as he raced to her house, praying she hadn't passed out because she wasn't answering his frantic shouts. When he'd arrived, the police and ambulance were already there, her front door busted open, and Mom carefully strapped to the stretcher.

"She'll be okay," an ambulance attendant had told him while he fought back his tears and silently prayed for her to open her eyes. "She's unconscious but breathing normally. We're headed to Mackenzie Richmond Hill Hospital and immediately into surgery."

He had nodded, too stunned to speak. As everyone started to pack up and leave, Mark had a disturbing thought. "You two," he called out to the remaining officers on the scene. "I want to run a standard check through the house, make sure everything's as it should be."

They had stood guard at the front door while Mark looked around for…something. Mom wasn't the kind of person to just fall down the stairs—she was usually so sure-footed. While nothing seemed out of place, he'd called the best forensics investigator to beg for her help.

Cynthia Cornwall had been there in record time, and less than two hours later had the fingerprints in her lab. What she'd told him was disturbing.

His father had been in Mom's house, and more than once, if the amount of fingerprints Cynthia had found was correct—and she was almost never wrong. But was he there because Mom had invited him? Or had he decided to ignore the restraining order and sneak in when she wasn't around?

Mark had a lot of questions. But so far, his father hadn't been found, and his subtle inquiries with Mom resulted in her adamant replies that she'd had an accident, end of story.

"Well, *chérie*, your new, esteemed customer was more than thrilled to see us today, I think."

Britt nodded, her excitement so strong she almost squealed with glee. She had been starstruck when they arrived at the rap artist's mansion in the Bridle Path. "Can you believe he saw the lineup at the bakery one morning and sent his housekeeper to investigate?" She laughed at the image in her head—a middle-aged woman snooping around the store, asking customers questions and sitting in a corner, taking in everything. She could have worn a trench coat and fedora, and Britt wouldn't have noticed. "I guess he gave us a thumbs-up."

"But of course he did!" Jacques drove the company van around the block to get to their parking spot behind the store. "Why would you think otherwise?"

He was right, of course. Britt had a bad habit of not giving herself credit. In fact, she was her own worst critic. "Thanks for coming with me to help set up."

"*Avec plaisir*, with pleasure. Sometimes, it is good to get out of the kitchen."

He parked the van, and Britt stepped out, her mind on what to grab out of the back.

"I'll take care of the bags, Britt. Go inside and see how everyone is doing."

"Thanks, Jacques." He knew her mind was constantly on the bakery—that was one of the many things she had learned on her journey to becoming an entrepreneur. Her business absorbed almost all her waking moments, and she was constantly planning ways to stay one step ahead of her competitors. Moments of pure luck, such as attracting the rap singer's attention, helped, but it was increasing her steady stream of regulars that brought the money in, paid her staff well and kept her reputation in good standing.

She entered the store through the back and made her way to her small office located opposite the display counter and cash register. As she walked through the kitchen door, Britt was surprised at how many customers were inside. Jasmine and Oliver seemed to be keeping things moving, but she'd get out there and help as soon as she checked a few things.

Their website had been busy, too—orders were coming in for the next few weeks. Summer was their busiest time, but Britt refused to extend the store hours. She couldn't afford another full-time person yet, and Jacques and Thomas could only do so much, even with Betty's help. She had to think of their well-being, and not allow her staff to overextend themselves.

Right, better get out there.

She was greeted by enthusiastic people who sang praises about her bakery, the food and her staff. She grew embarrassed from all the attention and soon hid behind the counter, helping with orders and ringing up sales. At one point, she headed back to the kitchen, where Jacques was moving almost too fast for the eye to follow. Thomas was at the sink, chugging back a large glass of water. "How's everything back here, Jacques?"

He turned and gave her the okay signal with thumb and forefinger. "Thomas did a fantastic job with the prepping. We'll have more pastries in thirty minutes."

"Thank you." She smiled at Thomas, who had hurried back to his station. "Both of you."

She couldn't be happier with her little team, and especially Jacques—she'd really lucked out when she hired him.

The head baker brought out a tray of cinnamon rolls while Thomas carried one filled with Danishes, and a cheer went up from the crowd. She stayed out of the way as the chefs slid the desserts into the display case with ease before hustling back to the kitchen.

That was when she spied Mark standing by the window. He had a small paper bag with handles in one hand and a large takeout cup of coffee in the other, which he saluted her with. Smiling, she wove her way through a sea of people until she got to his side and wasn't ready when he suddenly kissed her full on the lips. She raised her hand to her mouth, surprised.

"It's more fun than just saying hi." His mouth curled up in a shy smile.

Damn it, how could Mark be so…well, damn cute?

He looked around the store in awe. "Do you play linebacker every time this happens?" he asked.

Britt leaned against the wall beside him. It had only been a couple of hours since arriving at the store this morning. She knew it would be busy, but this… "Pretty much. Usually it's more organized than this. I suspect we had more new customers today walking in off the street. My regulars aren't this rowdy."

"All of you handle it like professionals." He moved close enough that Britt felt the warmth from his body. He was a dangerous distraction, and if she wasn't careful, Britt could easily fall under his spell.

That was a sobering thought.

She tilted her chin at the bag. "Did you get what you wanted?"

Mark nodded. "I waited until there was a bit of a lull, then dived in. My mom wants to try your chocolate croissants."

"Oh, I hope she likes them."

"I would have brought her, but…" His expression clouded over. "She's in the hospital."

"Damn, Mark, I'm sorry. Is she okay?"

"Her doctor said another week to ten days. She's getting better, though, thank you for asking."

"Of course." Britt knew the importance of family. Her parents and younger sister still lived in Norway, and she missed them. "Did you want any other pastries? I can get something else for her to try. A cinnamon bun, maybe?"

"I'm good." He shook his bag. "But thank you." He sipped his coffee, but Britt noticed his eyebrows drawn into a frown as he looked across the tide of customers. "Oh, I wanted to tell you." He leaned in close. "I heard some customers chatting among themselves. It seems that there's some kind of event on social media to boycott Mighty Big Bakery."

She frowned. One thing Britt kept abreast of was news on the competition. Britt had nothing against another bakery opening nearby. No two stores were exactly the same, and in her studies, she found that customers in smaller neighborhoods loved the variety. But as for Mr. Ferguson's behemoth of a bakery… "I hadn't heard about that."

"I get the feeling people are upset that a Mighty Big Bakery is opening almost across the street from you, and someone did take their anger out on Mr. Ferguson, so…" He shrugged.

"Seems almost inevitable, don't you think?" Britt didn't

condone violence of any kind, but she did believe in karma. "He must have known that his…less-than-desirable business tactics would get him into trouble."

"Justifying the assault doesn't make it right, though."

Britt decided to tell Mark the story behind her peace bond. "When I decided to lease this property, there were no other bakeries in the area. It was a prime spot—lots of foot traffic, nearby neighborhoods, other stores. Mr. Ferguson's construction site was originally a fruit and vegetable store, a butcher shop, and a clothing store that also sold flowers." Her hands clenched in frustration. "Those stores had been here for close to forty years, and Ferguson bullied them into selling out."

"How did he do that?"

Britt closed her eyes. That incident had been nine months ago, but it felt like only yesterday. "I had arrived earlier than usual one day to get started on an order. Jacques was already waiting at the front door. He said he saw three teenagers come out of the butcher shop carrying baseball bats. The grocery store had already been vandalized the week before, but no one saw anything. He managed to get pictures of the kids and turned them in to the police."

He nodded slowly. "I think I remember that. It caught our attention because the boys confessed some rich man had paid them a lot of money to wreck those stores."

"It didn't matter, did it?" Britt felt the anger bloom within her body. "Those teenagers were only issued a fine and released to their parents. As for Mr. Ferguson, the police couldn't track the payment back to him.

"In the end, he got what he wanted. He paid the owners of those stores enough money for them to retire comfortably." Britt blew out a loud sigh. "A lot of the neighbors, including myself, hoped the owners wouldn't sell, but in the end, I couldn't blame them. They were older and their kids weren't interested in taking over. It just feels…" She stopped, thinking of her own situation.

"Like they gave up?"

She looked at Mark, his gaze observant. "It sounds harsh, doesn't it?"

"In the end, it was their choice."

She bit her lip. Mark's conclusion made sense, of course. Every businessperson that came into contact with Mr. Ferguson made their choices, whether they were bullied or not. She'd made hers. "I should tell you that he came after me, too."

Something changed in Mark's demeanor. Britt saw the tensed jawline and the frown that made her step back in concern. The air around her cooled considerably. "What?" he exclaimed.

"I couldn't prove it was Ferguson. I had to use the back door that morning, and I saw it had been forced open and the security camera smashed." That memory was still fresh in her mind. "I hid behind a dumpster and called the police and kept my phone out in case I got lucky enough to take pictures. The cops didn't find anyone, and some stuff got broken, but nothing else. I was lucky."

She blew out a breath. "The next morning, there was graffiti scrawled all over my storefront with the letters *MBB*. I couldn't prove anything. All I could do was repaint." Britt smiled. "The pink basically screams *screw you* at him."

"Hey." Mark stroked a finger across her cheek. "In the end, you did what you felt was right. Not everyone has a steel backbone like my Nordic princess."

Man, he had a way with words, but he made her feel special each and every time. "*Takk.* Thank you."

"Listen, I have to run, but maybe we can talk later?"

"I sure hope so." This time, Britt initiated the kiss, and muffled a squeal of indignation when he pinched her backside. "I'll get you for that," she seethed between clenched teeth.

His expression gave her goose bumps. "I sure hope so," he said, his voice deep. He brushed past her, so close that their bodies touched from chest to thigh, and was out the door before she managed to collect her wits.

Oh yes, he was a very dangerous distraction.

Mark's second visit with his mom was short, because he had to make more progress on his case before his meeting with Captain Fraust tomorrow.

"I see work is more important than your own mother," she sniffed.

His body tensed in annoyance. "That's not fair," he growled. "I was here this morning, and I'm visiting you again because I wanted to bring a chocolate croissant for you. But my work shouldn't come as a surprise anymore."

Mom arched a brow. "And you should know better. Did you really think I was serious?"

Mark backed off, surprised and confused.

"Hmph, you did. Shame on you. I know you have an important job."

He blew out a frustrated breath. "Sorry, that wasn't like me."

"You're right. You sounded like your father."

Mark held his breath as his stomach twisted into a painful knot. He'd promised himself and his mother that he'd never be like that man. To hear her say those words… "That hurts, Mom."

"I'm sorry, baby. But you did ask me to tell you if or when you acted like your dad."

Mark had worked so hard to burn his father's abusive tendencies out of his life. When he was growing up, it had never occurred to Mark that he'd been doing anything wrong. *Angry friends are weak friends*, Dad used to say.

High school had been his turning point. No one was afraid to tell him he acted like a jerk. Mom had never said anything, until he told her that he needed to change—and then she'd become almost a different person. Her encouragement and support helped him become a better version of himself.

"I'm sorry, too, Mom. I don't know why…" He stopped, racking his brain to figure out what caused his relapse.

"I think you're more stressed than you realize. How is your case progressing?"

"Slowly. I need to talk to a couple of witnesses today."

She looked at him, her brows raised. "What are your plans for the rest of the day? I hope you're going to relax. All this work…" She paused.

Mark wasn't going to tell her about his surprise visit to Mr. Ferguson then, that was for sure. Instead, he said, "I had a dinner date last night."

"What?" Her excitement filled the room. "Why didn't you start your conversation with this? Now I know why your visits are short. Another woman's taking my baby's attention away from me."

"Mom," he warned, but her mischievous smile stopped him. "My God, you're doing it again."

"You're going to have to get used to it. If not me, then someone else."

"I know." Mark remembered Timmins's jokes about

Jenny the construction worker, but he hadn't been upset, more annoyed.

"May I ask a question?"

He looked at her serious expression. What was wrong now? "Go for it."

"I'm just curious. Do you act so stoic at work?"

What was Mom getting at? "I don't believe so."

"No one teases you on the job?"

He nodded. "They do, but I try not to react to it. I guess I'm worried about…" He didn't look at her, suddenly realizing that his deliberate act of being unaware only masked the real problem. He shuddered. "I don't think I'm handling this the right way." He looked at her, hoping she'd see his concern. "Do you have any suggestions?"

She nodded, as if realizing something. "Maybe you should ease up a bit."

"With my case? Mom, that's not going to happen."

"That's not what I meant. I mean lighten up. Have fun but be humble, too. You say you want to be better than your dad, so I'm challenging you to open up a little. Who knows, maybe your date will be the one to stick that Cupid's arrow into your heart."

Ah, if you only knew. He smiled. "I didn't know you were a romantic."

"Always have been." She rubbed her leg, now out of its cast and secured with a metal brace. "Always will be."

Mark watched her expression, but she gave nothing away. He really hoped she wasn't talking about Dad. "I have to go. Enjoy your treats."

"Oh, I plan to. Thank you for bringing some for me." She patted the paper bag that sat beside her. "I'm going to have one now and save the others for tomorrow. I'll see you soon?"

"You bet." He smooched her cheek several times, gave her a tight hug and headed out.

Evelyn was at the nurses station and looked up when he approached. "Everything good?"

"Yeah, thanks. Mom's in a good mood." He hesitated, worried that Dad might have tried to see her.

"He hasn't been here. Don't worry, I've got it covered." She gave him an impish smile. "Christie's taught us some basic self-defense moves."

He grinned—when Evelyn said she'd be ready for anything, she wasn't joking. "You're something else."

"I do my best." She reached into a drawer, and her hand came back into view with an envelope. "This came for your mom."

He pursed his lips and took it from her. The envelope was empty. "What was in it?"

"A letter. Your dad's name wasn't on it, but then after I gave it to her, I wondered… Well, I thought, what if he faked his name, but your mom recognized the handwriting as his?"

Mark looked for that now, turning the envelope over in his hands. This wasn't Dad's writing. "Nothing to worry about," he said, tucking it into his jacket pocket. "But I'll have it scanned for fingerprints."

"What would you like me to do if another envelope comes in for her?"

He sighed. He had no right to hold back Mom's correspondence, but if there was a slight chance it *was* Dad… "Keep it in a plastic bag so it doesn't get touched by too many hands, then give me a call or send a text. I'll let you know."

Chapter 5

Edward Ferguson lived on High Point Road within the Bridle Path, a very ritzy and expensive neighborhood located in the north end of Toronto. Mansions were surrounded by wide lawns and high decorative concrete walls, and all were barred with thick metal security gates.

Mark turned right at the third driveway and stopped his car before a set of barred gates and beside an intercom embedded within a stone pillar. He opened the window and reached out to press a button. It took just over a minute before he heard an audible click, and then a woman's voice. "Yes? Who is it?"

"This is Detective Mark Hawthorne from York Regional Police 4 District," he announced. "I'm the lead investigator on Mr. Ferguson's case. I'd like to talk to him."

A short pause. "He's currently working in his home office. May I ask if you have an appointment with him?"

An appointment? On a Sunday? "No, I do not."

Another pause, and Mark wondered if the woman was discussing the situation with the CEO in the background. He drummed his fingers on the windowsill, refusing to let his impatience get the best of him.

"May I see your badge, Detective?"

"Of course." He dug it out of his pocket and held it up in front of the intercom.

"Thank you. I'd like to verify your identity. It'll take a few minutes."

"I'm not going anywhere."

Mark didn't understand why Ferguson didn't just let him in. It was obvious the intercom had a camera—the CEO could have looked out and told the woman it was okay to let him inside.

Oh well, it wasn't worth burning through brain cells to try and figure out what Ferguson was thinking.

A cool breeze scented with flowers wafted into his car, and Mark took a deep breath. He closed his eyes and listened to the sounds surrounding him—birdsong, the rustle of leaves, the buzzing noise of a lawnmower in the distance. Sometimes, he'd forget that a few minutes of quiet solitude was enough to ease his jostling thoughts. Work would always be there, but he also had to balance it with self-care. He felt his body relax, and he inhaled again, letting his breath out in a slow exhale.

The intercom clicked. "Thank you for waiting, Detective Hawthorne. Please come in."

The thick iron gates swung open, and Mark slowly drove along a curved driveway toward the front of the house. He parked the car and got out, letting his gaze scan over the manicured landscape. A large fountain with a Cupid statue at its center gurgled with water as it flowed from a stone pitcher into the basin. Hedges and tall trees planted in front of the surrounding walls bordering the property offered natural privacy and dampened any sounds from the main street. He imagined himself sitting out here reading a good book.

Mark approached the pair of huge dark-stained doors

and pressed the doorbell, curious as to why no one was already here to greet him. He stuck his hands in his pockets and casually strolled the length of the porch, spying the four security cameras—one over the front entrance and three others over the stretch of windows on the ground floor. He wouldn't be surprised if more surrounded the house. There was also another intercom embedded in the brickwork beside the door.

He blew out a frustrated breath, wondering if the CEO was deliberately making him wait. Mark would bet his next cup of coffee that Ferguson was looking at him even now through the security camera.

Annoyance bubbled through him, but Mark wasn't going to let it boil over. Instead, he stepped off the porch and walked across the impeccable lawn, stopping occasionally to smell the beds of flowers surrounding it. The lavender bushes that bordered the property were tall and lush with flowers, and he pinched several to release their heady fragrance.

Mark didn't experience a lot of moments like these—he was either buried in work, playing hard sports with friends or at home, trying to restore his energy after dealing with cases that tore at his emotions. He had few minutes to slow down, and he enjoyed these precious scenarios whenever he could.

His thoughts drifted to the woman who had entered his life, the stunning Nordic princess who had completely ensnared him with her voice, her looks, her eyes. Those eyes—such a bright, clear, sparkling green. He could stare into Britt's eyes all day and not notice the time going by. How could Mark ignore such beauty? He knew he was damn lucky that his reaction to her seemed to be mutual.

"Detective Hawthorne," a voice called out.

He turned around. A woman dressed in a housekeeper's uniform stood at the doorway, her hands clinging together. "I'm sorry for the wait."

He nodded, and walked across the lawn again towards her, noticing her anxious expression as she glanced down at his feet. Mark had deduced that Ferguson wouldn't like anyone touching his stuff unless they had permission. Stepping on his near-perfect lawn and manhandling his shrubbery would bother the CEO a lot. As soon as he placed a foot over Ferguson's imaginary boundary, Mark knew the man would get angry and put a stop to it.

The CEO should have just let him in, instead of testing Mark's patience.

As he climbed the stairs, the housekeeper, who looked to be in her late thirties, smiled. "I apologize. Ever since those robberies last year, Mr. Ferguson has insisted on extra precautions."

"Of course. I understand." Timmins and Solberg had worked on that case until they caught a woman impersonating a courier. For some reason, women often weren't suspected as criminals until it was too late. "Better to play it safe."

When he stepped inside, Mark let out a low whistle of appreciation. The foyer, covered in black and white tile, was almost the size of his condo. Marble statues were displayed in four niches, two on each side of the wide space. The walls were a pastel green, making the area feel bigger than it looked. A grand staircase led to the second-floor landing.

"If you'll come this way." The housekeeper turned right and opened a door that led into a large study. Books graced two walls, while a heavy mahogany desk dominated the room. A wide bank of windows looked out onto the front landscape.

She pointed to a pair of leather chairs in front of the desk. "Please have a seat. Mr. Ferguson is just finishing up his business. He should be here in a few minutes."

More waiting, but there was no use in getting mad about it. Mark sat in the plush high-back chair and crossed his legs.

The housekeeper seemed so nervous that Mark was worried she'd faint. "Would you like anything? Coffee, tea, snacks?"

He almost said no, then changed his mind. If Ferguson was going to make him cool his heels, he might as well enjoy it. "Yes, thank you."

Mark had finished his first cup of coffee and had popped a mini quiche into his mouth when he heard Mr. Ferguson's voice. Moments later, the bakery CEO strode in. "Sorry about that," he apologized. "If you'd let me know you were coming in advance, I would have made sure I had cleared my calendar."

"This is an impromptu visit." Mark stood and shook hands. "Everything good?"

The CEO looked surprised at the question. "Yes, yes, of course."

Mark watched as Mr. Ferguson settled in, grabbed a cup of coffee and a snack for himself, then sat down behind his desk. "So, Officer, how can I help out today? I would have thought you'd have Sundays off."

Mark hid his expression behind the coffee cup until he was sure he could keep a neutral face. "The law doesn't sleep, Mr. Ferguson, and my colleagues do rotations so that each of us can have a decent weekend off. It's called teamwork."

Mr. Ferguson pursed his lips but didn't reply.

"How are you feeling, by the way?"

"I saw the doctor yesterday and he gave me the all clear." He leaned back in his chair. "Thankfully, no concussion, broken bones or internal bleeding. Just a lot of bruises that'll take some time to go away. The swelling in my lip is already gone." He unbuttoned his shirt cuff and rolled up the sleeve to expose a large piece of gauze. "I don't remember it happening, but I got cut by something sharp. I had to get stitches." He rolled the sleeve back down and shot Mark a sharp look. "Any news on the scumbag who attacked me?"

"I have a couple of promising leads I'm looking into." He brought out his work phone, hit Record and placed it on the desk between them. "I wanted to ask some additional questions."

"Sure, that's why you're here."

Mark put his cup back on the serving tray and mirrored Ferguson's reclining posture. He wanted to observe the man's reactions without being distracted. "How long have you owned the Mighty Big Bakery?"

"Let's see." The CEO tilted his head back. "About thirty-five years. Well, I've been owner and CEO since that time. My father started it back in the 1950s."

"Was it called MBB back then?"

"No." He shook his head for extra emphasis. "Just Ferguson's. The original neighborhood loved the store—it offered a bit of everything."

Mark noticed the nostalgic expression on the CEO's face. "Why the name change?"

"The chain needed something more distinct, more powerful. I had plans for what I wanted to do—grow the business until everyone heard about it, bake the best of everything, beat out the competition."

"I've heard you had some problems considering that last statement." Mark decided to jump on that first, since he had an opening. "It seems that there are some people who aren't thrilled with your way of doing things."

Mr. Ferguson snorted. "What do you want me to do, huh? I'm running a business. My goal is to have a Mighty Big Bakery in every city and town of Ontario." He shrugged. "After that, I'll move on to bigger things. That's how business works, son."

"I get it, but you're steamrolling over small businesses using tactics that aren't, shall we say, ethical."

The CEO stared at him. "Are you pulling the bleeding-heart sob story on me?" He laughed. "Give me a break."

Mark linked his fingers together and rested them on his lap because he didn't want Ferguson to see the clenched fists he really wanted to show. This man sounded a little too much like his father. "Just saying what I've heard from others."

Mr. Ferguson sat up in his chair and leaned across the desk. "I offered the best deals when I bought out those businesses. If the owners turned it down, that was their choice."

"It wasn't their choice to be bullied when they stood up to you."

He sat back and blinked. "I don't know anything about that."

"Oh, I think you do, but you're too smart a man to admit to it." Damn it, Mark had to stop mouthing off before he got in trouble with the captain.

Mr. Ferguson frowned. "Are you accusing me of something, young man?"

"No, sir." Mark stood, knowing he wouldn't get any kind of confession out of the guy. He grabbed his phone from the desk and stuck it in his pocket. "Thanks for seeing me today."

"Of course." Mr. Ferguson followed him to the front door. "I'll help in any way I can. Maybe I'll put in a call to Captain Fraust, let her know how cooperative and efficient you've been."

Mark hoped the surprise didn't show on his face. "Thank you. Enjoy the rest of your Sunday."

Outside, Mark gulped mouthfuls of fresh air as he walked slowly to his car. His plan to catch the CEO off guard hadn't worked. If Ferguson was hiding something, he was doing a damn good job of it. Also, the man's discreet threat that he knew the captain threw Mark for a loop—he hadn't expected that. He knew he needed to finish up any leftover work on his case today before updating Captain Fraust tomorrow morning with his findings.

Mark hoped the second item on his list—bringing in the suspect with the different-sized feet—would go off without a hitch and make up for his lack of progress with Ferguson.

When Mark and Timmins pulled their car into Henry Toussaint's driveway, the older detective hooked a thumb towards his window. "I just noticed the curtains moving."

"Good, that means someone's home." Mark hopped out of the car and strode toward the front door. Similar to Ferguson's house, there was a security camera above the entrance.

Mark pressed the doorbell then stepped back, giving the homeowner a clear view of him. "Mr. Toussaint, I'm

Detective Mark Hawthorne with York Regional Police 4 District. We'd like to talk to you."

He heard a steady clicking as someone approached the front door. As it opened, a security chain blocked any entry, only allowing about three inches of free space to speak through. On the other side, a silver-haired woman almost as tall as him looked defiant. "What do you want?" she demanded.

It wasn't a greeting Mark expected, and it instantly put him on alert. "Good afternoon." He pulled out his badge, and Timmins did the same. "I wanted to ask if Henry Toussaint was at home?"

"I don't know where Henry is right now." It didn't seem like she was going to be cooperative.

"Does he have a day job?" Mark kept his voice pleasant-sounding. He hated going into situations like this when people immediately got their hackles up and became combative.

"What has he done?"

"We'd like to ask him some questions about an assault last Friday evening."

"He doesn't work." Her frustrated expression gave Mark a clue that she wasn't happy about Henry's lack of employment.

Mark pulled out a notepad and a pen. "And you have no idea where he might be today?"

"Henry's an adult. He does whatever the hell he wants. I'm not his secretary."

"I understand. We'll come back later on today to see if he's returned."

The woman frowned. "You can't come into my home unless you have a search warrant."

Interesting—was she hiding something? "We only want

to talk to Henry—I don't need a search warrant for that."
Mark glanced at Timmins, who gave a slight nod—time
to take it up a notch. "However, I can get one within a
couple of hours. The next time I'm here, I'm allowed to
come in, and you won't be able to say anything about it."

The woman looked surprised at that, but she didn't
back down. "Fine," she sniffed. "Bring your search warrant. You won't find Henry here, and he's done nothing
wrong."

"Fair enough. Have a good day." He turned on his heel
and walked casually back to the car, but inside, he trembled with adrenaline. He felt certain Henry Toussaint lay
hidden within the house.

He and Timmins would wait him out.

They drove onto Cunningham Drive, made a U-turn
and parked one block from the entrance to Sierra Court.
"I'm sure he's hiding in the house," Timmins stated.

Mark nodded. He didn't think Henry Toussaint would
be hiding unless he had done something. "I have no idea
how desperate this guy is," he murmured.

"We should call for backup just in case."

"Good idea." He listened as Timmins made the request,
telling the dispatcher to inform the officers to stay at a
distance so that the suspect couldn't see them until it was
too late.

Unfortunately, the waiting game gave Mark too much
time to think. Everyone he had talked to, including Britt,
suspected the Mighty Big Bakery CEO of illegal activities that should have gotten him arrested. The fact that
Ferguson still bullied victims to this day meant he'd never
been caught or received more than a slap on the wrist.
Was someone protecting his interests? Or did he just have

a team of shrewd lawyers that got the CEO out of any tainted situation he found himself in?

Mark wouldn't be surprised at all. The man was like an eel, slipping out of any dirty kind of muck that surrounded him. If he could find any kind of evidence that would stick...

The police radio crackled. "Detective Hawthorne, we're in position."

Mark glanced over his shoulder. A squad car was parked about half a block behind him.

"And not a moment too soon. There's someone coming," Timmins said.

Mark stared at a man who came to a halt on the sidewalk across the street. He was tall, taller than him, and very fit. He wore a red-and-white soccer jersey with Toronto's team logo emblazoned on the front, black track pants, and smart-looking red, white and black hi-top sneakers. He stood at the corner of Sierra Court and Cunningham Drive and looked around. His gaze lingered on the police car a bit longer than necessary, making Mark twitch with excitement.

After a few minutes, the man turned and walked in the opposite direction.

"I'll follow him." Mark was halfway out the car.

Timmins scooted into the driver's seat. "Don't do anything heroic."

Mark jogged across the street and walked at a fast pace until he was about half a block behind the man. There were few cars and fewer pedestrians at this time of day, so he knew if the guy kept an eye on him, Mark would lose the chance to take him by surprise.

They walked for a few minutes, Mark matching his pace to the man's. Suddenly, the guy made a left-hand turn into a field of tall grass. His pace had quickened.

"Damn it." Mark managed to keep the same distance between them. He didn't dare glance over his shoulder to see where Timmins was, but he was certain his partner was close. He spied the wide half-hidden path and got on it, spotting his target in the distance. Timmins and the others would have to follow him on foot.

He was sure this was Henry Toussaint.

Mark's cell phone rang, and he answered it.

"Where the hell is this guy going?" Timmins demanded.

"Don't know. Just the fact that he came this way where I can barely see him is already suspicious. There's a large pond to the right behind all this grass, and up ahead is a huge park."

"He's going to try and lose us at one of those spots." Timmins swore over the phone. "I'll follow you, but I'm sending the officers parallel to the pond, see if they can get ahead and cut him off."

Mark craned his head. The guy managed to get farther away—shit, he was fast. "Tell them to move like Olympic sprinters or we'll lose him."

There were more people here—mothers with children, joggers, seniors out for a stroll. Mark remembered the children's play areas. He wanted to take the guy down before they got too close to people. If the suspect became desperate…

He caught a flash of white to his right—the officers had just passed him, moving quickly through the foliage. Mark hurried as well, his quickened steps turning into a sprint as he heard one of the officers shout out a command to stop.

When he came around a curve in the path, both officers had the man restrained. "What the hell is going on?"

the suspect shouted. He didn't fight back and allowed the handcuffs to be snapped around his wrists. "Hey, I asked you a question!"

"Detective Mark Hawthorne with York Regional Police 4 District." He showed his badge. "What's your name?"

"I don't have to tell you shit!"

"Pat him down." Mark waited as the officers quickly checked the man over. Timmins had caught up, and was directing traffic, telling people to move on. A couple stood several feet away, recording the arrest on their phone—great, just what he didn't need.

"Here's his wallet, sir." One of the officers tossed it to him.

Mark caught it in one hand and opened it. Sure enough, it was their man—Henry Toussaint. Mark advised the man of his rights. "I need you to come with us to the precinct to answer some questions."

"And if I refuse?"

He had every right to do so and request a lawyer. Mark shrugged. "I'll talk to you one way or another. But it might seem like you saying no means you have something to hide."

"You've got nothing on me," Toussaint sneered. "I'll go with you, just to prove you're wrong."

Mark loved nothing more than a challenge. "Okay then. Prepare to be mistaken."

Mark, Toussaint and an officer waited while Timmins and the second officer brought their vehicles. The suspect was seated in the back of the squad car while Mark hopped in beside Timmins. Despite driving as fast as possible back to the precinct, Mark was impatient. "I can't wait to hear what this asshole has to say for himself."

"I get it, but don't get too cocky, either," Timmins

warned. "The suspect could pull a fast one on you and you'd have no way to dig yourself out of that hole."

"I know, I know." At a stoplight, Mark cracked his knuckles. "Did you see his feet? One is definitely bigger than the other."

"And if his fingerprints match those found at the crime scene, we've got him."

At the precinct, Toussaint was taken down to interrogation. Mark had called Myrna along the way, and she was waiting for him in front of his office. "Here's his wallet," he told her, providing the evidence nestled within a plastic baggie. "See if you can lift a viable fingerprint from any of his cards in there. Pray that we get a match to those at the crime scene."

"Gotcha." She ran off.

When Mark arrived downstairs, Constable Turnbull was sitting in the recording room. "Sir, all set when you are."

He nodded and watched as Toussaint was seated at the metal table, his wrists unbound. He decided not to hand-cuff the suspect to the table, on the very slim chance he wasn't their guy. If he was, however, Timmins would be in the room with Mark, and the two officers who had arrested him would be standing just outside the door.

He remembered Timmins's warning as he walked in and sat down. "Mr. Toussaint, I'm Detective Mark Hawthorne. Detective Walter Timmins is here as well to listen to your statement. As I said, I have a few questions for you."

"What's this about?" Toussaint wasn't quite belligerent, but his slouched stance in the chair said otherwise.

It did give Mark a chance to study the man's feet. "Your right shoe is bigger than your left."

"Yeah. What about it?"

"Just noticing. I haven't seen that before."

Toussaint shrugged. "An anomaly among many in this world. What's that got to do with why I'm here?"

"If I'm lucky, a lot." Mark had brought his notes with him and started shuffling through pages until he found the picture with the shoe prints. "Do you remember the story about the high-priced sneakers that got recalled because its symbol on the sole of the shoe resembled a holy Arabic word?"

"Man, I got the sneakers before they got pulled." Toussaint sat up. "I put them up on a sellers' website just to see how much I could get for them. The price got up to over ten thousand dollars. No one cared they were different sizes."

"That's a nice chunk of change for a pair of kicks. How did you manage to get different sizes? Most stores wouldn't sell shoes like that."

"I got lucky." He picked up a foot and brushed his fingers against his sneaker, as if to wipe away something. "Some guy in the Middle East has the same problem as me, but the opposite feet. Worked out perfectly for us."

It worked out perfectly for Mark, too. "That's some story."

"Sure is. The ladies get a kick out of it." He grinned. "Pun intended."

Mark laughed, but not at the bad joke. "Then you'll be fascinated with what I have to show you." Mark slid the picture across. "Imagine the coincidence of finding the same shoe prints at a crime scene. Oh, and the right foot is bigger than the left. And the print matches that infamous symbol."

Mark watched Toussaint's face become slack-jawed and tried not to grin in triumph. "How about telling us why you were trespassing at a construction site, and waiting for Mr. Edward Ferguson, CEO of Mighty Big Bakery, so you could beat the crap out of him?"

Toussaint licked his lips and looked around. His eyes, wide and dark, flickered from Timmins to the door and back again. Mark sincerely hoped the young man wasn't thinking of fighting his way out. "What makes you think it was me?"

"Please." Mark tapped the photo. "Like you said, an anomaly. Plus, some old-fashioned detective work."

"Excuse me, Detective Hawthorne." Turnbull's voice came over the speaker. "Walsh is here. She says the fingerprints found in the suspect's wallet are a match for those found on the piece of wood used to beat the victim. The same fingerprints also match those found on the gas canister at the construction site."

Mark smiled. "Another coincidence. Your prints match those at the crime scene."

Toussaint wiped his hands over his face—he knew he was cornered. "Look, it's not what you're thinking," he said quietly.

Mark eased forward in the chair, his body tense with anticipation. "Then how about explaining what happened that night?"

"If I do, will I go free?"

"Maybe you should think about whether to do the right thing and tell us why you were there."

Toussaint's attitude had completely changed. He looked defeated.

"Help me understand why you would take your anger out on Mr. Ferguson. And bring a gas canister to the site. You were going to burn the building down."

"Not with people still inside!" Toussaint got up and

paced a tight path between the table and Timmins. "Look, I know it's going to sound outrageous, but here's the truth, I swear."

He came back and sat down. "You know who Mr. Ferguson is. Big-name CEO of those bakeries. He hurt a lot of people when he bought out the small businesses. A real scumbag."

Jeez, Ferguson had really made a bad reputation for himself. "I've heard the stories," Mark said.

"A friend of mine told me about someone who was holding rallies to speak out against Ferguson's tactics. The first one I went to was about two weeks ago."

"A rally? Isn't that unusual?" And why hadn't Mark heard of it? Rallies were usually logged so that they could obtain police security. Unless… "Or do you mean a protest?"

"Does it matter? It was undercover, though. My friend picked me up, and we had to follow these weird instructions to get to the place."

"So that you couldn't report them to the police when the time came," Timmins chimed in.

Toussaint nodded. "All I know is that it was near the rail yard."

Mark frowned. "How do you know that?"

"I could hear the trains stopping and starting. You know, when they make those big clanging noises."

"Sounds like train cars being hooked together."

Toussaint nodded. "Yeah, like that. We went to a small building. The inside smelled of grease and metal, but I could barely see anything. There was a guy standing on a box, dissing Ferguson and saying that we should stop him."

"How many people were there?"

Toussaint shrugged. "Maybe a dozen? I don't know.

But listening to the guy talk, he had a way of getting us riled up, to do something against Ferguson, you know?"

There was nothing more dangerous than a leader with charm and incentive. Under the right circumstances, that leader could send a frenzied mob to do whatever he asked. "Did this leader provide instructions on what to do?"

"A few. A popular one was graffiti on the Mighty Big Bakeries, but someone yelled that spray-painting the stores wasn't enough. I heard another person saying something about torching the bakeries. Then some other guy shouted that we should beat up the employees." Toussaint shook his head. "It was getting out of control, but somehow the leader managed to calm everyone down."

"Could you see his face?"

"No, man, he wore a mask that covered the bottom of his face and a baseball cap."

Mark jotted some notes down. "So you decided to burn down the new Mighty Big Bakery store that's going up nearby?"

"No, that was my friend's idea. She was more excited than I was. She said she could get me onto the construction site with no problem."

A coil of anger wove up Mark's back until it hit him square in the face. If it was her... "How did she manage to do that?" he said through gritted teeth.

Toussaint gave him a weird look. "How else? She's a construction worker. Jenny was all for taking that bakery down. Now I want to talk to my lawyer."

Chapter 6

Britt read Mark's text and wondered what the hell had happened to him.

Have you ever wondered how it would feel to just stay home all day and IGNORE EVERYONE? Cuz I wish I had done that today.

Instead of texting back, she called. "Hey, Mr. Detective."

"Hi, Britt."

Okay, that did *not* sound like him. Work must have been especially stressful today. "Is everything all right? What's going on?"

A sigh. "Too much, but I think I have a handle on it now."

She didn't think looking for Mr. Ferguson's attacker would take that much effort, but what did she know about police investigations? "Excellent. That means we can have dinner together."

He was silent on the other end, and Britt mentally smacked herself. Mark must be exhausted. "I'm sorry," she started. "I shouldn't have presumed…"

"Are you kidding? Spending time with my Nordic princess is the perfect ending to a day like this."

"Mr. Detective, flattery will get you everywhere. Where would you like to go?"

"How about you make the choice? I'll be at your place to pick you up in about half an hour?"

"It's a date."

It was going to be a warm night. Britt chose her blue maxi dress, as she loved how it flowed around her legs. A small purse and comfortable sandals finished the outfit. She thought about leaving her hair down, but hated how it got easily tangled around things, so she swept it up into her usual ponytail. A bit of lipstick, and she was ready to go.

As she waited in the lobby downstairs, Britt thought of what she'd normally be doing right now, which would have been making dinner and watching another repeat show on television. Or work. She noticed she had picked up the bad habit of checking her laptop for customer emails during her downtime. Once, she had told herself it was necessary to stay one step ahead, but now she knew it was to fill in the long evenings until the next day arrived.

She had to be honest. Work had started to take up too much of her time. Oh, Britt loved it and wouldn't give it up, but she knew there was more to life than that. She had no problem being alone, but being lonely? That sucked.

Several times, she had thought about moving back to Norway. Her family would have been thrilled, and she could return to a familiar routine with no problem. Britt wouldn't be alone, but that was not what she needed. Independence was a critical part of her existence, supported by family, friends and work. She had all of that, but she'd realized something was still missing—a person to fill the remaining void in her heart.

Britt had been so busy building a life for herself, she'd forgotten about everything else. But she'd needed to do something—anything—to get her mind off the pain and humiliation she'd suffered before creating Konditori. She had built her dream from scratch—learning, failing and learning again had been the catalyst she needed to realize that she was capable of anything, and no one could tell her different.

However, Britt also believed in the Nordic Fates, that everyone's life was woven to follow one particular destiny. Was Mark one of the threads to be woven into her life's journey? Britt didn't know yet, since they'd only met a couple of days ago. However, their instant connection was something she'd never experienced before. It had been solid, never wavered, and if the gods were smiling down on her, it would last.

A horn beeped twice, and she mentally shook herself out of the past and into an exciting present. Mark was already out of the car and holding the passenger door open for her. "How are you, *vakker*?" he asked in a deep tone before managing to sneak a kiss on her cheek.

God, his voice... She smiled. "Starving. Oh, and happy to see you, too."

He raised a brow at that. "I'm not sure I'm convinced."

Oh, he needed convincing, huh? Britt grabbed his face and pulled him down so she could mold her mouth to his. Damn, he tasted good, like something rich and delectable. She backed away before she got too mesmerized. "I hope that helped."

His expression made her insides tie up in knots. "What's that look for?" she demanded.

His gaze traveled slowly down to her feet, then back up. Britt's nerves were lighting up and tingling. "Are you sure you want dinner? Or are you hungry for something else?"

She swallowed the lump that formed in her throat, knowing exactly what he meant and fighting to keep herself in check. "You are a very naughty boy," she whispered, "making suggestions like that."

"You don't seem shocked."

He noticed that? Damn it, Britt, of course he did—he's a detective. "You're very observant."

"With you? Yes, I can't help myself."

She didn't have a comeback. Instead, with a shaky smile, Britt slid into the car.

"Where would you like to go?" he asked.

"Do you like sushi?"

"Love it."

"I was hoping you'd say that. I found a great place on Yonge Street, just north of Highway 401."

They parked at a corner close to the restaurant. After Mark helped her out of the car, he didn't release her hand. With his fingers closed over hers, that strange feeling of belonging hit her again, along with something else—she was relaxed and content. And damn if that didn't feel wonderful.

The restaurant wasn't busy yet, and the hostess and staff greeted them in Japanese before taking them to a booth that offered a view of the sunset and the gradual uptick of nightlife.

"This is a nice place," Mark said. "I haven't been here yet."

Dark paneled wood covered the walls, which were decorated with bright prints of Japanese figures. The sushi kitchen was at the other end of the spacious room, with the chefs hurrying around each other as they made the meals. Soothing Japanese music played in the background. "Oh? Were you planning on trying it out?"

"Eventually. I worked a burglary case in the area a few months ago." He stopped as a waitress brought green tea and two cups, then poured for them. "I came in here to ask questions, and the hostess at the time had valuable information that led to the perp's arrest. She was very observant."

"That's amazing." They clinked their cups, and she took a sip. The tea was hot and refreshing. "So, how was your day? You sounded pretty stressed over the phone."

"Busy. But I'll have a final report for my captain tomorrow."

The only police procedures Britt knew were from the reality shows on television. They were real but didn't have the same impact as actually talking to a live person. "I don't want to sound nosy, and you can stop me whenever you want. Did you find Mr. Ferguson's attacker?"

"Yeah."

Short and to the point. "And the person will be charged?"

"There are a few steps in between, but yes, he'll be formally charged with assault."

Britt didn't think she could do Mark's job. It seemed like there was too much emotional back-and-forth. "I guess Mr. Ferguson could sue the attacker, too."

"If he wanted. I'd rather he backed off, but…" Mark didn't say anything.

Damn it, Britt, think of something else! "How's your mother doing?"

"Much better, thank you. She'll have months of physical rehab, though." His expression grew clouded. "I hope she's up for it."

"Why wouldn't she be? I'm sure your mom will have excellent help from the nurses." On an impulse, Britt rested her hand over his. "Maybe you can go to her follow-up appointments and encourage her."

He turned his hand over and laced his fingers with

hers. "Thank you, I needed to hear that." He grinned. "She loves your pastries by the way, and it takes a lot to impress her."

She smiled back. Britt sensed that Mark loved his mother very much.

The waitress had returned, and they placed their order.

Britt kept their conversation light and away from work as much as possible. "Do you watch cartoons?" she asked.

He gave her a weird look.

"You're kidding, right?" she demanded. "Everyone should watch cartoons. There's too much serious shit going on in the world, and I don't think that's going to change. I find watching cartoons makes me remember how funny life can be sometimes."

"Which ones do you watch? And if you say the coyote and weird-looking bird with the long legs, I might walk out."

She burst out laughing. "It's one of my favorites!"

Mark made a move as if to get up, but she grabbed his arm. "Hear me out," she demanded. "Since you know the cartoon, tell me—have you ever seen a more motivated individual? He goes after what he wants and nothing gets in his way."

Mark cocked a brow, which put her on the defensive.

"You know it's true," she insisted. "Okay, how about the two mice? The really smart one that wants to take over the world? That's what I call dedication."

Mark shook his head. "You sure are something else."

"And what's that supposed to mean?"

"I mean you're different. Your bakery is your job, but I sense it's a lot more than that."

Britt sat back, watching him. "It's my passion. I love what I do. And I think that's allowed me to look at life a little differently, too. Life's too short to, I don't know, worry about mortgages or what people think of me. If I enjoy it, that's what counts."

He nodded slowly, as if thinking.

Their dinner arrived—miso soup, salad, two different kinds of sushi rolls and tempura vegetables. "This looks delicious," she said in a singsong voice, moving several pieces onto her plate. She grabbed a piece of spicy tuna sushi and popped it into her mouth. "So good!" she groaned, as she chewed. "I never would have thought I'd love sushi until a friend introduced me to it."

"Have you tried a lot of different things?"

"Before I became an entrepreneur, yes." She started ticking items off her fingers. "I wanted to be a ballet dancer, but I hated the training and the eating lifestyle. I couldn't eat sushi if I kept it up. And I was in the army."

"Seriously?" Mark's brown gaze widened in awe. "How old were you?"

"Nineteen. All Norwegians are mustered at that age. Then I took the military's compulsory training. That was nineteen months of hard work."

"So, wait a minute. If there's a war, are you called back?"

She shook her head. "I don't know… I think it's possible."

"Shit." He looked upset.

"Hey, let's hope it doesn't happen. Trust me, if it did, I'd look for an administrative job." Damn it, she hadn't meant for the conversation to head in this direction. Maybe it had been her conscience telling her to warn him of the possibility? *Yeah, thanks, brain.* "Then I decided on politics. That didn't go so well." Just thinking about it made her a little sick to her stomach.

"What happened?"

Britt knew Mark would ask the question, but she wasn't ready to tell him. "A lot of crap that could have been avoided." She started eating again to keep her mouth busy—she didn't want to get into it. Except… "Now you see why I love cartoons. Oh! And anime. Japanese anime movies are just so beautiful."

He remained quiet but watched her while he ate, which made her squirm in her seat.

The restaurant started to fill with more customers, and the noise from their conversations got too loud. As the waitress returned, Britt had an idea. "Did you want to stay? Or maybe we could go for a walk?"

"Yeah, I'd like that."

The sidewalks were filled with people. It was a warm evening, and it seemed everyone wanted to take advantage of it.

Mark saw Britt glance back at the restaurant, as if she missed its atmosphere. "Come on, I know just the place." He grasped her hand and tucked it beneath his arm. At the next block, he turned right and entered the neighborhood just beyond the busy atmosphere of Yonge Street. He breathed in the scented air and felt himself relax as the quiet settled around them.

"I never knew about this," she murmured. As they crossed another street, a large park appeared between the stand of tall trees bordering it. The security lights came on as the sky grew darker, illuminating a group of kids playing soccer. Town houses and large older homes stood side by side and stretched out into the distance.

"You need to explore the city more often. I came through here because—what else? Another case." It felt like Mark only found out about hidden areas of the city when he was working. He led them into the park and walked to its edge, then stopped and offered her a bow. "Shall we take a turn, my lady?"

Britt giggled and curtsied. "You are too kind, milord."

Unlike on Yonge Street, the only other sounds here were songbirds and the children's laughter. They walked the length of the park in comfortable silence, not hurrying, and Mark suddenly realized this was what he needed—time to himself, not rushing headlong to his next case.

The thrill and excitement of his job was great—he had no complaints. He loved the adrenaline rush, hanging out with the guys during their downtime, or collaborating and throwing out theories over a complex investigation. But his colleagues had something else that, if he was honest, made him jealous. Solberg and Cynthia were dating now, and Timmins was married. Occasionally, the guys would talk about their significant others, their plans, their futures. Mark wanted that for himself.

He had no problem meeting women and had been on plenty of dates. However, there was always something missing. He couldn't explain it, but he felt it. Mom once told him he'd know when a woman was "the one." He had scoffed at the idea, but now...

He looked at Britt while she talked and pointed out things that interested her. Her body was warm against his, and Mark felt that same sizzle of awareness as when he'd seen her the first time. He knew it was too early to decide if she would be the woman in his life, but she'd certainly made one hell of an impression on him.

So far, so good.

They had almost reached the other end of the park. A

soccer ball rolled toward them, but one of the boys intercepted it and kicked it back to his friends.

"Mark, could I ask you something?"

He looked down into her ocean-green gaze, those sparkling eyes that filled him with an emotion that ached in his chest. "Only if you let me kiss you first."

"Ah, you're not above bribery then." She tilted her face up to his, her full lips puckered and making smooching noises that had him snorting with laughter.

"Will you stop that?" he told her.

"Make me."

That was a challenge he would not pass up. He molded his mouth to hers, trying to get past the humor of her kiss until she suddenly relaxed against him. Her lips parted, and he gently delved his tongue into her warmth, exploring every bit until she groaned softly. The sound almost had him begging for more.

He reluctantly backed away, and that's when he heard the kids whistling, hooting and howling wolf calls.

Britt blushed a deep shade of pink. "Mind your own business! I thought you were playing soccer!"

"This is a family park, lady!" a tall boy yelled out. "Go find a room!"

Amid the jeering, Mark finally settled on her question. "What did you want to know, Britt?"

They reached the second corner and turned right. Their stroll took them past a small playground. Moms helped their kids onto the swings, caught them as they reached the bottom of the slide and called out when one got too ambitious on the monkey bars.

"How did you become a police detective?"

He expected the question. He just wasn't sure how much to say. "My family used to live in British Columbia," he started as they walked back. "Mom and I loved it there, but Dad was too much of a nomad. He'd travel for work and leave Mom and me a lot."

That wasn't exactly how he wanted to start the conversation. "I got into a lot of trouble as a kid. Getting into fights, picking on the smaller kids. Mom tried her best and finally got me to settle down, but I didn't want to do anything. I didn't have an interest in school."

Mark remembered those days and wished he could take them back. "When I got to high school, I had a difficult time with my courses, and nothing grabbed my attention. I know Mom was worried, and I tried to apply myself, but nothing worked."

He bit his lip against the pain and anguish swelling within him. He remembered hearing Mom crying one night in her room after a heated argument they'd had, and him storming out of the house. He had never meant to hurt her, but Mark had been too angry at himself to notice until that night.

"What did you do?" Britt asked quietly. They had reached the end of their walk and stood beneath the trees.

"Someone came to my rescue. My phys ed coach. He must have found out about my failing grades from one of my teachers. Gave me a swift kick in the ass first, then mentored me through high school. He was exactly what I needed."

Stanley Tucker had saved him from a life of regrets. "Next thing I knew, I got high grades and earned a scholarship. I studied law enforcement because I wanted to do what Stanley did for me, helping others." He looked at her. "Mom was proud of me, but I needed to be proud of myself or I was going nowhere."

"That's an amazing story, Mr. Detective. You've really impressed me."

Suddenly a voice yelled out. Mark approached the soccer ball bouncing in their direction and his competitive streak kicked in. He juggled it with his feet to the delight of the young boys, before kicking it out toward them.

"I see you like sports as well."

"It helps me release a lot of pent-up energy."

"Are you on any sports teams?"

He shook his head, looking out at the boys as they raced across the field. "Just too busy."

Britt moved up to him until their bodies touched. Jesus, he wanted to explore the woman beneath the clothing, discover her secrets and desires. Her flirtations were making it hard for him to concentrate on her as a person. "I think I did say that life was too short to not enjoy what you love." She caressed his cheek with her hand. "You should consider it."

He turned his head slightly and pressed his lips to her palm. "I will, *vakker.*"

"God, I love how you say that. It almost makes me want to do anything."

He stared at her, thinking of the delicious things he'd love to do with her. "Really?"

"Mmm-hmm."

It felt like the air around them had stilled, as if holding its breath. His finger touched her chin, but he didn't move—he waited. He wanted Britt to be sure that this was a moment of no looking back, to know that he wasn't going anywhere, that he wanted her with every fiber of his being.

Her lips parted in a slight gasp. He wondered if she was

thinking the same thoughts, but then his brain shut down when she leaned in and brushed her mouth across his.

He uttered an unintelligible sound and wrapped his arms around her, dying to caress her body with his eager hands and fighting against the urge. Standing in a park with kids watching was not the ideal spot. But when her arms came around his neck and he felt her fingers grab his hair, he almost lost it. He gently grasped her bottom lip with his teeth and was rewarded with her soft sound of desire.

This moment felt right. He had no other way to explain it. His Nordic princess wanted him just as much, and when the time was right, he would lavish all his attention upon her like the true goddess she was.

Chapter 7

Sunlight was pouring through the window when Britt woke up, yawning and feeling refreshed. She'd slept through the night.

She stayed in bed, hugging the pillow to her chest as she reminisced about her dinner date with Mark. She imagined herself in one of those romantic movies, where the couple strolled around a city at night, looking at the bright lights and staring into each other's eyes. She wasn't one for clichéd plotlines, but now that she had experienced it for herself…

Britt stared at the ceiling. She hadn't wanted last night to end, and if she read Mark's actions correctly, he hadn't wanted to stop, either. But she wasn't quite ready to take the next step. Things were moving pretty quickly, and despite the swirl of euphoria that still rushed through her, she wanted to take things just a little easy.

Mark had more or less indicated the same thing, although while he was driving her home, his hand couldn't stop touching her arm and thigh. Which sure as hell didn't help. By the time they got to her place, she was ready to drag him upstairs, but she'd convinced her lust to calm down.

Maybe next time.

Giggling, she went to the bathroom to get a shower. Today was a new day. Mark had warned her about his busy work schedule, so Britt would have to daydream about last night until she could see him again.

But man, to have him kiss her like that...

She turned the tap to Cold to allow the water to wake her up and hopefully cool off the very sexy thoughts roiling around in her head. She had a business to run.

The bus ride gave her time to check her emails. She had received a couple more party requests for her pastries for this coming weekend. If this kept up, she'd need to consider hiring extra help. She hadn't wanted the bakery to grow too fast—she wanted to keep the small-business charm intact. It was something she'd need to discuss with her staff, especially Jacques and Thomas. She refused to overwork them.

When Britt arrived at her stop, other people were also hurrying to work. It was almost nine, but the bakery opened at eight during the workweek to take advantage of the early-morning crowd. As she approached the store, she noticed a couple of customers peering in through the window, and as she reached the door, Britt was shocked to discover how busy it was inside.

"Helvete." Hell. What was going on?

She hurried around the side of the store, intent on using the back entrance so that she could get inside and help out. However, as she turned the corner, she almost bumped into someone who looked like...

"Ms. Gronlund." Mr. Ferguson was almost unrecognizable, wearing blue jeans and a white shirt instead of his usual two-piece business suit. But it was his expression that made her take a step back—he was furious. "I couldn't get into your bakery this morning. You certainly have loyal customers and staff."

"What are you doing here? Have you forgotten about the peace bond and what it means?" He was the last person she expected to see. "It means stay away from my shop."

Britt glanced over her shoulder—she was about six feet from the sidewalk. The odd person glanced in her direction and kept going, not seeing anything wrong. But if she decided to scream…

Suddenly, his hand clamped over her wrist. "I can see what you're thinking," he growled. "I just want to talk."

"We've talked enough." Britt tried to wrench her arm free, but no luck. "Get your hand off me."

"Why didn't you sell your business? I offered top dollar. Do you want more? I'm sure we can come to an agreement."

"And I already told you where you could stick your offer." Mr. Ferguson was stronger than Britt expected, but she wasn't a lightweight, either.

"Name your price."

"Why?" She waved her other hand at the construction site across the street. "You got what you wanted. Leave me alone."

"No, I didn't. I've never had anyone refuse my offers. Tell me your price." He actually bared his teeth in a snarl.

"How about this?" She set her stance, then swung one leg up, aiming her foot at his crotch.

Mr. Ferguson howled in pain and let go of her hand to clutch his manhood with both of his.

"Stay away from me and my bakery!" She took off down the short alleyway. At the back, she scrabbled for the key that opened the back door, and after what felt like agonizing minutes, managed to grasp it between her shaking fingers. Moments later, she was inside, the thick metal door between her and that creep. She fought to slow her rapid breathing, but it was hard. The adrenaline had kicked in, and it would take some time before it wore off.

How dare he? Mr. Ferguson had some nerve, coming to her business like that. Competition she understood, but this—this smelled of desperation. She wondered about the CEO's comment of being refused entry into the bakery. Did he finally understand that trust and loyalty were the two things necessary to run a successful business?

"Nah," she told herself. He just resented it when a competitor was doing better than him.

As she walked through the large kitchen, she saw Jacques and Thomas moving quickly through the space like two synchronized partners. As she watched, Britt wondered with a bit of awe how they never bumped into each other.

"Ah, Britt, *bon matin*, good morning!" Jacques called out. He said something to his assistant, then hurried over to her, wiping his hands on his apron. "Our pastries are selling faster than we can bake them today! What has happened?"

"Konditori becoming popular is what happened. I couldn't get in through the front door. I had to come in the back way."

"*Mince!* Damn." Jacques wiped his sweaty brow with a dishcloth, then threw it into the laundry basket behind him. "This frenzied pace, *chérie*. I love the excitement, but…"

She grasped his arm. "I know. We'll need to have a meeting. I have a couple of ideas, but I want to hear from all of you, too." She'd also have to tell them about Mr. Ferguson threatening her in the alleyway. Her staff was going to be infuriated.

Britt joined Betty and Kevin in serving the customers, and about an hour later, it finally slowed down.

"Britt, you gotta stop with the billboard advertising," Betty said with a laugh.

This time, her fast breathing came from excitement. "Seriously, I haven't done anything different."

"It's word of mouth," Kevin said. "And those party pastry trays we set up. We hear what the customers are saying—they love this place. And it's getting around."

She nodded slowly, knowing Kevin was right, but she'd never expected this kind of popularity so soon. She'd have to decide on that fine line between expanding and keeping the coziness of the bakery.

Thankfully, the rest of the day was manageable. Britt finally had a chance to sit down in her office and let her body go limp. As she let her brain process the day, she realized she hadn't told her staff about her encounter with Mr. Ferguson. It was probably better this way.

"What have you got for me, Hawthorne?"

"Captain." Mark hadn't been able to get a read on Captain Michelle Fraust since she took over two months ago. Late forties, no-nonsense, and with a list of awards for her leadership and competency, she was one of the youngest officers to make the captain's list.

There had been speculation—and gossip—about her in the precinct. It was expected. But, Mark surmised, unless Fraust decided to suddenly open up about her personal life, all they had were guesses and theories.

He pulled out his notes from the thick folder he had brought with him. "After confirming that Mr. Ferguson was okay, Forensic Investigator Walsh and I collected evidence at the crime scene. Initially, the suspect's fingerprints were found and processed, but the database hadn't provided any positive hits. However, we found distinctive shoe prints in the area that helped to considerably narrow down our search."

"How so?" She sat on the other side of the meeting table, back straight in the chair, with no sign of emotion on her face. It was like talking to a statue, which creeped him out a little.

Mark summarized for the captain the work involved in locating the suspect who owned the limited-edition sneakers.

"And how did you find the right suspect? Shoe size?"

"Not just shoe size." Mark pointed at the left and right footprint. "Do you see the distinction?"

She frowned for only a moment before her blue eyes widened in surprise. "Different-sized feet?"

"Yes, ma'am. On Saturday I went to several stores until I got a hit. I found Henry Toussaint Sunday afternoon and brought him in for questioning. He didn't admit to the assault despite the evidence pointing to him. However, he told me that someone else came up with the plan to commit the arson." Mark still wanted to kick himself for missing that. "Jenny, the construction worker who first reported the incident."

Her ice-blue gaze riveted him in his seat. "Has Mr. Toussaint been charged?"

"No, ma'am." Mark thought carefully on how to phrase his next words. "I think Toussaint has been getting directions from Jenny. I also think Jenny knows pertinent information about these anti-Ferguson protests. If she's in hiding, I'll never find her. But with Toussaint out there..."

"He should lead you to her. A little unorthodox, but I understand your reasoning." She paused. "Mr. Ferguson may want to press charges against Toussaint and Jenny once they're arrested, but we'll wait and see if that happens. Was there anything else?"

Mark kept his expression neutral—he knew what she meant, but he was going to take a risk and feign ignorance. "No, Captain."

Fraust rose and slowly paced the room. "I received a call from Mr. Ferguson first thing this morning," she started. The captain looked over her shoulder. "He complimented you on being thorough with the investigation."

"I'm glad to hear it, ma'am." He was waiting for the other shoe to drop.

"However, you paid him an unexpected visit at his home Sunday morning." She came back to the table but remained standing. "Was there a reason for that?"

"More a gut feeling. I didn't feel that Mr. Ferguson had told me everything that had happened."

"I see." She sat down again. "What was the result of your surprise interview?"

"Not a damn thing." He should have known better than to think a shrewd businessman like Ferguson would accidentally disclose information about his business tactics.

"You should know that Mr. Ferguson is not a man to be taken lightly."

Surprised, Mark looked at his boss. "I understand, Captain."

"Do you?" Her smile was dangerous. "He didn't climb his corporate ladder with just grit and determination. He did so with a ruthless ambition that would scare off CEOs running the best-known global conglomerates."

Captain Fraust was giving him a hint, and Mark got it—if he was going to accuse Mr. Ferguson of his unethical business dealings with small-business owners, he'd better be damn sure he had everything lined up.

"I'm going to provide an update to the media, but you don't need to be there. My statement will be short, with some diplomatic phrasing that we're still investigating."

"Thank you, Captain."

"Good work so far, Hawthorne, both you and Walsh. Keep me updated. Dismissed."

Mark got on the elevator and hit the button for his floor. That had gone a lot smoother than he'd anticipated. He had felt sure Captain Fraust would browbeat him for suspecting a crime victim, especially a high-level CEO.

Maybe she knew something about Mr. Ferguson that shouldn't be known.

"Huh." Maybe, if he had time, he might poke around to see what he could find. There was no way Ferguson could threaten people and destroy property without suffering some of the consequences.

His personal phone pinged with a text, and Mark glanced at the short, humorous note from Britt.

Hey, how's it going? How was your meeting with the dreaded captain?

Mark couldn't get over Britt's choice of words. He texted her back.

I'm not walking the plank.

Chapter 8

Britt sipped her tea. "I'm telling you, Joyce, seeing Mr. Ferguson in the alley like that freaked me out."

Before the bakery had closed, her friend Joyce came in to say hi. Britt felt guilty for not keeping in touch with her, but between the CEO's threats, a busy bakery and Mark's sudden appearance in her life, she felt like she'd been stretched in too many different directions.

"Did you report it?" Joyce Mathurin had been hired to do the interior design of the bakery. In her thirties, she was a beautiful dark-skinned Torontonian with roots in Saint Lucia, and the two of them had hit it off almost immediately. Because of their busy schedules, getting together to socialize had been hard, so they made the most of each personal visit.

They were sitting in Britt's office. The bakery had now closed for the day, but she told Joyce to wait in the office while she and the staff cleaned up. The store sat in darkness except for the one lamp in the room, and the security lights located at the front and back of the building.

"No. I know I should, but it feels like I'm not getting anywhere with the police. I took it upon myself to let the man know how much I didn't like him."

Joyce's eyes widened with curiosity.

"I kicked him in the nuts."

Tea spewed from her friend's mouth as her laughter rang through the small office. Britt calmly handed her a napkin. "Are you kidding? Oh gosh, I wish I'd seen that!"

"I think it was more instinct than anything else. I just reacted."

"Hey," Joyce said suddenly, pointing at her. "Where's your bracelet?"

Confused, Britt looked at her left wrist. It wasn't there. "I'm sure I had it on today."

"I only noticed when you handed me the napkin. Maybe you forgot to put it on this morning?"

"Maybe." The rune bracelet had been a birthday present from her family—she rarely left home without it. "I've been distracted lately."

Joyce nodded and bit into a mini cinnamon roll. "I remember you saying you had a lot on your mind, and now this Ferguson guy is ignoring your peace bond. It's too bad you didn't have him in your security footage. I'll bet the police would have done something more."

Britt sat up. "You know what? I just might." Mr. Ferguson had told her he tried to get in the store, but the customers had blocked his way. Her laptop was still on, so she clicked on the security app and used the arrows to slide back to the time just before she arrived.

The scene she watched was chaotic. Several customers jostled in the tight space in front of the door, and in the middle, Mr. Ferguson was using his arms to protect himself from the shoving. Someone landed a punch on his chest.

"The bastard lied. He was actually inside my store," Britt whispered, her voice trembling with anger.

"Holy crap," Joyce breathed. "I can't believe that guy had the balls to walk in here."

"I admit to being more nervous that Mr. Ferguson might charge me with assault."

"You? But you didn't do anything—you were defending yourself!"

"It happened on store property." Britt sighed. "But, with the peace bond still in force, he shouldn't stand a chance if he tried to charge me."

They continued watching until Mr. Ferguson was forcefully shoved out of the store. He shook his fist and yelled something, then straightened his clothing. At that moment, a bus arrived at the nearby stop.

"I'm sure that's the bus I was on," Britt murmured.

The CEO looked over his shoulder, then hurried away and out of the camera's view. A minute later, Britt appeared on screen, opened the front door, looked inside, then left.

"That's when I realized I couldn't get in." She closed the app and shut the laptop.

"So it was coincidence when the two of you saw each other." Joyce wiped her hands on a paper napkin.

"A coincidence that I don't want repeated. How the hell am I supposed to keep this guy away from me and my staff if he deliberately ignores the peace bond?"

Joyce shook her head. "I honestly don't know. If you report it and provide this footage, the police should charge him with a criminal offense."

Britt snorted with disdain. "As if. With his slimy lawyers, Ferguson will only get another slap on the wrist."

"You've done the right things, Britt. The only other idea I have is moving your location."

"Like hell I will." Britt refused to be scared off.

Joyce laughed. "That's what I wanted to hear." She leaned forward in her chair. "So," she said, dragging out the word. "Anything else going on in your life?"

Britt looked at her friend's inquisitive expression and tried not to smile. "Just me and work."

"Mmm-hmm." Joyce picked up her mug. "Work must be more fascinating than usual. Other than dealing with Edward Ferguson of Mighty Big Bastard."

"Oh my God, did you just say that? That phrase is going to be stuck in my mind now." She laughed, enjoying the sound and how it made her feel. She could always depend on Joyce to find the humor in everything.

"So, tell me—what has made you look so glowy?"

"What?" Britt tried to act naive, but by the look on Joyce's face, that wasn't going to work anymore. "All right, you found me out. I met a guy last Friday."

"Oooh, good for you! Who is he? Give me all the deets."

"Well, he's a detective with York Regional Police."

"He's in law enforcement? How intriguing." Joyce propped her chin on her hands. "How did you meet him?"

"Would you believe me if I said our eyes locked on each other from across the street?"

Joyce frowned. "Sounds like something from a movie."

"Right? But that's what happened. I saw him as he was going to his car, and my eyes just went *boing*! You know, like how it happens in the cartoons when their eyes bug out?"

Her friend chuckled. "You and the cartoons...but I know exactly what you mean. Have you been on a date?"

"A couple, actually."

"Girl, you're not wasting any time—I love it! What kind of a kisser is he?"

Britt felt her cheeks heat up in a blush. "A thorough one."

"I'm liking this more and more." Joyce waggled her brows.

"That's as far as we got. I…" She realized that she didn't want to mess this up. Not because she hadn't been on a date in a long time, but because Mark meant much more than that to her. "I don't want to rush things."

"Totally get that. You're being smart. What does he look like?"

"Over six feet. Thick, beautiful hair—it's so soft. Brown eyes with these gold flecks I can see when I'm close enough. I'm pretty sure he's built, but I haven't had the chance to check out under the hood, so to speak."

Joyce laughed and clapped her hands. "Don't worry, you will. I'm so happy for you! I know the store has been your focus, but you need to live your life, too."

Britt couldn't have put it better herself.

"We should get going." Joyce looked at her watch. "Time flies when you're—"

The sudden noise of shattering glass reverberated through the office. "What the hell…?" Britt started to say.

"Someone's breaking in!" Joyce sprang to her feet and peeked out while Britt grabbed her laptop and stuffed it into her purse. Her friend shut and locked the door. "There's three guys, all with baseball bats," Joyce whispered urgently. "We need to hide."

"Joyce, they're going to destroy my bakery!"

"Better that than hurting you. Come on, where can we hide?"

Britt thought furiously. "Not in here, especially if they break the door down." She turned, trying not to panic as several loud voices traveled through the air toward them. "The window. It's our only chance. Hurry!"

Britt slid it open. Although she had installed security lights in the alley, she worried that one wrong move could spell injury for her and Joyce, or alert the intruders.

Joyce climbed out first, displaying her strength as she slid over the windowsill with ease. "Give me your stuff," she said, while holding her hands through the window.

Britt gave her the purse, then proceeded to perch her butt on the sill. Another loud crash, closer this time, caught her attention—they were destroying the display counter.

"Come on!" Joyce called.

She swung her legs over the sill and, grasping her friend's hands, eased down into the narrow alley. "If they get in the office and see the open window, they'll know I was here," Britt said, her voice trembling.

"I'll give you a boost up." Joyce linked her fingers together to form a makeshift step. Britt took her shoe off and stepped into her friend's hands, and held onto the sill while she was slowly lifted upward. Whatever Joyce was doing to stay in shape, Britt needed some of that.

She reached the edge of the window and pulled it down. She couldn't lock it from this side, but she wouldn't worry about that—she was going to call the police as soon as she and Joyce put some distance behind them and the intruders. Britt got her shoe back on. "We have to get out of here." She hurried toward the main street.

"Not that way." Joyce grabbed her arm. "They might have a lookout. Stay close to me."

They hurried down the walkway. At the back of the bakery, Joyce peered around the corner.

"Come on," Joyce whispered, taking the lead. Britt was

right behind her, trying not to imagine what those thugs were doing to her bakery.

They had to be careful in the rear alley. While several streetlights helped them to navigate the uneven surface, there were still pools of darkness to walk through. Add the broken, chipped concrete, and it made for a treacherous path. At one point, Britt cried out as she stumbled and fell to her knees on the hard surface.

"Shit, are you okay?" Joyce wrapped an arm beneath her shoulders and got her to her feet. "Give me your bag. We're almost there."

Britt leaned heavily on her friend, her knees burning with pain. Her feet dragged like lead weights, and she used all her energy to move one foot in front of the other. Her hands throbbed painfully from certain cuts. "Joyce, I don't know—" She gasped.

"Yes, you can. Just a few more steps. We're almost on Melville Avenue. We'll call the police then."

It felt like hours later before they finally sat on a sidewalk bench. Joyce had wanted to have at least a block between them and the burglars before stopping. "Hang on, I'll call them," Joyce told her.

"Wait." Britt was fighting to catch her breath. "Ask for Detective Mark Hawthorne if he's still at work. He'll bring the troops."

"The man who makes you go *boing*? Gotcha." Joyce hit a button on her cell, then started talking.

Beneath the streetlight, Britt assessed the damage. The skin on her knees was torn, and blood dripped down her legs. She tried to pick the debris out of her wounds, but it wasn't easy. Her palms were in better shape, just scraped a little, but they hurt like hell. She'd have to go to the hospital.

"They're on their way." Joyce sat beside her, then looked around. "Less than five minutes."

True to their word, three police cars sped toward them, their sirens off. Two vehicles raced by and turned the corner at full speed, while the third screeched to a stop in front of them. Mark literally jumped out of the car. "Britt!" he yelled, running toward her. "*Vakker*, are you all right?"

"Yeah," she said quietly, then hissed when the pain in her knees started to pulse up into her thighs. "I think so."

"Damn it. Hey, get me the first aid kit!" he yelled at the officer who was with him. "What the hell happened?" he demanded.

"Tried to run in heels down a dark alleyway." She smiled at Joyce. "But my friend got us out safely. That's what matters. Sorry," she apologized. "Mark, this is Joyce. She did the interior design for Konditori."

"Pleased to meet you." Mark shook hands. "And I'm glad the both of you are okay."

"That makes two of us," Joyce replied dryly.

Suddenly, a loud static noise came from a walkie-talkie on the officer's belt. "We're at the store," a voice called out. "No one's here. Repeat, the place is empty."

"Son of a bitch!" Britt's anger made her temporarily forget the pain. "They were just there!"

Mark looked at the officer waiting with him. "Tell them to make a sweep of the area, see if anyone's hanging around." He turned to Joyce. "Any idea what they look like?" he asked.

Joyce shook her head. "I managed a peek out the office door but didn't waste any time trying to see their faces. I locked it and got us out the window."

"Smart move." He broke open the kit and pulled out a tube and some gauze. "I'm taking you to the hospital," he mentioned. "But I want to at least get some of this on you and bandage it up." He popped the top off the tube. "I'm going to put this antibacterial ointment directly on your wounds. It's going to sting. You ready?"

Britt nodded, then bit her tongue as the cream burned her skin. "Holy crap, that hurts!"

"Sorry." His hands were comforting and gentle as he carefully taped gauze over both of her knees while the other officer held a powerful flashlight over them. He used the ointment on her hands as well, and after careful inspection, taped gauze over them as well.

Joyce insisted on riding in the front seat, giving Britt a coy wink as she slid into the police vehicle. Mark helped her inside, then sat beside her. "Check in with the others," he said, his voice demanding. "See if they found anyone."

As Britt listened to the officer's conversation over the radio, Mark shifted until he was up close and personal. "You're sure you're okay?" he asked quietly. Under the car's interior light, his worried expression made her heart thump hard in her chest.

She nodded. There was no way Joyce or the other officer could miss the intimate tête-à-tête going on behind them. "Yeah, I'm good. Just really mad that Ferguson sent more assholes to bust up my shop."

He raised a brow. "What makes you think Ferguson is responsible?"

"You mean besides the other time my bakery got vandalized?" She hadn't meant to sound sarcastic, but it was obvious to her the CEO was involved. But Mark also didn't know about her other unpleasant visit. "He was here this morning, trying to get into the store, but the customers kicked him out. I had the misfortune of running into him when I arrived."

She told him what had happened as the police car sped toward the hospital. "He's really pushing the boundaries," Mark growled. "Until we can prove Ferguson's responsible for the breaking and entering, the police can't do much."

"He's violated the peace bond Britt put on him. And Britt's customers are doing more than you guys," Joyce called out from the front seat. "If that Ferguson guy shows up again, something worse could happen. Shouldn't you all put a stop to it?"

"Trust me, I agree with you. But without hard evidence, I can't do anything."

"Mr. Ferguson is recorded on my security footage from this morning," Britt told him. "That should be enough?"

He nodded. "Yeah, that would do. But let's look after you first."

They arrived at the hospital within minutes, and Mark carried her into the emergency room. "I can walk," Britt complained, wiggling in his tight grasp. "You don't have to do this."

"What? Caring for you? What if I told you I want to?"

That shut her up. Mark had come charging in like a knight in shining armor and taken over. In the back of her mind, Britt quickly realized she didn't mind at all. She'd spent so much time doing everything herself that having someone else look after her made her feel comfortable, protected. And with Mark, she liked it—a lot.

An hour later, her knees and hands were thoroughly cleaned and bandaged. "I need to get to the bakery," she said as she slowly limped beside him and Joyce. The crutches felt alien in her hands. "I have to see what damage they've caused."

"I'll do that, Britt. It's a crime scene now. If you have

the security footage on Ferguson and the B and E, it would certainly help."

"I'll email that to you tonight. And I'll text my staff and tell them to stay home tomorrow." It was a serious blow, to both her business and her pride. If there was any shred of proof that Mr. Ferguson was responsible for the destruction of her store, she'd make sure he suffered for it.

"Britt, call me when you get in and settled, so I know you're all right." Joyce sent a meaningful glance in Mark's direction.

She almost laughed at her friend's expression. "I will. And thanks again for saving my butt."

"What are friends for? I'll call tomorrow to see how you're doing." She shook Mark's hand. "Thanks for getting us out of there so fast. Look after her." Joyce hurried to a nearby taxi parked at the curb.

It was just the two of them, and the tension built up in the air.

"Are you sure you're okay?" Mark asked her quietly.

His voice was a beautiful deep rumble, full of emotion. Britt couldn't help herself and turned to face him. "Yeah, thank you." She shook her head. "I can't believe I fell and skinned my knees, though. I know how to walk in my heels."

"You certainly do."

She knew her eyebrows went up at that. "What do you mean?"

"I've seen you walking in them." He leaned close and whispered in her ear. "And it's sexy as hell."

So, he'd been observing her from behind? Britt smiled. "I'm glad you noticed."

"I'd better get you home." He helped her to the police car and held out his arm as a brace while she hung on and lowered herself into the seat. This time, he rode in the front, talking to the officer and getting updates from the others still at the bakery. A jolt of disappointment hit her, but Britt understood the importance of Mark displaying leadership to his colleagues.

He did take her up to her apartment. "I'm sorry, I have to run."

"Mark, it's fine. You did so much more than I expected." She leaned the crutches against the wall and hobbled close to him, then grabbed his shirt collar to keep herself from falling flat on her face.

He prevented that easily enough, wrapping his arms tight around her. He rested his head against her shoulder. "I'm just relieved you're all right."

Britt relaxed against his warmth and inhaled the scent that was uniquely him. To be in his arms… It was so comforting, like sitting in a favorite chair with a wonderful book and a cup of hot tea. She didn't want it to end.

But Mark finally released her, slowly, and his hands rested on her hips. "I'll call you tomorrow and let you know what's going on," he said, his gaze intent as he stared at her. "And if you need anything—anything—call me."

"Sure." Britt caressed his face, feeling the slight stubble from a day's growth of beard. She leaned in and kissed him, her lips just touching his, hoping he sensed how grateful she was for his help.

He angled his head and molded his mouth to hers. Damn, he tasted good, and when his arms went around her again and tightened, she couldn't help herself. Her own arms encircled his neck as she melted into his embrace, her emotions weaving a spell around her that she didn't want to break. All this still felt like a dream.

Hmm… She reached down and pinched Mark's butt.

He backed away quickly, uttering a loud yelp of surprise. "What the heck?"

"Sorry. Well, not really. That was payback."

And confirmation that Mark was definitely real.

Britt didn't call Joyce right away because she needed to email her staff the bad news. As soon as she sat on her bed, she lay down and slept right through the night—she'd been that tired.

The next morning, she sent Mark a file of the security footage from the day before. Britt still didn't think Mr. Ferguson would be charged despite breaking the peace bond. As for the burglars, she saw they had worn masks—fat chance being able to identify them.

Finally, Britt called her friend after settling on her couch with a mug of tea.

"So, any news about the break and enter?" Joyce asked over the phone.

"Nothing yet, and I don't want to bother Mark, either. My staff wasn't happy about it when I emailed them last night."

"How are you feeling?"

"Much better. A little stiff in the legs, but I'll walk around to loosen them up."

"Awesome. So…that was the detective, huh?"

She laughed. "Yes."

"Very handsome. And attentive. I know it's none of my business, but what do you think?"

Britt knew what Joyce meant. "I want to be sure, so I'm taking things slow right now."

"Best decision to make. But I saw the way he looked at you. That detective gives me the impression he'll hang around if you give him half a chance."

Britt swallowed the sudden lump that lodged in her throat. "I thought that, too," she said quietly.

"I don't have to go into work until eleven, so if you want, I can come over and…" Joyce's voice trailed off into silence.

"Joyce? You there?" Nothing. "Joyce!"

"Yeah, sorry." A pause. "You'd better turn on the television."

"Why? What's going on?" She grabbed the remote and clicked the television to life. "What am I looking for?"

"Any national station. I'm sure all of them are covering the story."

"Joyce, you can be such a mysterious drama queen…" Britt's own voice stuttered to a stop as she watched the breaking news.

Edward Ferguson, Mighty Big Bakery's CEO, had been found dead in his backyard early that morning.

Chapter 9

Talk about being up shit creek without a paddle.

Mark stood on an expansive back porch made of fragrant cedar. Off to one side, furniture and a large BBQ dominated the space, while the other side was bare except for flowers that decorated the railing and roof beams. Directly in front of him, a set of stairs led down to a wide stone patio, and beyond, an in-ground swimming pool was surrounded by a spacious green lawn. More flowers and mature shrubbery bordered the high stone wall that he could just see between the slim gaps created by the tall hedge that offered additional privacy.

Edward Ferguson lay sprawled at the back entrance to the three-car garage, to the left of the porch. He was face down, his head resting against the flagstone. The back of his head showed blunt-force trauma. He'd been hit so hard that a trail of blood had oozed several feet toward the fence.

Mark couldn't say that he was surprised by what happened, but it still bothered him. The bakery CEO seemed to have made a lot of enemies, judging by what Mark had discovered during this investigation. He had hinted at something similar to Captain Fraust during his last update. Somehow, the media had gotten their greedy hands on the story before he arrived, and it had already been broadcast on the morning news.

Myrna was prowling the backyard looking for clues. Several officers were posted around the house to provide security.

He glanced over his shoulder. Ferguson's wife and the housekeeper were in the kitchen, and he could hear their grief echoing through the room.

This wouldn't be easy.

"Keep an eye out for nosy neighbors," he told the two officers that stood beside him. "The coroner should be here within the hour."

Mark had kept his arrival as low-key as possible. Along with his car, which he and Myrna had driven in, two police vehicles were parked on the curb about a half block away. It was possible that someone had spotted them going up to Mr. Ferguson's door, but he hoped that everyone would keep to themselves and not grow curious. As for the coroner van, Mark had asked that they drive straight in, and an officer would direct them to the back. He suspected the media would make another appearance and made sure the other four officers who arrived with him were advised to keep the gates closed and the area clear. It was the best he could do.

He approached Myrna, who was kneeling to one side of Ferguson's body. "Need any help?" he asked.

"I did a sweep of the backyard, but I'm pretty sure the attack happened around here." She lowered herself until she was almost at the level of the body. "I can see strangulation marks around his neck," she stated. "I can't tell if there are any fingerprints, but I'll check in with the coroner after he's finished examining the body."

Mark nodded. Mr. Ferguson was dressed in his usual

business suit, which could mean he'd been heading to work. One of the garage doors was open, revealing a dark green luxury sports car. Mark walked inside in a wide arc so as not to disturb anything, even though he had plastic booties on. Turning on his flashlight, he ran it over the car's gleaming surface. He saw some smudging, but nothing that looked like a print—still, he'd let Myrna know.

The other side had something interesting—a long scratch down the driver's side of the car. "I've got something here," he called out.

She looked up. "I saw that. Got pictures, too, but I can't find the keys."

Although he trusted his forensic investigator to be thorough, Mark knew he'd feel better if he reviewed the lay of the land so that it was clear in his mind. He did a slow walk around the perimeter of the backyard, stopping each time he thought he noticed something, then moving on. It wasn't until he almost reached Myrna on the other side that he noticed something between a pair of thick hedges. "Did you see the footprints?" he called out.

"What?" She jumped to her feet and hurried over. "Where?"

"They're actually behind that row of hydrangea." He only spotted them because he was particularly searching for footprints. "You have your kit with you?"

"Yep. Can't believe I missed that," she grumbled as she pulled out her tools, took photographs of the evidence in question and made a cast of the impressions. "How did you find them?"

"I was looking for them. I'm hoping they belong to Toussaint."

"With the different-sized feet? It would make our lives easier."

The cast had already dried, and Myrna carefully lifted it out. "Great," she said, placing it on top of a plastic bag. "And not so great."

"What happened? Did it crack?" Mark looked over her shoulder and swore in disbelief. "Those footprints don't belong to Toussaint. They're actually smaller..." He paused, his brain firing off a possible answer that made him want to throw something. "Son of a bitch!"

Myrna watched him, a quizzical expression on her face. "Care to clue me in?"

"Jenny."

She frowned. "The construction worker?"

He nodded. "She's been playing me from the beginning. Not anymore."

"Mrs. Ferguson."

The woman looked up from her pile of tissues. She was in her early fifties, with black hair and green eyes. She wore a silk pajama set beneath a thick, plush white robe.

"Do you think you can talk to me now?"

She nodded and blew her nose.

Mark sat down opposite her. She'd been crying—her eyes were red and swollen, and her mouth compressed into a thin line. He could tell she was trying hard to remain composed, but her trembling body spoke otherwise. "Can you tell me what happened?"

"Normally, I'd wake up before Edward around seven. But when the alarm rang, I didn't see him." She shrugged. "I thought he'd gotten up early to go to a meeting."

"Does he tell you his daily schedule?"

She nodded. "Or he'd have it written on a calendar in the kitchen." She frowned.

"Is that the calendar over there?" Mark pointed. She

looked over her shoulder. "I don't see anything written down for today."

"And he didn't mention anything to me or Gloria, our housekeeper. But he had his business suit on. The good one."

"What does that mean?"

"Oh." She waved a hand. "Edward wears the really good suits when he's taking over a business."

Mrs. Ferguson said that nonchalantly, but Mark could feel his temper starting to rise. He fought to control it. "He dresses up to take over someone else's company?"

"A weird habit, I know. It shouldn't matter what he wears. The ending is still the same."

Shit, she sounded just like her husband. "What did you do next?"

"I came downstairs. My housekeeper had already come in."

"Does she have a house key?"

"Yes, and she knows the security code."

He nodded to encourage her to continue.

"Gloria—my housekeeper—and I talked for a bit in the front hall while she put away her things, then we both headed for the kitchen. I turned on the television while she tidied up and made coffee."

"And Mr. Ferguson wasn't in the house."

"No."

His next question was critical. "How did you find him?"

Her hands scrunched the tissues, but that was the only movement he saw. "Gloria opened the kitchen blinds, then stepped out to look at the plants. She noticed the garage door was open, which was odd, and when she stepped down to the patio, she saw Edward lying on the ground." She shuddered. "Her screams were so loud they echoed into the kitchen. When I got outside and saw him…" She paused and dabbed at her eyes. "I pushed Gloria back into the house and told her to call 911. I tried to turn him over, but he was too heavy, and I—I couldn't…"

"It's okay. You did your best." Finding a critically ill or deceased loved one so unexpectedly was a fear Mark had lived with for too long. When Dad's abuse became more violent, he was scared that he'd find Mom on the ground every time he came home from school. Their divorce gave him peace of mind until that day when he'd found her at the bottom of the stairs with the broken leg and hip. "You can't blame yourself." But he knew she did—just like how he felt guilty every time he left Mom alone with that devil. "Did you notice anything odd about him? Or anything on the property?"

"No. I thought someone was trying to steal one of the cars since the garage door was open."

Made sense. "I'm going to talk to the housekeeper. If you need anything, let one of the officers know."

He found Gloria sitting on an ornate wooden bench in the hallway. Compared to Mrs. Ferguson, the housekeeper's grief seemed more palpable. He sat down beside her. "How are you holding up?" he asked gently.

In answer, her face twisted in pain, and a loud sob broke free. He gave her a few minutes to calm down before trying again. "What happened, Gloria?"

She blew her nose, then shook her head. "I don't know. Nothing seemed out of place."

"Tell me what you remember from this morning."

The housekeeper gave the same information as Mrs. Ferguson, except… "His briefcase was missing."

"Missing?" Mark pictured the area around the garage in his mind. She was right. "Did you look for it?"

"No. I was…" She waved a hand helplessly.

"Maybe it's in his car. We'll look for it. What does it look like?"

She blew her nose. "It's a metal briefcase. I think it's the fancy one that can withstand a lot of heat."

Damn, if it's the case Mark thought it was, it could do a lot of damage to a person's skull. On a hunch, he asked, "Any idea what might be in it?"

Something—a flicker of recognition—skimmed across her face. "Not at all."

He sensed a lie. "Are you sure?" he pressed. "It's possible whoever murdered Mr. Ferguson was after whatever was inside this briefcase."

"I don't know what you're talking about." The housekeeper rose. "If you'll excuse me, I'd like to tend to Mrs. Ferguson."

Mark got up as well. "Of course." As he watched her hurry toward the kitchen, he knew there was more going on than what the housekeeper was admitting to. He would need to question the ladies further anyway, and then he would sniff out the secrets Gloria was obviously hiding.

Back outside, the coroner had arrived. Mark mentioned the missing item to Myrna. "His briefcase?" She frowned. "I haven't seen anything lying around. Maybe it's in his car?"

"We'll need to see if the keys are in his pockets."

"Let me ask. I didn't want to turn the body over until they got here to supervise." She approached the coroner and after a moment, he and his assistant had deftly flipped Mr. Ferguson onto his back.

Mark grimaced. The CEO's face had turned an ugly shade of purple and blue and was horribly swollen. Which made him wonder… "How long do you think his body has been lying there?" he called out.

Both Myrna and the coroner looked up. "Judging by the body's state of rigor mortis," the coroner answered in a dull voice, "the male victim has been dead since very early this morning. Say, between one and five in the morning."

So, Mr. Ferguson would have gotten out of bed while his wife was sound asleep. The housekeeper wasn't a live-in, so he could sneak out and be back before Mrs. Ferguson knew. But what would prompt the CEO to go out at that time of night?

Mrs. Ferguson did say the suit her husband had on was only worn when he was about to conquer a business. What kind of business deal was so critical that he had to sneak out to complete it?

"Mark, here are his car keys." Myrna held them up with a gloved hand.

They opened the car door, but after searching the interior, didn't find the briefcase. Mark had just climbed out when he noticed a soft glint of something sitting on the dash. When he took a closer look, the blood chilled in his veins. It couldn't be…

Britt's bracelet.

"Myrna, can you collect that?" He pointed at the piece of unique jewelry, watching his hand shake. Confused, angry, hurt—he wasn't sure how he felt at the moment.

"It's pretty." She held it up and looked at it closely. "Huh. They're small Nordic runes, and it looks like they spell out a name. B, R, I…"

"Britt."

She squinted. "Yeah, you're right." Myrna looked at him with wide eyes. "And you know this because…?"

He chewed the inside of his cheek. "It belongs to someone I know."

* * *

Captain Fraust had her back turned to him as Mark updated her on his findings at the murder scene. "So you don't believe this Toussaint had anything to do with Mr. Ferguson's death." It was a statement, not a question.

"No, ma'am. The evidence at Ferguson's house doesn't support it."

"And this Jenny, the construction worker? Why did you bring her up?"

Mark tried not to bite his tongue in frustration. "Toussaint said she thought of the arson idea. I don't know if she's capable of murder, but the footprints we found were about her size, and the brand name stamped on the soles of the boots belongs to a well-known clothing company that specializes in construction gear."

She turned around, her brows raised. "You understand that you can't make that kind of assumption without additional hard evidence?"

"I know, ma'am, but it's one plausible answer. I'm going to bring her in on the premise that I have further questions. If Jenny gives any hint that she's responsible for the arson attempt or knows the identity of the murderer, I'll have her charged. Maybe sitting in a jail cell will get her to talk. I know it smells of desperation, but I think she'll provide the information I need."

Fraust cocked a brow. "This is highly unusual of you, Hawthorne."

"Yes, ma'am. But the two viable suspects I found are not talking." Mark paused, feeling unsure of himself. "I'm also afraid that if I let Jenny go after questioning her, she'll dig a hole so deep we'll never find her again."

The captain nodded. "Normally, I wouldn't endorse this kind of thing, and would recite all the reasons why it's wrong. But after listening to your theories, I'm going to let you go ahead. However," she warned. "Remember her rights."

"Yes, ma'am." Mark's gamble had paid off.

"What have you found out at the house?"

Mark felt like he was back in school, with the teacher singling him out to answer a particularly difficult question. "I believe the housekeeper knows more than she's letting on. I found out from Myrna—Investigator Walsh—that the coroner told her the method of death. The murderer strangled Ferguson first, then hit him in the back of the head several times. Approximate time of death was between the hours of one and five in the morning. We also can't find his briefcase."

She nodded. "The only way the murderer could even get close to Mr. Ferguson at that time…" Fraust let her voice trail off.

But Mark got the hint, and as he came to the most logical conclusion, he smacked the table, causing the papers to flutter. "Son of a bitch, the suspect arranged it. Must have called Ferguson and told him a lie so big that it made the CEO put on his best suit in the middle of the night to meet him."

"Agreed. We'll need to find out what business deal Mr. Ferguson had arranged that would make him go off schedule." She paused. "Anything else?"

Britt's jewelry burned a hole in his mind. For God's sake, why the hell was it even in the CEO's car? "We haven't located the suspects who pulled that B and E on the Konditori bakery," he said instead. "We received security footage, but the burglars were wearing masks. However, I believe they were hired by Ferguson to destroy it."

"It seems a moot point now. However, we can't let destruction like this go unpunished. Someone in Mr. Ferguson's small circle must know something. I want them flushed out."

"Yes, ma'am." Mark gathered his things and headed to his office. He should have thought of the suspect getting in touch with Mr. Ferguson. Honestly, he couldn't stop thinking of Britt's possible involvement. Her bracelet was a damning piece of evidence in the middle of this murder investigation.

Timmins was in the office when Mark walked in. "Hawthorne, you haven't told me what happened at the murder scene. How did the search go?"

He gave the older detective a rundown of his findings.

"Shit. An attack like that would need strong upper body strength."

And it was probable Jenny possessed that kind of power to cause lethal damage.

Mark couldn't stall any longer. Both women had a lot of explaining to do.

Mark just hoped Britt had nothing to do with the bakery CEO's death.

Chapter 10

Britt climbed out of the taxi, her injuries almost healed, though her knees were still stiff from not moving much yesterday. She walked the few steps to Konditori, her gaze scanning over the building. Her insurance company had been here since this morning, evaluating the property damage alongside the police, and they had called an hour ago to tell her they would help pay for the renovations. It wasn't as bad as it looked. Someone would be at the store tomorrow morning to give her the key to the padlock, and she could start cleaning up the pieces of her bakery.

The large picture window was completely smashed. Wooden boards had replaced it to keep the curious and the thieves at bay. The front door was sealed tight with a large padlock and covered in a crisscross of bright yellow tape with the words DO NOT CROSS.

The letters *MBB* were sprayed across the storefront multiple times with black paint, leaving only small glimpses of pink through the mess.

She hated to think what she might find inside and began to doubt her insurance company's reassurances.

She walked down the alley, remembering Mr. Ferguson's skulking form half-hidden in the shadows. His anger at her refusal to sell couldn't match the fury Britt felt deep in her stomach. That pretentious dickhead hadn't cared who he hurt—he had steamrolled over small businesses, families and innocent people to get what he wanted.

He wouldn't be doing that anymore.

Britt peeked around the corner before walking toward the rear exit—she didn't know if those jerks might still be around. There was no damage to the steel door or the windows here. It seemed that the police had arrived before the thugs could do anything else.

She completed her circuit, her emotions jumbled, but her anxiety was sitting pretty high. She would need to find additional money to make repairs. Even though her insurance said they would cover most of it, until she got inside, Britt didn't know what would need to be replaced. If the expensive kitchen equipment had been damaged…

She sighed. There wasn't much she could do.

Her cell phone pinged with a text. It was an officer from York Regional Police 4 District, advising her that their investigation was complete, and she could go into her store. Thank God for that.

Britt looked across the street to where Mr. Ferguson's latest bakery sat partially finished. Despite the CEO's death, she was sure his company would continue building, while she would scramble to make ends meet.

Her one consolation was the loyalty of her staff and customers. She had received emails that offered their condolences, reassuring her that they would return as soon as she got back on her feet. She had almost cried while reading those comforting notes, never realizing how she made an impact on strangers. Joyce had already insisted on helping her get Konditori back on its feet, and Britt could pay her back when she had the funds.

Britt sighed. Mark. She hadn't talked to him at all

today—he had to be busy working on Mr. Ferguson's murder investigation. She pulled out her phone, focused on calling to find out how he was.

He picked up on the second ring. "Britt, how are you?"

His voice sounded different—a bit strained, tired. "I'm fine. I managed to see my doctor this morning. My knees look good, just a bit raw and achy. How are you?"

"Okay. It's been a long day."

He didn't sound all right, though. In fact, he sounded like a stranger, not the warm, attentive man she had gotten to know over the last few days. "You don't sound okay," she said gently, hoping everything was fine. Did his mom take a turn for the worse? "Maybe you'd like to come over later? I could make us dinner." Those words came out of nowhere, but to her, they felt right. Mark had begun to bring out a portion of herself she hadn't seen in a long time.

"I'd like that, but…" He stopped.

This wasn't like him. In fact, this whole conversation felt wrong. "Mark, what is it? Talk to me."

"Are you home?"

She was sitting on a sidewalk bench near the store. Her knees weren't bothering her—Mark's strange attitude was. "I got restless. I'm at my bakery, assessing the damage from the outside."

"You are?" A moment passed. "You're not trying to sneak in to take a look, I hope."

"I did get the go-ahead from both the insurance company and the police. An officer just texted me with clearance, so I can finally get organized." Knowing this offered some closure. It meant she could move forward with plans, get her staff back up and running. They'd been anxious, worried they'd have to find other jobs to make ends meet.

She'd also toyed with the idea of renting out another, smaller space nearby to get Konditori back on its feet while repairs were being made to the original bakery. In fact, she might have to look into that, depending on what she found inside…

"I…need to ask you something, Britt."

All her senses were instantly on alert. Mark's voice sounded professional, almost distant. "Yes?"

"I have to ask you to come to the station."

Was that all? Did he want to give her a tour of his workplace, maybe introduce her to his colleagues? She rubbed her chin—Mark was taking their relationship a little too fast. "Mark, it's sweet that you want me to meet your fellow officers, but I don't think that's—"

"No, that's not what I meant." His voice had gotten quieter, and now he sighed. "I need you to come down to the station in order to ask you some questions about Mr. Ferguson."

Did she hear him correctly? "Mark, what are you talking about?"

She heard a car door slam. "Stay at the bakery. I'm coming now to pick you up."

"Mark, you'd better explain what you mean by that." She rubbed her stomach at the ache that flared inside. Something was horribly wrong, and Mark wasn't giving her any answers. "What's going on?"

"I'm almost there. Give me a minute."

The urge to run off and hide had Britt on her feet, even though she knew she hadn't done anything wrong. She could easily meld into the early-evening rush-hour crowd and lose him until she got home. Or maybe stay with Joyce until she could figure out why he needed to question her about a dead man who had threatened her hard-won business.

Too late. Mark pulled up in front of her. As he got out of the car, Britt moved to keep the bench between them. "What's this about?" she demanded, drawing stares from nearby pedestrians.

He stopped, his expression a mix of confusion and hurt, touched with a bit of anger. "Maybe you'd like to explain this to me."

He held up a plastic bag, and as she peered at its contents, her breath caught in her throat. It was her runic bracelet, a birthday present from her parents. "Where did you get that?" she asked, automatically rubbing her left wrist.

"Would you like to get in the car and I can tell you privately, or shall I announce it for everyone around us to hear?"

His anger sent a shock wave of trepidation coursing through every part of her limbs. She should have escaped when she had the chance.

Refusing to cause a scene, Britt came around the bench and quickly got into the car, slamming the door hard so that he got the hint she was frustrated with him. He climbed in, tossed the bracelet on the dashboard and gunned the motor. He waited until she got her seat belt on before driving off and merging with the busy evening traffic. Britt saw how tense his body was, from the white knuckles gripping the steering wheel to his clenched jaw. "Mark, talk to me. What's bothering you?" she asked.

His gaze hovered over her bracelet before he returned his attention to driving.

"My bracelet?" How did Mark find it anyway? She reached for the baggie.

"Please don't touch it, Britt."

Her hand froze in midair from the shock of his words. "Why not?" she whispered. "What does my bracelet have to do with Mr. Ferguson?"

She watched his expression, unsure what he was feeling. "Your bracelet was found in Mr. Ferguson's car."

There was a moment of pure disbelief before she burst out laughing. "Jeez, Mark, for a moment there you terrified me."

He frowned. "I found it in his car, Britt. I'll show you the evidence when we get to the precinct."

No hint of a smile or anything to portray that he was joking. And she suddenly realized he wasn't.

When they reached the precinct, Britt immediately got out of the car and walked to the front doors. Inside, she had to take Mark's lead and followed him onto an elevator at the back of the building. He hit a button two floors down, then turned to her. "Look, I'm sorry to do this to you…"

"No, you're not." During the ride to the police station, she had time to think about Mark's allegation. "You're doing your job—I get that. What I don't understand is how my bracelet ended up in Mr. Ferguson's car—it's not like I gave it to him. And in case you haven't noticed, you're making me nervous."

The elevator pinged. When the doors opened, they were in a brightly lit hallway, and stretching to either side were square rooms. She saw an officer open one of the doors and step inside. "Where are we?" she asked.

"These are the interrogation rooms." He guided her to the same room the officer stepped into. When she hesitated on the threshold, Mark said, "Step inside, please."

He indicated a chair. Jeez, he wasn't even going to be

a gentleman and pull it out for her as he usually did. With a huff of disdain, she dropped her butt onto the hard seat.

Mark looked at her for a moment, and she stared back, hoping he'd see her furious expression. He bit his lip, then turned back to the door. An older officer had come in and sat in a chair behind her.

Britt glanced over her shoulder, then looked back at Mark, willing herself to relax. She told herself again that she'd done nothing wrong, and this was just a simple Q&A Mark had to do as part of his job. She would wait until he started talking.

"Britt Gronlund, I'm Detective Mark Hawthorne with York Regional Police 4 District." His introduction was cold, unfeeling. "Behind you is Detective Walter Timmins, who is my backup."

She nodded and wrapped her arms around herself.

"I'm investigating the murder of Mr. Edward Ferguson, CEO of Mighty Big Bakery." He had a small pile of documents in front of him, and he shuffled through them until he pulled out a picture. When he slid it over, Britt looked at it and frowned. That was her bracelet, sitting on someone's car dashboard.

He then reached for the piece of jewelry, still in its plastic bag. "Does this item belong to you?"

She almost snapped at him. Of course Mark knew the bracelet belonged to her. However, she held back, and after taking a deep breath, she settled her emotions into a kind of calm detachment. "Yes."

He placed it to one side and wrote something down. "I need to advise you that during my investigation at Mr. Ferguson's home, your bracelet was found in his car."

She blinked, still not believing what she'd heard, but

remained silent, waiting to see if Mark would add any further context.

He looked at her, his brow raised. "Can you explain how your bracelet got into Mr. Ferguson's car?"

Mark wasn't seriously thinking... "I have no idea how my jewelry got into that jerk's car."

A small smile ghosted his lips before it disappeared.

"Are you saying you weren't in Mr. Ferguson's car at all, Ms. Gronlund?"

She turned to stare at the older man who had asked the question. "Not at all."

He gave her a look that had *I don't believe you* written all over it.

"Can you explain how it might have gotten into Mr. Ferguson's car?" Mark asked.

Britt kept her gaze on Mark. "On Monday morning, I arrived at my bakery, but it was filled with customers—I couldn't get in. I went around to the alley to go through the back door, and Mr. Ferguson was there." The angry look on the man's face still gave her the creeps. "He told me the customers threw him out when he tried to come in, and for some reason, he hung around until I showed up.

"He went through his usual spiel of trying to buy my business. I told him it wasn't for sale. He got angry and grabbed me."

A dark shadow crossed Mark's face. She hadn't told him that part because she knew she could handle the CEO. Besides, there were plenty of pedestrians at the time—a few high-pitched screams would have brought someone running to help her.

"What happened next?"

"I kicked him in the balls and left him there. I had a business to run."

This time, a full smile lit up Mark's features. "Very proactive of you."

Britt kept her professional stance up, despite the warm feeling seeping through her at Mark's grin. "I can only think that Mr. Ferguson pulled my bracelet off when he grabbed me. It makes the most sense."

"Do you think he planned on returning it to you?"

"I hope so. Although I wouldn't put it past him if he tried to bribe me with it. The bracelet has a lot of sentimental value."

"Can you tell us the rest of your day?"

Britt explained in detail up until Joyce had called the police. "The rest you already know, Detective Hawthorne. Thank you for assisting my friend and I last night." Being detached and polite worked both ways.

"We'll need to hang on to your bracelet for the duration of our investigation." Mark slid the picture back into his stack of documentation and placed her bracelet on top, then stood. "Thank you for your cooperation. We may need to call you in for further questioning."

She nodded, biting the inside of her cheek, only because she wondered what Mark was playing at.

He glanced over her shoulder. "I'd like to escort Ms. Gronlund outside, Timmins. Would you mind taking my notes to the office?"

Glancing at the other detective, who had grabbed Mark's stuff and was heading out, she finally surmised he probably had to be professional when questioning her. Still, he could have warned her.

When they got outside, he took her elbow and led her to his car, remaining quiet until they got in. He breathed a loud sigh of relief. "*Vakker*, I can't tell you how sorry I am for putting you through that."

Britt twisted her hands in her lap. "You're a real jerk, Mark Hawthorne."

He jumped in his seat, his eyes wide with surprise. "Britt, I mean it…"

"I get it. You were playing detective—can't get too close to the witness. Gotta keep it professional."

"Britt, that's not fair." He got the car started.

"No? Was treating me like a criminal fair?"

"I didn't do…" He stopped, his breath loud and harsh within the car interior. "We found your bracelet in Ferguson's car. How else did you expect me to treat it? And you?"

"You could have simply asked, instead of dragging me through a police interrogation and embarrassing me."

"No, Britt, I couldn't. Your jewelry was found at a murder scene. Think on that. If I treated you any differently to the other witnesses I'd brought in, Detective Timmins and the officers outside that room would have questioned my motives. I can't play favorites in this job." He drove out into the busy traffic. "If I'd given you any hint about what was going on, you wouldn't have been surprised or upset. That would have tipped off Timmins for sure. He's an old pro at this. He would have given me a world of grief."

Britt listened as Mark explained his actions. She understood the intent, but it didn't quite make her feel better. "Did you really think I killed Mr. Ferguson?"

"No!" His voice was firm, assuring. "You would beat him up, but not kill him. I knew you would think Ferguson wasn't worth going to jail for."

"You got that right." At least they were on the same page with that. She started to calm down, thinking through everything Mark had said, and coming to the conclusion that, yes, he was doing his job. She knew she was innocent and had nothing to worry about.

"Why didn't you tell me about Ferguson grabbing you in the alley?" he asked.

"Because I knew how you would react. Besides, he didn't expect me to know self-defense maneuvers."

"Wish I'd seen that." His smile was his own, filled with humor. "And how are your knees?" He rested a hand on one. "I noticed you didn't have trouble walking."

Britt had worried she'd flinch, considering what he'd put her through. But her anger had almost melted away, and the warmth from his touch felt good. "A lot better, thank you." She thought of something. "Have you found out anything about those jackasses that broke into my store?"

"No. Thanks for the security footage, by the way. Unfortunately, it doesn't help since the thugs were disguised. Myrna, my forensics investigator, did find some fingerprints, but she didn't get any hits."

"I wonder what they'll do now that Mr. Ferguson's dead."

"Best scenario? Stop trashing people's businesses."

For some unexplained reason, she didn't think that would happen. "Do you honestly believe that?"

Another sigh, but he sounded tired. "I don't know. Until I can collect more information, I can't do anything."

Britt noticed he was taking her back to her place. "Listen, do you want to grab a bite to eat? I'm starving."

"Great idea. So am I."

They found a well-known sandwich shop. It was empty, which Britt was glad for. In her gut, she felt that they needed to discuss some things—not just what had happened with Mr. Ferguson, but themselves, especially her.

She hadn't opened up about her past because she hadn't been ready to revisit the pain and humiliation. Britt knew that if she didn't get it out of her system, it would continue to fester like an untreated wound, and she couldn't move forward with her life. It seemed the best time to talk to Mark about it.

They sat at a table near the front window. Despite the noise of traffic, it was unusually quiet in the shop. "Other than interrogating me," she started, "how was your day?"

Mark frowned and twisted his mouth. "Frustrating."

"Can you talk about any of it? Or is it confidential? Maybe I can help."

His look was curious. "You have enough going on with the bakery. I don't want to add to that. Besides, it's part of my job to be pissed off when the clues don't come together."

"But you must discuss investigations with your colleagues, right? Just think of me as one of them." She imitated Detective Timmins's stance, crossing her arms and attempting to make a stern face. "Come on, Hawthorne," she growled in a deep voice. "Let's hear what you've got."

His widening grin burst into a loud snort of laughter. "That was almost perfect. Thank you for that."

Their meals arrived, and Britt stared at the smoked salmon and cream cheese specialty she had ordered— the sandwich was big, and it came with a salad and a chocolate-almond croissant for dessert. She could take half of it home to have for lunch tomorrow. She glanced at Mark's, inhaling the scent of steak, cheese and onions. "Oh my God, that smells delicious."

"I'll give you a piece." He used a fork and knife to deftly cut off a corner and put it on her plate. *"Bon appétit."*

They spent a few minutes enjoying their meal. By the time Britt came up for air, she'd finished her sandwich and half of her salad. "Crap," she mumbled, wiping her mouth with a napkin. "I didn't realize how hungry I was."

"I've heard that stress can increase one's appetite," he murmured.

"Oh, great." She eyed the croissant with disdain. Ah, what the hell. She took a bite of the sweet, flaky pastry. "Mmm, this is good. Maybe I should ask Jacques to come up with a similar recipe, Norwegian style."

Mark stirred his cappuccino. "How did you two meet each other?"

His question meant talking about her past, and it was as good a time as any. "I had Konditori all planned out. I found the perfect spot for it and hired Joyce to do the interior design. I started looking for staff, and Jacques answered me the day I posted the job, and I was honestly shocked at his experience. He worked at a Michelin-starred restaurant while living in France, before moving to Toronto."

His brows rose. "Why would he move from France?"

"He said better opportunities. He never talked about it, but my hunch is, he wants to open his own business someday."

Mark nodded. "You might lose a great baker."

"I know. But I'm not going to begrudge his ambitions. He'll do what's right for him." She paused, thinking of herself.

"How did you become a bakery owner, Britt? I don't think I asked you that."

Britt took a breath as her muscles wove into tense, painful knots. Here it was, her opportunity to clear out her past.

He grabbed her hand and squeezed it. "Hey, if you don't want to talk about it…"

"I have to." The words rushed out of her. "Because if I don't, I'll feel like I'm keeping secrets from you, which isn't fair to either of us."

His eyes widened, sparkling beneath the lights in the shop.

"When I was in university, I majored in economics with the goal of becoming a parliamentary secretary. My ultimate dream was to become a member of Parliament. I wanted to try to change some of the things going on in the country."

"A lofty goal."

"But achievable. I graduated with honors and was determined to find a position within a year." Back then, her ambitions were laser-focused. "I had my pick of various jobs everywhere from Fisheries and Oceans Canada to the federal security agency.

"I finally decided on working with the minister of international trade. That was five years ago. I loved it. I learned so much from Minister Frank Strathmore. But I started hearing strange rumors about the minister's mannerisms, especially toward women."

Mark's face darkened with anger, which she expected. "I found out the world of politics was still a man's domain, and of course, they like to do things their way. Minister Strathmore was no different. When he became a little too friendly, I accused him of assault. He just laughed in my face."

The awful, familiar feelings of humiliation and embarrassment reared their ugly heads, demanding that she acknowledge them. This time, Britt did, but chose not to let those emotions make her feel bad or ashamed. She fought them back, showing that she was in control, that she was sick and tired of feeling guilty for standing up for herself. "I learned quickly that every man and woman had to fend for themselves. After I reported the minister's actions, nothing was done. In fact, I was told to suck it up and be proud that Minister Strathmore was giving me 'personal support,' as Human Resources called it."

"Jesus," Mark breathed. He squeezed her hand. "One of my female colleagues at work talked about that. She had to prove her worth almost twice as much as the men. I used to think of her as aggressive, but when she told us what she went through…" He stopped. "Did you quit the job?"

"I thought about it—many times. But I wanted to put Minister Strathmore's head on a platter first.

"I collected evidence over a six-month period. Photos, calls, video, text messages, to support myself and the other women he'd been harassing. I called HR out on their crap, and next thing I knew, I was being summoned to defend my actions." She sighed. "Those were the worst five weeks of my life." Britt could see the scenes in her mind—the courtroom, the minister and his friends giving her the evil eye, the women who said they would support her instead looking at their hands while she testified.

"I had enough physical evidence to get him fired from his position, that's all. And the next time I heard his name, Minister Strathmore had somehow become an independent member in the Parliament of Canada." She chewed the inside of her cheek. "Just goes to show you what a person can do with enough clout."

Mark hadn't moved or said anything while she talked, but his being there helped to keep the demons away. "My ability to trust took a serious nosedive," she concluded. "I became introverted, closed myself off after the trial.

Thank God I was too stubborn to stay that way. So I pivoted and worked on my next dream job, which was owning my own bakery. Now here I am, making Nordic pastries and comparison shopping for supplies."

"But you love it. That's what counts."

"Sure do. And getting the all-clear from the insurance company to rebuild has taken a weight off my shoulders. My staff and I can start cleaning up tomorrow."

"That's great news, Britt." He finished his cappuccino. "Maybe I'll swing by to visit."

His cell phone pinged with a text. As he read it, she noticed his worried look. "Is everything all right?" she asked.

"Yeah." He raised his hand to get the waiter's attention. "It's my mom. She wants me to come to the hospital to visit."

"I hope she's doing well." They headed for the car.

Mark grasped her hand in his as they strolled down the sidewalk, and Britt could easily get used to this. To not just have a man in her life, but someone who was also in her corner, to provide support and encouragement. She'd love to return the favor. However, his line of work may not offer a chance to provide ideas or theories that could help in his cases. She could certainly ask. "You know, if you need a sounding board during your investigations, you can let me know. I won't tell anyone anything."

He raised her hand to his lips. "Thank you, *vakker*. That means a lot."

At the door to her condo, she wrapped her arms around his neck. "I'm not sure if I should even kiss you," she whispered, a breath away from his lips. "You thought I was a criminal."

He cocked a brow. "No. I thought you were up to something with that bastard."

"Ewww." She pulled at his ear. "I can't believe you'd think that!"

"No, I didn't mean it that way. I meant…" He paused. "I was worried you had changed your mind about selling your bakery."

"If there's one thing you should remember, Mr. Detective, it's that I'm stubborn. I get what I want, but not by hurting others."

"Yup, that's my Nordic princess." His kiss was thorough, lingering. She didn't want it to end.

Another ping from his phone. He groaned as he slowly released her. "I'd better get going before Mom sends a hunting party out looking for me."

She grinned. "Your mom sounds like fun."

"Great sense of humor. I think you two would like each other." With a wink and another kiss, he disappeared down the hallway.

Britt had plans of her own to organize. She emailed her staff with the good news and told them to wait for her by the rear door so she could let them in. Then she called Joyce, who screamed with delight, and said she'd be there by ten o'clock tomorrow morning to assess what needed to be done.

All in all, a good day despite the vandalism hanging over her head. Britt was taking baby steps to move her life forward again, this time with Mark at her side.

Chapter 11

Mark had never felt so scared. He could handle mouthy dickheads with ease as he dragged their sorry asses to jail. No problem at all.

Britt, on the other hand… The drive to the precinct yesterday to interrogate her about her bracelet had him on pins and needles. He had no way to know how questioning her would turn out.

What hurt the most was remaining silent. She may not have noticed, but he heard the increasing note of panic in her voice as she demanded answers. Answers he couldn't provide until he got back to the police station.

Perhaps there was a better way of handling the situation. Mark certainly hadn't been thinking straight when he'd found her bracelet in Ferguson's car. Considering all that had happened these past few days, how else could he have viewed that damning piece of evidence?

But his instinct had told him how wrong he was. And while instinct was a great indicator, it was hard to ignore what was in front of him—Britt's bracelet, in the car of Mighty Big Bakery's dead CEO.

He remembered how the weight lifted off his shoulders when the interrogation was over, although he still had an angry Nordic princess chewing him out when they'd left the precinct.

Mark sat at his desk, piecing clues together, thinking on theories. The footprints at Mr. Ferguson's home and the fingerprints found on the CEO's body didn't match Henry Toussaint's as he'd first hoped, but he had to be sure. As for Jenny the construction worker, she had already lied to him once, so he'd have to be ready for any tricks, including that flirtatious manner of hers. If she was the killer, she would do everything possible not to get caught.

Mark still believed he hadn't received all the truth from Toussaint, either. He thought the young man might know who the protest leader was, but scratched that idea. Since it was Jenny who drove them to the secret protest site, Mark might have a better chance of obtaining that information from her.

Now all he had to do was locate her.

As for the housekeeper and Mrs. Ferguson… Well, something definitely smelled fishy about Gloria. He would explore that after talking to the construction worker.

His first visit, to the partially built Mighty Big Bakery, yielded no results. Mr. Smith, the supervisor who was still in charge of the site, told him that Jenny got called to another location. "Damn pain in my ass," he grumbled. "How the hell am I supposed to stay on schedule when I'm down a person?"

"Is that normal?" Mark asked.

"No, it's not. And with Mr. Ferguson dead, I don't know who's taking over this project."

The comment made Mark's ears perk up. That was right—there should be a succession plan in case the owner couldn't direct anymore. He'd have to pay a visit to the MBB head office. "No one called?"

"Not a peep. I'll keep going until I hear otherwise."

"Thanks." He headed back to his car, thinking. Toussaint no doubt told Jenny about his interrogation with the police, and she was probably in hiding. He had her address, which wasn't far from the sushi restaurant he and Britt had gone to.

It was an old duplex apartment, which blended in with the large houses on the street. He hit the buzzer twice, and when he didn't get an answer, tried calling her cell phone. It went immediately to voice mail. He left a message, asking her to call as soon as possible, then slowly went down the stairs. He turned around to look up at the apartment. The blinds were shut—maybe she was sleeping in and had turned her phone off.

Maybe…

Mark hopped back up the stairs and hit the buzzer for the other apartment. This time, a dog barked furiously but went quiet when a stern voice hushed it. The inner door opened to reveal a man in his late fifties. "Yes? You looking for someone?"

"Good morning." He showed his badge. "I wanted to ask if you'd seen Jenny recently."

"The young lady lives here, but I haven't seen her today. Might be with that boyfriend of hers."

Mark felt like a first-class douchebag—why hadn't he put two and two together? "Don't tell me, Henry?"

He nodded. "Yeah, that's the name. He came by around five or so yesterday. Jenny gets home about that time. Did the horizontal mambo for a couple of hours before taking off. I don't know where."

Mark had his suspicions. "Thank you, sir."

This time, no more Mr. Nice Guy.

With a search warrant in his pocket, Mark pounded on

Henry Toussaint's door. "Open up! York Regional Police 4 District! I know Henry Toussaint's in there!"

Timmins, his hand resting on a stun gun, glanced at him. "What do you think?"

"I think they'll make a run for it. Ergo, officers watching the back door and windows."

The front door finally opened, and the woman he had met a few days ago appeared. "Oh, it's you again," she sneered. "Henry's not here."

"Now you're just bullshitting me." Mark's temper was getting hot, but he wasn't going to lose it.

The woman's surprised expression morphed into anger. "How dare you talk—"

"Where's Henry?" He pushed against the door, but the woman held her ground. "Look, Mrs. Toussaint, I have a warrant to search the premises and bring Henry and his girlfriend in for further questioning."

"Henry doesn't have a girlfriend," she spat.

"Well, you're in for a surprise." The woman was strong, but not enough to keep him and Timmins out. "Unless you want my partner and me to thoroughly search through the house for your son," he warned, "I suggest you tell him to make an appearance." He took the warrant out and waved it in the air. "Your call."

The expression on her face would have scared off a grizzly bear. "Henry!" she yelled out. Damn, she had a powerful voice. "Henry! Get down here, now!"

No answer. She frowned, then turned back to him. "He's not home. What's this about anyway?"

Mark knew his brow went up at that. "He hasn't told you?" He glanced at Timmins, and at his nod, barged in and raced for the stairs.

"Hey! What are you doing?"

Mark got on his walkie-talkie. "This is Hawthorne. Anyone show up?"

"No, sir, the windows are clear."

"One of you get to the garage. Bust the back door down if you have to."

With the older detective at his back, they checked each of the rooms on the second floor but couldn't locate Henry or Jenny. "Team, tell me you have them!" he said into the walkie-talkie, running back downstairs.

"Negative, sir. No one's out here."

He and Timmins checked the rooms on the main floor before Mark stepped up to Mrs. Toussaint. "If you don't tell me where Henry is, I'll arrest you for obstruction," he growled out.

"As if. Henry hasn't done anything wrong."

"Your precious Henry beat up the CEO of Mighty Big Bakery," Timmins chimed in. "And now the man is dead."

Whoa, Mark hadn't expected Timmins to be so blunt. But maybe it would get Mrs. Toussaint to open her eyes and help them find her son and Jenny.

She grasped the front of her blouse, and Mark watched with growing concern as her face turned a ghastly shade of white. Her mouth trembled, but nothing came out.

"Mrs. Toussaint," he said gently. "We need to find your son and take him and Jenny in for questioning. We believe they haven't given us their full story."

Every minute the woman remained quiet was another minute that Henry and Jenny could escape. Mark snapped his fingers in front of her face, concerned that she'd gone into shock. "Mrs. Toussaint."

She blinked slowly, as if waking up from a dream. But then her face screwed up in anger, and he was now worried she wouldn't help at all.

"Follow me." She headed toward the back of the house.

He eyed Timmins, who shrugged, then hurried to catch up to Mrs. Toussaint. "This is Hawthorne," he called over the walkie-talkie. "Maintain position. Repeat, maintain your posts."

They followed her into a spacious kitchen. Wide, ceiling-high windows let in plenty of sunshine and offered an amazing view of the expansive backyard, with a swimming pool and BBQ patio. She veered to the left, then stopped in front of a door. "This leads to the family room in the basement," she told them. "He's down there."

"Is there any way for him to escape?" Mark asked, eyeing the entrance.

"There's a door that leads into the backyard. I guess if he was desperate, he could crawl through a window that faces the front."

"Would you mind calling him out, Mrs. Toussaint? I'd like to conduct this with the least resistance."

"If you need to knock him about the head, I don't mind."

Mark kept his surprise in check as she indicated to him and Timmins to stand around the corner. Mrs. Toussaint opened the door. "Henry! Get your ass up here!"

Timmins gripped his stun gun in one hand. Mark had debated taking out his weapon but held back—this could get ugly really quick. "Stand by," he whispered into the walkie-talkie. He noticed two officers at the back door and hurried over to quietly slide it open. "Stand with Timmins," he told them. "Suspect's coming upstairs from the basement."

They remained silent, the tension building.

"I'm busy, Mom," Henry called out.

"I don't give a shit. Just get up here. I need you for something."

Mark indicated to the officers to have their stun guns ready.

"I told you I didn't want to be bothered," Henry told her. His voice held a hint of frustration. "Come back later."

Wow. He saw Timmins rolling his eyes.

When Mrs. Toussaint glanced at him, Mark nodded in encouragement.

"Henry, we've talked about you living here, remember? If you don't pay rent, you have to help around the house, that was the deal. Now I need your help with something."

Mark backed away and radioed the rest of his team. "Keep an eye on the garage and backyard for the female," he whispered.

Footsteps stomped on the stairs. Mark motioned for Mrs. Toussaint to stand away from the door so that she didn't get caught in the middle. "You had to bring that up, huh? I've been trying to find a job for weeks."

"Which tells me how much effort you're putting into it," she retorted. She appeared at the corner and continued backing up, keeping her gaze on Henry.

As soon as he stepped into view, the two officers jumped him. Henry yelled out in surprise and fought, kicking out and landing a bare foot against an officer's knee. The officer's grip loosened, and Henry pushed him away, before turning his attention to the second cop, throwing punches into his face.

"Henry!" Mark shouted. He managed to grab and pin the man's arm and held on tight as the first officer cuffed him. Damn, this guy was strong. Mark kept his legs together as Henry tried to kick him in the balls. "Hey, calm down!"

The young man continued to struggle. "Get your hands off me!" he yelled.

It wasn't working. "Henry, if you don't calm down you'll leave me no choice but to stun you," Mark warned. "Do you want me to Tase you in front of your mother?"

That seemed to do the trick. Henry finally stopped thrashing around. "Get him in the car," Mark demanded. "And read him his rights."

He moved to stand at the top of the basement stairs. "Jenny, I know you're down there," he called out. "We've got Henry. Don't make this hard on yourself."

A couple of minutes went by. "Detective Hawthorne, I didn't see anyone come in with Henry," Mrs. Toussaint said.

"He might have sneaked her in through that back door you told me about." He tried again. "I'd better not have to come down there to flush you out. The house is surrounded. You won't get away."

He tensed at the sound of a door. He was about to call in to the officers when a person appeared at the bottom of the stairs—Jenny, with her hands raised in the air.

"Get up here," he shouted, and backed away as she reached the top. "Turn around."

She complied, and an officer slipped the cuffs on her. "Aren't you going to read me my rights?" she asked, sounding cheerful, for the love of God.

"The officer taking you to the police car will do that." Mark was still trembling with adrenaline after the scuffle with Henry.

As the construction worker was led out of the house, he turned to Henry's mother. "Mrs. Toussaint, I need to find Henry's sneakers."

"He keeps them lined up downstairs in the closet. Second door to your left."

When Mark opened the door, he couldn't believe his

eyes. There were eight pairs of limited-edition sneakers, as clean as if they'd come out of the box. He pulled on a pair of gloves and grabbed the ones he needed, noticing smudges of dirt in the creases and more stuck to the sole. He dropped them into an evidence bag and headed back upstairs.

He and Timmins were the last to leave. "I'm sorry, Mrs. Toussaint," he apologized. "I had a feeling Henry might have resisted the arrest, but I didn't think he'd actually start fighting. Are you okay?"

She nodded, her expression sad. "Henry never said anything to me about this. It happened last Friday night?"

"Yes." How did she know?

"When he came home, there was mud on his clothes and his best sneakers." She frowned. "He treated those shoes like they were his pets. When I asked him what happened, he ignored me and hid in the family room for most of the weekend until you showed up on Sunday." She shook her head. "I don't know what's gotten into him recently."

"That's what we hope to find out. An officer will call with an update." Mark didn't know what else to say, so he nodded at her before leaving.

At the precinct, Mark was all business. "Henry and Jenny in their own interrogation rooms," Mark demanded. "I'm getting tired of the bullshit."

A cheer went up when Britt turned the corner. All her staff were waiting at the rear entrance. "Good morning, everyone."

"Chérie." Jacques grasped her shoulders and kissed both cheeks. "We heard what happened to you. Are you all right?"

"Yes, thanks to Joyce." His worried expression tugged at her heart, and she placed her hand on his cheek. "I'm fine, Jacques. See? The scrapes have almost healed. My calf muscles are just a little stiff, that's all." She moved past the rest of her employees. Betty gave her an impromptu hug, while Kevin, Jasmine and Oliver gave her big smiles. Thomas, Jacques's assistant, tilted his head in a nod—he'd always been shy and quiet around her.

Inside, everyone was silent as Britt led them to the kitchen. As she went through the swing doors and took one look at the room, she breathed a sigh of relief.

Everything looked to be in place. The door leading to the front had been knocked off its hinges, but as they moved farther in, she didn't see anything out of place or smashed on the floor. "Thank God they didn't get in here before the police arrived," she breathed. "Jacques, can you and Thomas go through everything carefully and let me know?"

"*Bien sûr*, of course." He took off his jacket and talked to Thomas about how to inspect the kitchen properly.

The front of the bakery was where the most damage had occurred. The display cases were destroyed, tables and chairs thrown about, the bookshelf shattered on the floor. Some of the books had been torn to shreds and the pages strewed everywhere. The office door had been kicked but had held in place.

It had been a scary night—Britt was so glad Joyce had been with her. Without her friend's support, she might have done something unthinkable, like confront the jerks.

"I honestly thought it was going to be a lot worse than this." Britt turned in a slow circle, glass crunching under her feet. "Let's get this cleaned up," she announced. She got her key in the lock to the office, but it took a bit of persuading before it opened. The room was undamaged.

She put her things in the desk drawer and got her laptop fired up to check for messages. Other than Joyce reconfirming her arrival, her new emails were from customers, reiterating their support and good wishes.

Britt wanted to cry she was so happy. This was what she loved the most—the loyalty and trust from almost perfect strangers. Many of them stated they would wait until Konditori reopened, as they didn't want to spend their money anywhere else.

She called everyone into the office and read some of the emails out loud. "Wow, now that is something," Betty exclaimed. "I hadn't realized how much our customers loved the bakery."

"And the staff," Kevin added. "Without Britt, I think we'd just be another bakery like MBB."

"Bite your tongue, young man." Jacques trembled. "That will never happen."

"How does the kitchen look, Jacques?" Britt asked, worried there might have been damage that she'd missed.

He kissed his fingers. "The criminals didn't have a chance to destroy the appliances, but everything is covered in dust and debris. The power had been turned off, no doubt during the police investigation, but *merde*, they could have turned it back on when they were finished. Everything is spoiled in the fridge and freezer."

"The food is the least of my worries, and honestly, I'm glad everything was turned off. Heaven help me if a fire started in here."

They got to work. Britt grabbed a large broom and carefully swept the glass to one corner while Kevin and Oliver stacked the broken pieces of the bookshelf in another. Betty managed to stack the chairs, then Britt, Oliver and Kevin helped manhandle the tables until they, too, were stacked on top of each other.

Suddenly, there was a loud knock on the door, followed by the sound of the padlock being opened. The makeshift door swung open. "Good morning. Is Britt Gronlund here?"

That must be the insurance representative. "Hi, that's me."

The representative stepped inside carefully and put the padlock down on the windowsill. "I've brought an extra key for you," she said, holding it out and giving it to her. "I'm glad my insurance company was able to help you."

"So am I. The payment will cover everything that needs to be replaced."

"Oh, speaking of which." The woman opened her purse and pulled out an envelope. "You'll receive two insurance payments instead of four. You're a longtime client, and we want to help get you back on your feet as soon as possible."

Frowning, Britt opened the envelope and stared at the number on the check. "Seriously?"

"Uh-huh." The rep smiled. "I'll have to come down one day and try your pastries. I've heard a lot of wonderful things about the bakery. The second payment should arrive in the next two to three weeks."

Britt squeezed her eyes shut to keep the tears from flowing. "Thank you," she whispered.

"You're most welcome. Good luck." And just like that, the rep was gone.

Joyce arrived about a half hour later. "Shit, the storefront looks like it got hit with a bomb."

"I'm glad those assholes didn't come up with that kind of plan." Britt swept her arm around the room. "The kitchen is in one piece—I have the Fates to thank for that.

Jacques and Thomas are cleaning it up now. As for here, well, you see what we're dealing with."

Joyce swept her gaze around the room. "Honestly, sweetie, this won't take long to fix up. I'm glad it's just this space. Replacing the kitchen would have cost you a pretty penny."

"Tell me about it." She showed her friend the check.

"Whoa, I didn't expect that much."

"The insurance company decided on giving us two payments within a month. I can get the bakery up and running in that time."

"Then we should go shopping. I brought my laptop, so I'll show you the latest styles I have in furniture, paint and fabrics." She looked at the walls. "Do you still want to keep the same colors?"

"Absolutely."

For the next hour, they worked out a plan for rejuvenating Konditori. "I can have a team here in a couple of hours. We can start work on replacing the display cabinets and front door, getting glass for the windows and giving the walls a power wash and a fresh coat of paint. I still have all the original measurements, so it won't take as long."

Britt nodded—she couldn't speak she was so grateful.

As Joyce made her calls, Britt went into the kitchen to see if Jacques needed any help, but her staff was already there, working under Jacques's exacting demands. The back door was open to let in fresh air, and it looked like everything was under control.

Britt returned to her office and dropped into her chair, mentally exhausted. Things were moving faster than she had anticipated, all because of a few people who cared about her bakery. She wanted to call Mark to give him the good news. Instead, she grabbed her phone and sent a text, knowing he was probably busy with Mr. Ferguson's murder.

Goose bumps prickled her arms as she thought about her reaction when Mark had held up her bracelet. Joyce had noticed it was missing, and for the life of her, Britt hadn't remembered whether she'd put it on or not that morning. The simple move of clasping it over her wrist was so automatic, she never thought about it. She had never noticed it coming off during her scuffle with Mr. Ferguson, and because she'd been so upset with everything else, she'd completely forgotten about it until she got home and started looking for it. She was only glad that it had been found—it was a custom-made birthday gift from her parents.

There was another loud knock at the front door to the bakery. She rose and watched as Kevin scooted across the space and opened it. "Yes?"

"Hi there." It was a woman in her fifties, and Britt recognized her as a regular customer. "Will Konditori be open again soon?"

"We're hoping in the next few days."

"Thank God!" She waved at someone. "I told you I saw someone coming in here!"

Britt watched in fascination as several people crowded around on the sidewalk. "What's everyone doing here?" she asked.

"We hadn't heard anything about the bakery since that horrible break-in," the woman told her. "And we were worried that Mighty Big Bakery had bought you out."

"No, that won't happen." It felt good to say that with certainty, although horrifying that Mr. Ferguson had to pay with his life. She shook her head at the senseless loss, wondering if he had a wife, family, friends.

"We're glad you're reopening," a young man called out from the crowd. "I miss my morning Danish!"

Everyone laughed, and at a gentle push from Kevin, Britt stepped into the animated crowd, shaking hands and answering questions. As she turned, Mighty Big Bakery's construction site across the street came into view, but now, she wasn't worried. With an incredible staff, wonderful friends and customers who stood by her, Britt believed she had turned a page in her life. The next chapter held new opportunities, including a man who had literally swept her off her feet, and the future looked glorious.

Chapter 12

Mark had left Henry and Jenny to cool their heels in separate interrogation rooms while he sat at his desk, thinking. Some of the clues he had found didn't make sense, such as the footprints behind the shrubbery in Ferguson's backyard, the missing briefcase, and the fingerprints that didn't match Henry's or Jenny's. Evidence that had been found at the construction site only led to Henry, despite the young man's admission that Jenny was the mastermind behind the attempted arson.

"You okay, Hawthorne?"

He glanced at Timmins, who was leaning back in his chair, hands clasped behind his head. He knew the older detective would help him if asked, but sometimes, Mark's stubborn streak got in the way. "Just trying to sort everything out."

"Let's hear it. I know you're eager to get at those two downstairs. But go over what you've got out loud, and I'll chime in if necessary."

Mark rehashed everything from the beginning, starting with Mr. Ferguson's assault. "The one thing that has remained consistent is everyone's hatred for the CEO, and someone took it far enough to kill him." He looked at his list of potential suspects. "That could be anyone listed here."

"Who stands to gain the most from this?"

"Mrs. Ferguson, definitely. But she already has everything. Of course, if his business personality was the same as his personality at home…" Mark knew he had to get back out there to question her and the housekeeper.

"What else?"

Mark was glad to have Timmins hit him with questions—his mind had been a jumbled mess even with his notes all neatly organized in front of him. Too many pieces were not fitting together. "The housekeeper gave off a weird vibe when I asked about Ferguson's missing briefcase."

"Then you can ask the ladies to come in later today. As for those two downstairs, do you think they're capable of murdering Ferguson?"

He shook his head, more out of confusion. "I think Henry's capable of it, but not on his own."

"Agreed. What about Jenny?"

"I don't get the impression she'd get her hands dirty, but I can totally see her guiding someone into doing it. I'm not sensing that here, though."

Mark closed his eyes, a trick he used to block out everything around him and concentrate on one item. Henry and Jenny were his immediate focus. They had lied to him to cover their butts, that was now obvious. But why? To avoid being tied to Ferguson's murder or just avoid jail time for the beating and attempted arson? He believed it was the latter, but he would ask Myrna to reconfirm that the fingerprints found at the murder scene did not match either Henry's or Jenny's.

Mrs. Ferguson and the housekeeper were on a different level, being much closer to Mr. Ferguson. He couldn't see them attempting anything as risky as murder, but he couldn't rule them out either. Mark was sensitive to the fact that Mrs. Ferguson would be mourning, and bringing her to the precinct for questioning felt wrong. A visit to her home would be more sympathetic, and might yield better results.

It only took a couple of minutes. When Mark opened his eyes, he felt clearheaded and had a direction. He hit a button on his office phone. "Myrna, sorry to bother you. Can I ask you to compare our two suspects' fingerprints again with those at the murder scene? Yes, I do trust your results, just humor me, okay? Thanks. I'll be in the interrogation room with Jenny."

Five minutes later, he sat across from the construction worker with Timmins in the background. "You've already questioned me," she snapped, leaning forward in the metal chair. "What the hell am I here for now?"

So, she was going to be like that? "I'm waiting on confirmation that fingerprints found at Mr. Ferguson's murder scene match yours. My forensics investigator got clear fingerprints from your purse."

Yep, that got a terrified look out of her—even Timmins's jaw dropped. "No, no! There's no way. I didn't kill him!"

"Guess we'll wait and see." He kept his tone and stance professional, refusing to let her try to bait him into anger. "In the meantime, let's talk. You never mentioned that you and Henry were an item."

"More like friends with benefits." Her smile was crafty. "I was more into you."

He let that comment slide. "You're already implicated, in case Henry hasn't told you. Why did you want to burn down the new Mighty Big Bakery location?"

"I'm sure you already know the answer to that," she spat out.

"Humor me."

She sat back in her chair. "You saw what Mr. Ferguson was like. Arrogant, a bully, a first-class asshole. If he didn't get his way, he'd threaten, cheat and steal to get what he wanted. I never understood why the *police*—" she emphasized the word "—never arrested him."

"I don't know about the other precincts. As for us, we never had enough evidence to charge him."

"That's horseshit!"

Mark let that one go, too. "You haven't answered my question."

Jenny blew out a loud breath. "My friend and her family got caught in Ferguson's vicious net. That jerk sent his goons after them and trashed their store. When that didn't work, they upped their game and burned the business to the ground." She shook her head, upset. "I'm sure you've had your share of grieving witnesses. It was tough on them."

Mark knew exactly where Jenny was coming from, since he had seen what had happened to Britt and her bakery. His fury almost had him hunting down Ferguson, except that Britt's needs came first. "I know how you feel."

Her eyes blazed with rekindled anger. "Then you know why I did what I had to do. Get revenge. An eye for an eye. Why should my friend and others suffer the loss of their life's work, while that dickhead acted like he'd done nothing wrong?"

"If Mr. Ferguson had any involvement with the arson and B and Es, we haven't found any proof. We need facts, Jenny, not theories."

She shrugged. "Guess it doesn't matter anymore. He's dead, and good riddance."

Jenny explained how she got Henry inside the construction site by leaving the gate unlocked. She had provided him with a hard hat and a high-visibility safety jacket so that he'd blend in. The idea was to hide the container until everyone had left, then go back, spread the gasoline around and light it up. Unfortunately, when Henry saw Mr. Ferguson, he let his anger do the talking and gave the CEO a thorough beating.

Mark digested her story as he wrote his notes. "What about the leader of these anti-Ferguson protests? Do you know who he is?"

"Like I'd tell you if I knew. You'd just arrest him and do nothing about Mighty Big Bakery's abusive takeovers."

"Not true, but I know you don't believe me. For now, I'm charging you with attempted arson."

Jenny jumped up so fast, the chair went flying. "Are you shitting me?"

"Nope. If you want a lawyer, I'll arrange your phone call. You already know your rights." He stood up. "Be glad it's not worse. If I find out you had anything to do with Mr. Ferguson's murder, I'll make sure you won't get out."

The young woman screamed a litany of curses as he and Timmins left the room. Two officers who had been guarding the room hurried past them to subdue Jenny and take her to a cell.

"Well, Hawthorne," Timmins said as they approached the second interrogation room where Henry waited, "I didn't quite expect that."

"It got results. That's all I wanted."

Their talk with Henry didn't reveal anything new, other than his relationship with Jenny. He did blame her for coming up with the arson idea. "I had nothing to do with that," he complained.

"You went with her to a secret protest to find out how to piss off Mr. Ferguson," Mark told him. He jabbed a finger onto the table. "You impersonated a construction worker and carried a gasoline container onto the site. You deliberately hid it with the intent of burning down the building. But when you saw the CEO, you also beat him up because hey, why not." Mark wasn't going to waste any more time with the young man and rose. "You'll be charged with attempted arson, as well as assault."

"How can you charge me with assault if the man's dead?" Henry yelled.

"You'd better hope I don't find out you had anything to do with Mr. Ferguson's murder as well."

This time, Mark was ready. When Henry jumped out of his chair and dived over the table, Mark grabbed the young man's arm and put a knee into his back.

Henry yowled in pain. "Get off me!"

Timmins had let the officers inside, and they deftly took over, cuffing Henry and getting him on his feet.

"If you had hit me, that would have been a charge of assault on an officer," Mark told him in a flat voice. "Get him out of here."

So far, Mark had solved a part of the puzzle, but he worried it wouldn't be enough for Captain Fraust. He knew the captain wanted a murder suspect captured as soon as possible—hell, so did he. He dropped into his office chair and blew out a frustrated breath.

A knock on the door, followed by Myrna. "Hey," she called out. "Sorry to say, but my analysis still stands."

He scrubbed his face with a hand. "Thanks, Myrna. It was a long shot, but I was hoping. I hadn't meant to insult your work. Sorry."

She shrugged. "There's nothing wrong with double-checking."

"What's next?" Timmins asked.

"I need your help," Mark said. "Can you go to Ferguson's head office and find out who's next in line to take over?"

"Any reason why?"

Mark knew Timmins was testing his methods, and he appreciated it—it kept him on his toes. "It's possible the head office didn't like Ferguson's methods. Maybe someone there wanted to get rid of him?"

"Now you're thinking." Timmins rose and grabbed his satchel. "No time like the present. It'll throw them off if I suddenly show up."

Mark smiled. "Good idea."

His phone pinged. As he read the message from Britt, his body tingled with pleasure. She mentioned that she and her staff were inside the bakery, cleaning up. She then sent a second text.

If you'd like something sweet, why don't you come over and see me.

How could he ignore that invitation?

"What's got you smiling so big?" Myrna asked.

Startled, he put the phone back in his pocket. "Good news from a friend."

"You mean the blonde beauty you rescued a couple of nights ago?" Timmins chimed in with a wink.

"'Blonde beauty'?" Myrna demanded. "Who? What did I miss?"

"She's just someone I met last week." It was bound to happen that one of the guys would pick up on something, but Mark had hoped for a bit more time.

"I'll bet she is. Don't get distracted, Casanova. Let's get this case solved first."

Mark couldn't help himself, though. As soon as he got in his car, he drove straight to the bakery. He wanted to spend a few minutes with Britt to show his support before driving over to talk with Mrs. Ferguson and the housekeeper.

He parked a block away and walked quickly to the front door, which stood open. Inside, it was a chaotic blend of work, chatter and laughter as debris was cleaned up and furniture moved to one side. A couple of employees swept the floor.

One of the staff noticed him. "Hey, aren't you the guy that asked for Britt last weekend?"

Mark stuck out his hand. "Good eye. Yeah, I am. Is she around?"

"I'll grab her. Just be careful. There's glass everywhere."

Mark took a good look around. Anything that wasn't nailed down had been smashed to bits. Even the display case had a couple of holes where someone had kicked it in. The bookshelf was nothing but a pile of firewood, and even the books hadn't survived—they were torn to shreds. The letters *MBB* were scrawled on the bright storefront. It almost felt like…this was personal. The vandals had managed a lot of damage in the short amount of time they had.

"Hi, Mr. Detective."

He turned and smiled as Britt approached, wearing jeans and a white T-shirt. "Hey. I see you've already started getting things back together."

She nodded and looked around. "I was lucky. No one got into the kitchen. That's where the most expensive stuff is."

"Did your insurance pull through?"

"With flying colors."

She told him how much she received, and he whistled. "That's a healthy chunk of change."

"It'll go toward buying foodstuffs and replacing the glass in the windows and a new door." She looked around. "And giving the inside a good makeover. We'll hang on to the salvageable furniture until we receive the second payment."

"Sounds like you have everything in order, *vakker*." He stepped closer but watched her carefully. He was suspicious that Britt might not want to get too intimate in front of her staff, but he couldn't resist teasing. "How about a kiss before I go?"

Her eyes widened in surprise, but their color darkened as well, a deep emerald. He kept his gaze on her, waiting, because she hadn't said yes—or no.

"Damn you." She licked her bottom lip, and he drew in a sharp breath. How could he back away now? "I want to, I think a little too much, but…" She glanced over her shoulder and gasped.

He looked up and saw her friend Joyce standing at the doorway to the office, arms crossed and the biggest smirk on her face. "Hello, Detective Hawthorne." She came over. "I want to thank you again for saving us."

"Don't mention it." He glanced at Britt until her cheeks flushed a light pink—damn, she looked adorable. "And I have to commend you on your fast thinking. To go out the office window and through a dark alley? That's gutsy."

"No, that's desperation. I wasn't going to let us sit in the office and wait for those shitheads to break down the door." She paused, and Mark noticed her clenched hands. "Any news?"

"I haven't heard anything, but I'm not on the case. I'll follow up and let you know what I find out."

"Thanks, Mark." Britt raised her hand as if to clasp his, then let it fall.

Joyce made a noise. "Could you two go outside and, you know, make out? I'll hold the fort."

Britt led the way—she hadn't hesitated at all. Feeling encouraged, he was right behind her until they stood at the entrance to the alley. "Joyce knows you well."

She laughed, a joyous sound that rang free and happy. Britt seemed more at ease. "I didn't have to tell her anything. She figured it out before you came to rescue us."

He reached for her hand, and her fingers wrapped around his. "I might have been too protective that night," he whispered, kissing her hand.

Her smile was bright. "I loved every moment, even when you cleaned my knees."

He laughed. "Jeez, I felt like a guy trying to hold on to a condom, my hands were shaking so bad." He sobered. "Are you still mad at me about bringing you to the police station for questioning?"

"No. But you really caught me by surprise."

"That makes two of us. I'm sorry, Britt, but I had to be an officer. I didn't know what to expect."

"I get it. I'm just ticked that Mr. Ferguson had my bracelet, instead of me finding it in the alley or at home. Will I be able to get it back?"

"As soon as everything's over. Speaking of which, I have to go." Although he didn't want to—he wanted to drag Britt away and spend the night with her. "Duty calls."

"I understand." She came up to him and wrapped her arms around his neck. "Maybe you and I can do something fun when duty finally stops calling?"

"Oh, you mean I can have that sweet treat you teased me about?"

Her surprise lasted only for a moment. "Haven't you heard? Norwegian treats are the best."

He crushed his mouth to hers, trusting that his intent was clear. *I'm here for you,* vakker, *no matter what.*

Chapter 13

Mark hit the buzzer beside the main gate. At the same time, he got a text from Timmins.

Call me as soon as you're finished.

Intriguing.

"Yes. Who is it?" The housekeeper's voice echoed through the intercom.

"Detective Hawthorne." He held up his badge to the security camera. "I'd like to talk to Mrs. Ferguson."

"Well… Mrs. Ferguson has had a long day preparing for her husband's funeral."

"I'm really sorry, but I wouldn't be here unless it was urgent."

It remained silent for so long that he thought the housekeeper had hung up on him. Then she said, "Please enter through the small gate to your right."

He heard a faint buzz, then walked through and shut it behind him. It locked with a loud click.

The housekeeper was waiting at the door when he reached the front steps. "Detective, good evening." They shook hands. "Please come in. Mrs. Ferguson is waiting for you in the library."

"Thank you. Oh, and I'd like you to join us as well."

That got a reaction. "Oh? Well, I'm trying to get last-minute preparations ready for tomorrow."

"I won't be long, I promise." He indicated to her to lead the way.

She clearly wasn't happy about it but walked down the hallway and stopped at a door to their left. She knocked twice, then entered. "Detective Hawthorne is here, Mrs. Ferguson."

The widow sat in a plush high-backed chair. She wore a long-sleeved black dress and black slippers. Her hair was tied back into a fashionable bun. She seemed calm, poised, but on a closer look, Mark noticed the swollen red eyes and a faint trail of black smudge down one cheek. She'd recently been crying.

"Mrs. Ferguson, I'm so sorry for your loss."

She remained silent, but waved her hand at the seat opposite her.

"Actually, I've asked your housekeeper—Gloria, is that right?—to join us. Please." He pointed at the other chair.

Both women glanced at each other before the housekeeper sat down, back ramrod straight, clenched hands on her knees. She seemed nervous.

Mark had thought about what to say to the ladies, and finally decided he'd be blunt in explaining what he was looking for. "I want to thank you for seeing me unannounced. We've cataloged everything from the scene—" he wanted to be careful in his choice of words for Mrs. Ferguson's sake "—and we're working on some leads. There are two things I'm curious about." He paused, watching their faces.

The housekeeper refused to look at him. Mrs. Ferguson glanced up. "What is it?"

He slowly paced across the width of the room. "Mrs.

Ferguson, do you know who will inherit Mighty Big Bakery with your husband's death?"

"I do. I would have thought that was obvious."

He glanced at her. "I thought perhaps you had children, a son maybe, to run Mr. Ferguson's business."

"Oh." She paused. "No. We don't have children."

"So, as heiress, you'll take over?"

"I'll have Edward's leadership team continue with the day-to-day business operations, of course. I don't plan on changing any of that."

"And they'll hire a new CEO as well?"

"Yes. I'll need a crash course on understanding how to elect, but I'll be a part of that process with them as well."

"Thank you." Mark stopped in between the women. "My second concern is your husband's missing briefcase. Would you know if he had any important documents in it?"

Mrs. Ferguson shook her head. "Leaving the house at that time of night in one of his best suits, I think it might have been contracts to sign over whatever business he planned to buy. That's the only thing I can think of."

"I see. And what about you, Gloria?"

When she faced him, her frightened expression raised a red flag. "What about me?"

"Well, you were the one who told us about the missing briefcase. Did you look for it? It's possible he didn't take one with him. Maybe it's in his study or in the bedroom?"

"I—I don't know. I didn't search for it."

"You didn't?" Mark stared at her, another red flag waving in his face. "Why not?"

She shrugged. "It didn't seem important at the time."

"So here I am, under the impression that the briefcase was stolen, when in fact, it might be here? It's a crucial piece of evidence, Gloria. Now I'll have to bring the police in to look for it."

"Gloria, you told me Edward's briefcase wasn't in the house." Mrs. Ferguson's hands were wrapped around the armrests. She was shaking and angry.

Gloria glanced from her employer to him, then back again. "I'm sorry, Mrs. Ferguson. I didn't want you to worry about it."

"You're not in a position to tell me what to worry and not worry about! Because of you, Detective Hawthorne will be bringing in officers to search my home! While I'm grieving! And everyone in the neighborhood will see this! All because of your incompetence!" She started crying, loud sobs that filled the room and tore at Mark's feelings. Mrs. Ferguson no doubt had kept her emotions in check, but Gloria's admission broke it. "How can I trust you now?"

"Mrs. Ferguson, I'm sure Gloria meant well." He knelt by her chair and rested his hand on hers. "I'm probably breaking protocol, but how about I wait until after the funeral? And I'll only bring in about five officers. I'm sure with Gloria's help, we can get this done in about a couple of hours. And we'll be discreet—no police cars, no flashing lights, I promise."

She held a handful of tissues to her face as she struggled to calm down. It took a few minutes before she looked up. "Thank you, Detective. That means a lot to me."

"Of course." He glanced at Gloria. Her expression betrayed the guilt she felt, which was part of the plan. He wanted her to confess what she knew, but the housekeeper wouldn't do it in front of Mrs. Ferguson. He got to his feet. "I'll leave you alone, and I apologize again for coming at this difficult time. I'll call in a couple of days, and we can arrange a suitable time."

Gloria led him out, leaving Mrs. Ferguson crying quietly in the library. As they reached the front door, the housekeeper turned on him. "How dare you pull a heartless stunt like that!" she seethed through a clenched jaw.

Mark feigned surprise. "Heartless? You're the one who lied."

"So that Mrs. Ferguson wouldn't worry!" She placed her hand to her forehead. "And now she doesn't trust me."

"She will if you find the briefcase. Where is it?"

Her innocent wide-eyed expression had him on alert. "I don't know."

"I think you do. You either hid it in the house, or maybe…" The thought struck him. "Maybe you know the murderer and let him take it."

"That's preposterous!" she yelled, then quickly lowered her voice. "I had nothing to do with Mr. Ferguson's murder."

"Then prove it to me. Where's the briefcase and what's in it? You know something, Gloria. Talk to me, or I'll have to bring you in for questioning and still search the house."

"No, not that, please. It'll tear Mrs. Ferguson apart."

Mark waited and watched while the housekeeper seemed to struggle with a decision. "I know where the briefcase is," she said quietly.

"Why didn't you say something when my team and I were here?"

She tangled her hands together and looked over her shoulder where they left Mrs. Ferguson. "Because of what's inside it."

Silence. He waited while she fidgeted, but she didn't say anything more. "Gloria…" he warned.

"I can't get the briefcase now. If Mrs. Ferguson saw…" She stopped and took a deep breath. "Can you come back tomorrow morning, around eleven? I'll give you the brief-case then."

He frowned. "Isn't the funeral tomorrow?"

"Yes, but I'll get out of it. Mrs. Ferguson will have her two sisters and brother with her." Gloria pinched her lips together. "Besides, she doesn't trust me right now."

That had been a productive, though emotional, evening. His unexpected visit with Mrs. Ferguson filled him with mixed feelings of guilt and accomplishment. The only other good thing that came out of this was that he wouldn't need to bombard the woman's home with officers turning everything upside down to find that briefcase.

In the car, he checked his text messages. Timmins had obviously found something out, but that could wait a few minutes. He texted Britt, letting her know he was fin-ished for the night and asking if her offer still stood. As he waited for her to reply, he called his partner. "Hey, it's me. Before you start, just letting you know the house-keeper had the briefcase all this time."

"Say what?" Timmins yelled into the phone. "You're kidding me."

"Nope. She was acting strange, so I was expecting some-thing. Threw me for a loop. The housekeeper deliberately said to Mrs. Ferguson and me that she hadn't searched for the briefcase. When I told the ladies I would have to come back with officers to look for it, Mrs. Ferguson lost her cool and chewed out Gloria.

"The housekeeper and I had a private chat. Gloria fi-nally admitted to hiding the briefcase and said to come back Thursday morning to grab it, as she won't be going to Ferguson's funeral. I hope Myrna can lift some viable prints from it." Mark paused, reabsorbing the unexpected turn of events. "What did you find out?"

"Edward Ferguson's head office is a well-oiled engine," Timmins began. "His board of directors had instructions that in the event of his death, they would hold a vote among themselves, their shareholders and Mrs. Ferguson to see who would become the new CEO. That's ongoing, and they know Mrs. Ferguson will inherit the business. No surprises there.

"What caught me off guard was a couple of security guys. My guess is they were hired after Mr. Ferguson was assaulted. As I was leaving, one of them asked about the investigation. I told him it's moving along. Then he had the nerve to say that if we were doing our job, Mr. Ferguson would still be alive."

"I'll bet you weren't expecting that," Mark told him.

"Nope, but I took a page out of your book and kept quiet. But what concerned me was that these two had the smell of *bad guy* on them."

That caught Mark's attention. Timmins had been doing this job for years, and his instinct was never wrong. "What are you thinking?"

"Possible mercenary."

Whoa—that was taking it to a whole new level.

"The guy also had a strong accent. I couldn't place it. Then he says if he was looking for the killer, he would do whatever it took to find the bastard. When I got back to the precinct, I asked Myrna to run all the fingerprints from your love interest's bakery and the murder scene through Interpol's Automatic Fingerprint Identification System database. It's just a hunch, especially after listening to that muscle-head jerk, but—"

"No, that's a good call, spread the net wide. Thanks for checking it out, Timmins."

"You bet, but my day got even weirder. Found out that Jenny wants to cut a deal."

"What?" How many strange things could happen in one day? In this case, a lot. "Tell me."

"She said she could get you into one of those secret protest meetings she'd talked about. Get you close to the leader."

"What's the point of that? Ferguson's dead—that should be the end of it."

"Not in this leader's eyes. Mighty Big Bakery is still here, and as long as they continue to run over the little business, Jenny said her leader won't back down."

"Goddamn it." For every answer Mark found, two more questions popped up. He'd have to find a chance to sit down and get all of his shit together and rethink probabilities. Captain Fraust would be asking for an update, too, and he'd need to be ready for that. "All right, thanks, Timmins. I'll see you tomorrow."

When he checked his phone, Britt had sent a text.

You'd better show up or I'll hunt you down, but you might already know that.

He coughed out a laugh and replied.

There's that Nordic warrior coming out of you. I'll bring dinner as tribute.

Her reply was short and promising.

Just bring yourself.

* * *

"Thank you for bringing takeout," Britt said, licking her fingers. "That was delicious."

Mark had an odd look on his face. "My pleasure." His voice was deep, almost rough.

Nervous, she grabbed the dishes and headed for the kitchen. Britt knew what to expect—she had invited him over for goodness' sake—but the anticipation and awkwardness made her feel like a teenager.

A very excited teenager.

She rinsed the dishes and placed them in the dishwasher. "Mark, would you like anything to drink?" She turned around and squawked in surprise. He stood inches away, hands in his pockets, his dark gaze traveling slowly over her. "You startled me."

"Sorry." He reached out his hand.

She could almost see the wheels turning in his head. Honestly, she wondered if her thoughts matched his. Britt grasped his fingers and watched in wonder as he raised her hand to his lips. The touch was warm, but her whole body burned inside.

When he looked at her, his brown eyes held a light of their own. "What are you thinking, *vakker*?"

His question, though innocent, wrapped itself around her, a force she couldn't fight against. She knew exactly what she thought, what she wanted, and was sure Mark picked up on it.

The past four years after the debacle with Minister Strathmore had been difficult and lonely, despite building a new life around her bakery. But finding Mark… She closed her eyes, because staring at him made her heart ache.

Movement, and then the warmth of his body against hers. "Britt."

She opened her eyes and looked into the depths of his own. "I was thinking that I shouldn't have been such a chicken Friday night."

He touched her cheek, a soft caress. "I figured you had your reasons."

She nodded, trying to form her next words. "I was scared, I think. I was sure you were married or in a relationship or something."

"Nope. You have me all to yourself." He leaned in, his mouth barely brushing against hers.

She trembled, the force of this moment intense and electrifying. Without thinking—Britt didn't want to think, just go for it—she wrapped her arms around his neck, pressing her breasts against his hard chest. She was tired of tiptoeing around her uncertainty.

Mark's grip was so tight she could barely breathe. He picked her up and managed to get them into her bedroom. He let her go and grabbed her hands. "Are you sure?"

"Just shut up and kiss me."

Mark didn't hesitate, kissing her so thoroughly Britt thought she would pass out. His hands slipped beneath her T-shirt and massaged her breasts until she groaned into his mouth.

"Damn it, *vakker*, you're driving me crazy. Lift your arms."

She did so, and Mark had her top and bra off in moments. His hands rested lightly on her skin, skimming over her nipples until they hardened with a will of their own. "Absolutely gorgeous," he whispered in a hoarse voice.

Undaunted, Britt reached for his shirt, her fingers shaking as she unbuttoned it. She pushed the material off his shoulders, letting her hands travel over firm muscle. His upper body was wide and defined, and Britt trailed her fingers across his chest and down his abs.

He hissed. "If you keep this up, I don't know how much longer I can hold still."

Mark was fighting to keep his desire in check, and hearing that made her feel mischievous. "You mean I can't tease you?"

He arched a brow. "There could be consequences."

She bit her lower lip, and his gaze focused on the movement. She didn't want to tease—she just wanted him.

Britt reached for his belt, unhooking it while keeping her eyes on him. He glanced down at her busy hands but slowly raised his head, his gaze dark and focused as he studied her body. He rested his hands over hers as he pushed his clothing down to his ankles before kicking his pants and underwear off with a swift movement.

Britt held her breath. Now that Mark was completely naked, she could ogle to her heart's delight. His body was covered in thick, dense muscle courtesy of the sports he enjoyed playing. She ran her hands over his arms again.

He moved close enough to let her feel his manhood against her stomach. "Let's get you out of those leggings, shall we?"

He kneeled in front of her and grabbed the waistband, pulling both tights and panties down in a slow, torturous movement. Britt couldn't look, but she felt his warm breath on a spot just below her belly button. She lifted her feet to remove the clothing, but Mark hadn't gotten up yet. The tension built up within her as she realized he wasn't in any hurry. "Mark…"

"Shh."

His hands caressed her legs, moving up until he grabbed her backside in a firm grip that made her bite her tongue. She held her breath, wondering what he would do. "I think you're teasing now," she managed to say.

Silence, but then she inhaled sharply when his lips kissed just below her belly button. Without thinking, her hands grasped handfuls of his hair to steady her shaky legs.

He rose, and in one movement, swept her into his arms and laid her on the bed. He hovered over her, his mouth trailing hot kisses across her body until she squirmed, desire flushing her skin with heat.

He reached the delicate skin between her legs, and her body tensed, emotions conflicting with each other. He massaged her with firm, slow movements that finally allowed her body to relax. When his tongue touched her sensitive folds, Britt arched off the bed, crying out in surprise at the strong reaction. Heat pooled in her lower body, and fast breathing turned to quiet cries as Mark relentlessly probed at her. He touched a spot that sent her over the edge, and Britt gave in to her orgasm until she fell limp against the pillow.

He propped himself above her and kissed her face. "How are you, *vakker*?"

"Mmm, I'm not sure yet." She flicked her tongue along his mouth.

"Hold that thought." He scrambled off the bed and reached for something in his pants pocket—a condom.

"I might need to keep a few of those handy around here," she quipped as he rolled it on.

He gave her a heated look as he crawled into bed beside her. "That sounds like a hint."

It did, didn't it? Britt didn't want to dwell on that, not now. "Come over here," she whispered, reaching for him.

Mark held his body above hers, and she didn't need

any prompting, wrapping her legs around his waist as he pushed slowly into her. She hadn't realized she had held her breath until he looked at her, his expression concerned. "Are you all right?"

"Yes." Without thinking, her body rocked to its own beat, pushing away all thoughts until she only saw him, smelled his scent and tasted his sweat. Her soft whimpers in Mark's ear encouraged him, his own pace increasing until with a loud drawn-out cry, her body spasmed, leaving her no choice but to ride the waves of desire that overtook her.

Mark wasn't far behind. His grip around her tightened as he shook from the force of his own orgasm, his deep groan loud in her ear.

He rolled onto his side and kissed her so hard she thought she saw stars. His hand gently caressed her as he stared into her face, remaining quiet.

Britt wondered what he was thinking but didn't ask. "I've heard that the first time is always the best."

He frowned and propped himself up on an elbow. "And?"

"It doesn't make sense if you have the right person in your life."

He stroked her hair, damp from their lovemaking. "Is that what you believe, *vakker*?"

"Yeah," she whispered, her chest swelling with unknown emotions. "Yeah, I do."

Chapter 14

When Britt woke up, sunlight had eased into her bedroom, a gentle warmth against her bare skin. She yawned and reached over, ready to caress Mark's body. But he wasn't there.

Alert, she turned onto her side. An empty, wrinkled spot on the bed was all she saw.

For a moment, a sharp pang of bitter disappointment hit her chest. He'd already left, probably going back to his place to shower and change before work. Logically, it made sense, and yet…

A toilet flushed, and a minute later, Mark appeared, dressed only in his boxers. "Morning, *vakker*," he called out.

"Good morning." Glancing around her bedroom, she finally spied Mark's clothing neatly arranged on a chair, and felt a little embarrassed at thinking that Mark had taken off during the night.

"What's wrong?" He sat on the bed beside her.

She shook her head, not wanting to admit her rash thought.

He frowned, his brown eyes not leaving her face. "You didn't think I'd leave, did you?"

Britt shrugged, refusing to meet his gaze.

His finger touched her chin and gently tilted her face so that she was forced to look at him. "I was kicking myself when I didn't follow you that night. You think I'm going to screw up now?"

She swallowed the lump in her throat. Mark had a way with words that made her insides tie up in knots.

His smile was devilish. "Besides, how can I resist this hot body of yours?" He whipped the bedsheet aside before she could hang on to it.

"Mark!" She covered her breasts with her hands.

"Oh, no, none of that." He kissed every bit of skin he could reach until he stretched his body over hers. She giggled at a ticklish spot above her navel, and he hovered around it, taking advantage until she gasped from laughter and tried to fight him off.

"Stop, please!"

When he raised his head, his brow was cocked up at a high angle. "I hope you won't doubt my intentions again."

Her throat constricted so much she could hardly breathe. "I'm sorry," Britt whispered, fighting to hold back a sob. "It's just…well…"

"Hey." He kissed her nose, her forehead, then her lips. His gentleness pulled at her heart until she thought it would shatter into a million pieces. "I plan on hanging around. You won't get rid of me that easily."

Their lovemaking this time was slow, filled with whispered endearments and gentle caresses. Mark's gaze never left hers as he explored her body again, his hands smoothing over her skin until the heat built up inside and her body trembled with excitement. His encouragement and urgent desire mirrored her own and then, with a shudder, Britt's orgasm burned through her body until she felt turned inside out.

A peaceful bliss settled over her. She was relaxed, her skin still warm. She yawned and stretched her arms over her head, thinking she'd like to stay in bed with him all day.

But it wasn't meant to be. A cell phone rang, and with a muttered curse, Mark jumped out of bed and dug it out of his pants pocket. He talked quietly for several minutes, and Britt heard the word *case* a couple of times—it was work. She gathered the bedsheet around her and headed for the bathroom while Mark watched her. Just as she passed him, he reached out and wrapped his arm around her waist. "It's seven now," he said into the phone. "I'll be at the station in about an hour."

He hung up, then kissed her on the cheek. "Sorry— work," he apologized.

"That's okay." Smiling, she returned the gesture but kissed him full on the lips.

"Damn, I wish I could stay with you." He wrapped his arms around her waist and grabbed her ass. "I'd like nothing more than to ignore work and love you all morning."

Her heart smacked against her chest. Hearing Mark say that he'd rather be with her than doing his job… She swallowed, but didn't say anything.

He released her and got dressed, putting his keys, phone and wallet into various pockets. She followed him out of the room and to the front door. "Talk to you later?" he said.

Britt smiled. "You bet."

He gave her a lingering kiss, his lips warm, gentle. With a squeeze of his hand, he was gone.

She locked the door, then turned and leaned against it. If she had told herself two weeks ago that she would meet the man of her dreams on a busy street, she would have laughed so hard she'd scare her staff.

* * *

Mark found it hard to focus on work with Britt constantly on his mind.

He'd gone home to shower and change, and arrived at the precinct just after eight to add yesterday's surprising revelation to his notes. The captain would want another update for sure.

He wanted to think about Britt, spend time dreaming of what they could possibly have together, but right now, the job called out to him to defend the less fortunate, including a man like Ferguson. Work was his balm, his comfort. Mark wanted to excel—he loved solving his investigations and bringing closure. He knew he was good at his job. Dad was finally out of the picture, and his and Mom's relationship had become tighter. Mark had a good life, and when he was ready, he'd hoped to find a woman he could love unconditionally.

To say that karma had blessed him when he saw Britt at Konditori was an understatement. The chances of ever finding someone like his Nordic princess seemed slim to none. If she hadn't stopped to check him out, he never would have recognized her at the bakery.

He blinked, refocusing his thoughts. Britt was here, he had spent a passion-filled night with her and she hadn't pushed him away or told him it couldn't work. This was real—*she* was real, and Mark wanted to find out how far they could take their journey.

He sat at his desk, coffee mug in hand, and pulled out everything from his work bag. As he waited for the computer to boot up, he read through his notes again, looking for areas he could link together. They hadn't found the weapon used to kill Mr. Ferguson. It was possible the briefcase was used to hit the CEO over the head, but he'd have to wait until he got the item from Gloria, the housekeeper.

Mark also remembered Timmins's remark about using the international database to see if there were any hits on the fingerprints found at the murder scene and Britt's bakery. He buzzed Myrna.

"Good morning," she said in a cheerful voice. "I figured you'd want some answers to that age-old question, whodunit."

He smiled at her bad joke. "It sounds like you got somewhere."

"I certainly have. I was waiting on Timmins, but you're just the guy to see what I've got."

At that moment, Timmins walked in. "He's here now," Mark said. "We'll be down in a few."

As he and Timmins walked into Myrna's lab, the forensics investigator waved at them from the other end of the wide room. "Over here," she called out.

She sat in front of two large computer monitors. Blown up in detail on one of the screens was a fingerprint. On the other monitor were three pictures of a man from the chest up in various mug-shot poses.

"Did you get a hit?" Mark stared at the picture. The man looked to be in his early thirties, with a full black beard and thick curly hair tied back in a ponytail. His dark eyes were unfeeling, bottomless. "Who's this?"

"Now, that's a good question. He has so many aliases, I don't think anyone knows. What we do know is that he's one of the men who broke into and destroyed that bakery across from Ferguson's construction site. His fingerprints were all over the place."

"You don't say." He leaned in to get a closer look. This

dude did not look friendly at all. "Did you find an address?"

"No, but here's the interesting part. He had to provide fingerprints for his current job." She hit a few keys, and the picture of a high-level security card appeared, with the suspect's picture and current name. Beneath it was the name of the company he worked for.

"Mighty Big Bakery Inc.?" Mark said, incredulous.

Myrna smiled. "I knew you'd get a kick out of that."

"Do me a favor and print that for me." It was a small step forward, and Mark was cheering inside. "Any other surprises?"

"Why, yes." Myrna pulled up the second set of fingerprints found at Britt's store, then called up the corresponding picture. This second man was younger with a blond crew cut, thick eyebrows and a permanent scowl.

"Hey, that's the jerk who talked to me when I finished my interview with the MBB board of directors," Timmins exclaimed. "Nice, we're getting somewhere."

"And behind door number three…" Myrna retrieved the information on the third suspect.

"That was the other security guard," Timmins told them.

"We could collect their work records, just to see what they wrote down to get a security job at MBB," Myrna advised.

So, one part of the puzzle solved. Myrna provided him with pictures of the men and their prints.

"Thanks, Myrna. Great job."

She got up and offered a curtsy. "My pleasure."

Upstairs, Mark laid the additional information on top of his other papers.

"When are you grabbing the briefcase?" Timmins asked. "Want me to go with you?"

"No need. I'm just getting it and bringing it right back. However..." Mark wasn't sure that Gloria had told him everything. "I think I'll bring the housekeeper in as well for further questioning. Are you going to pick up those three security guys today?"

"Damn right I am."

Mark checked his watch. "I'm going to head out. It should be a full house when we get back."

"Oh, don't forget Jenny's offer."

He swore. "I'm wondering how much we can get out of it. I guess I'd better talk to her first."

He headed toward the jail cell and talked with the officer on duty. "Is Jenny awake?"

"Oh yes, and very impatient to see you. She's in the last cell on the left."

"Did she use her phone call?" Mark asked.

The officer shook his head. "She didn't want to—at least, not yet."

Jenny was pacing the small cell when he stopped in front of it. "Good morning."

She glared at him. "Easy for you to say. You're standing out there."

Mark refused to let her bait him. "My partner told me you wanted to cut a deal."

She smiled, but he sensed an underlying malice behind it. "That's right. You guys want to arrest the protest leader before he does more damage. I know where he's going to be today. Got a text from him before you busted Henry and me."

When she didn't continue, Mark crossed his arms. "And?"

"What do I get?"

He shrugged. "I don't know. I'll need to talk to Captain Fraust."

"Shit, maybe I should have asked for your captain instead." She approached the cell door and wrapped her hands around the bars. "How about a reduced sentence? And you haven't allowed me my phone call. What's up with that?"

"Not true. The officer who brought you in yesterday said you didn't ask for it, despite reading your rights. And I just asked the officer on duty. He said you didn't call your lawyer."

"Fine, I want that and a reduced sentence."

"You'll get your phone call. As for the sentence, I can't do anything. Maybe it'll depend on what you've got to offer." Mark knew she was playing a game, but he was all over that—he had no idea if Jenny's information would be any good.

"Mr. Ferguson's funeral is today, isn't it? At eleven?"

Mark fought not to react, but a cold finger of dread ran down his spine. "What about it?"

She walked to the other side of the cell. "The protest leader is going to show up there. I have no idea how many followers will be with him, but I don't think it's going to be pretty."

"Christ!" Mark ran down the hallway. "Call in every officer on duty!" he yelled at the startled cop. "Find out where Mr. Ferguson's funeral is being held and call it in!"

"Hey, what's going on?" the officer shouted as Mark raced past him.

"The protesters against Mighty Big Bakery. They're going to cause a riot!"

* * *

Timmins had already left for MBB's head office to arrest the three suspects whose fingerprints were all over Britt's bakery.

Two police cars had already raced off by the time Mark jumped into his car. He got on the radio. "All units, this is Detective Mark Hawthorne. The funeral is at Mount Pleasant Cemetery on Bayview Avenue. Sirens and lights on until we reach Bayview and Eglinton, then go silent. We'll reconvene at Bayview and Sutherland Drive to assess the situation."

He got moving, speeding through traffic as he raced with the others to their destination. Suddenly, his radio came alive. "Hawthorne, it's Fraust."

He picked up and gave her a quick summary of what was going on. "I want us to get there before the protesters," he told her. "Surround the area without anyone knowing. As soon as they show up, we'll take them down."

"This is going to be a large memorial—at least a hundred mourners. You'll need to keep your eyes and wits sharp."

"Yes, ma'am."

"How many officers are with you?"

"I won't know until I get there."

She cursed under her breath. "It may not be enough by the time you pull in. I'll send more but do the best you can." She signed off.

The cemetery encompassed a massive amount of land, surrounded by tall mature trees, condos and large, expensive homes. They parked on Sutherland Drive, and Mark quickly counted his men—nine officers in total. That was all he had to work with. He pulled everyone together into a tight circle. "I don't know what to expect," he told them.

"I've heard these protesters wear masks, but they might take them off and try to blend in with the crowd. If you spot the leader, try to arrest them or follow their movements at a safe distance and call for backup."

"That's going to be hard if we don't know what the leader looks like," one of them grumbled.

"He'll be the one up front. I know, it feels like a guessing game, but it's what we've got right now." If they messed this up, the protesters would scatter. "We've got one chance at this. Team up and arrest anyone who endangers the mourners."

Mark instructed them on the go, telling them to sneak toward the church located at the center of the cemetery and to stay hidden. He saw a couple of workers preparing a burial site and went to speak with them. "I'm with York Regional Police," he said quietly to the startled men, displaying his badge. "I understand Edward Ferguson's funeral is this morning. Do you know where he'll be buried?"

"Over there." The older man pointed at a small mausoleum located at the edge of a wooded area. "The service already started." He looked at his watch. "The procession to the mausoleum is supposed to start at eleven—about twenty minutes. What's going on?"

Mark looked around—the officers had surrounded the church at a safe distance and kept mostly out of sight. "We might have unwanted company." At the man's confused look, he added, "Protesters."

"Those anti-MBB bastards." The man spat on the ground. "I'm all for stating my opinion, but they take it too far. Are they really going to show up here?"

"I don't know. I hope not." He scanned around him—no one was in sight.

"You want us to help you with anything?" the other employee asked.

He shook his head. "Just stay out of the way."

Mark hid within the shrubbery close to the mausoleum and talked to the officers via walkie-talkie. No one suspicious had appeared so far, and he surmised the protesters would start something as Ferguson was being entombed.

The mourners had started filing out of the church in small groups. Mrs. Ferguson was in the center, wearing a wide-brimmed hat, a black veil pulled over her face. Two ladies stood on either side while a large man shadowed them; no doubt her siblings.

Mark's radio crackled to life. "Sir, there's a group of people heading this way, moving quickly."

It had to be them. "There's a mausoleum about two hundred feet east of the church," he advised. "Ferguson's to be buried in it. I'm just behind the building."

The coffin was finally brought out, carried by six pallbearers. The priest came next, and Mark watched as everyone slowly proceeded toward the mausoleum. The next five minutes were going to be tense.

As the procession came to a stop, he saw several people marching on the wide path, their faces covered in masks, heading straight toward the mausoleum. Several of the officers appeared from behind, forming a semicircle around the protesters.

As the priest intoned a final prayer, the leader of the protesters started shouting. "Your husband doesn't deserve a funeral—he deserves to rot in hell! He's got a lot to answer for!"

That was their cue. "Move in!" Mark shouted into his radio, then scrambled out of the bushes to confront the protesters. "York Regional Police! Stay where you are and get your hands up!"

Damn it. Instead of everyone holding still, a mass panic ensued. Mourners and protesters alike ran away in several directions, and in the confusion, Mark lost sight of the leader. "Go!" he shouted to the officers.

As planned, they teamed up in twos. Two officers ran west, the next two hurried east, the third pair traveled south and the last two went north. Mark and his partner surveyed the crowd in front of them. Mrs. Ferguson stood by her husband's coffin, with her family flanking either side. Meanwhile, the priest was trying to calm everyone in a loud, commanding voice.

Mark ran the crowd's perimeter, his partner encircling the opposite side, hoping to spot the man who had made the threat. But by the time he managed to find an opening and look around, the protesters were either too far away to chase down or had disappeared among the tombstones and large trees. Masks were scattered across the grass. "Son of a bitch!" he shouted and got on his radio. "All units, report."

"In pursuit of a protester," an officer yelled back, sounding out of breath. "Proceeding south on Bayview."

"Stay on it," he ordered.

The other officers reported in, stating they had lost their targets in busy pedestrian traffic.

"Get to your cars and follow the chase on Bayview," Mark demanded. "Don't lose them." He radioed the officers chasing their suspect. "We have backup coming. Stay on course."

Mark turned to face the mixed emotions of the mourners. He walked straight toward Mrs. Ferguson. "Are you all right?"

"What the hell was that about?" a middle-aged, large-boned man yelled at him. "You've ruined what little peace my sister managed to salvage. When I get back to—"

"Stop." Mrs. Ferguson grabbed the man's arm. "Just stop."

The big man glared at him but backed off.

Mark breathed a mental sigh of relief. "Are you okay, Mrs. Ferguson?"

"Yes. Those are the people who hate Edward?" She shook her head. "Jealousy and anger won't stop the business from running. I wish they would learn that. Now, if you'll excuse us."

"Of course." Mark retreated, silently paying his respects to the grieving family before running to his car. "Status," he commanded as he got in.

"Still in pursuit. Heading west on Moore Avenue. Shit, this guy can run."

There were neighborhoods the suspect could hide in. "You have to grab him before he gets to Moore Park Ravine or we'll lose him. Box him in, mount the curb if you have to." It was too late for him to join in the chase. Glancing at his watch, he needed to get that briefcase from Gloria before Mrs. Ferguson and her family returned to the house.

Mark got the car started and drove off, periodically receiving updates until he heard, "Suspect in custody."

"Yes!" He did a fist pump. "Excellent work. Bring him in."

Mark arrived at the Ferguson house just after eleven thirty. The gates were already open, and he drove up towards the front door. When he got out of the car, Gloria opened the door, as if she'd been sitting beside it. "You're late," she accused. "They'll be back soon."

"The protesters against Mighty Big Bakery showed up at the funeral. We have one in custody."

If Mark only had a camera to take a photo of Gloria's expression. Surprise, mixed with fear—she couldn't be more obvious. "Do you know who?"

"Nope, haven't questioned them yet. Where's the briefcase?"

She headed toward the kitchen. "I haven't touched it after hiding it in the garage."

The housekeeper opened one of the garage doors. "The briefcase was lying here." She pointed at a spot between two of the luxury cars. "I kicked it under the Jeep."

Mark wanted to knock his head against a pole. He'd been so distracted by Ferguson's corpse and finding certain clues, he hadn't thought to search in other areas beyond the crime scene. He got down on his knees and looked under the vehicle. Sure enough, a silver metal briefcase sat between the front tires. "Do you have a plastic bag?" he asked. "And something with a long handle."

In a few minutes, his evidence was out in the open. As he inspected it, Mark saw dark red stains on one corner— blood. He wrapped it carefully in the green garbage bag Gloria provided him, believing he was close to finding the answers he needed. There was still one problem... "Gloria, why did you hide this?"

That fearful look again. "I'm not sure what you're—"

"You know exactly what I mean. Obstructing a crime scene, hiding evidence and lying to an officer."

She looked around, as if expecting someone to appear. "No, Detective. It's not like that."

"It is, and you're coming with me."

Gloria backed away, "I can't. Mrs. Ferguson will need me when she returns."

"You should have thought of that before pulling this stunt."

The precinct was full. Between Timmins's arrests, the officers' capture of one of the protesters and Mark bringing in the housekeeper, Mark didn't know which way was up. On top of that, Britt had left him a couple of voice mails, and he hadn't yet found time to answer her, not with everything else going on.

He immediately took Gloria to an interrogation room and handed an excited Myrna the briefcase and its combination code on a piece of paper. "Give me a miracle," he told her.

"I'll let you know in an hour." She practically ran to her laboratory.

"I think we'd better divide and conquer," he told Timmins when they met up in their office. "I'll question the housekeeper. Who can help you with those security guards and the protester?"

"I'll get Solberg to talk to the protester and one guard. He's in between cases at the moment. I'll handle the other two."

Ten minutes later, Mark sat opposite the housekeeper. "I believe you were read your rights," he told her, setting pen and paper before him. "You refused your phone call, but if you change your mind…"

"I won't. Let's get on with it."

Her demeanor had changed, and now Gloria looked defeated. "Why did you hide the briefcase?" he started.

"I wanted you to think it'd been stolen." Her voice was calm.

"Why?"

"Because I needed to get something out of it."

"What did you think was inside?"

The housekeeper paused. "A contract to buy a business from…someone."

She hesitated on the last word, and Mark pounced on it. "Who? The more information you provide, the better I can help you."

She chewed her lower lip. "A relative. They own a place called Levi's Bread & Bakery on Bathurst and Lawrence Avenue. It's been there for over fifty years."

Mark knew the area. It had been run-down for the past ten years before the city started renovating it, tearing down derelict buildings and putting up condos and multimillion-dollar homes. He also knew the bakery—three generations of the family worked there, fighting against the rapid change of their neighborhood. "Did Mr. Ferguson offer to buy the bakery out?"

"He didn't offer—he threatened. Someone else wanted to buy the business, and Mr. Ferguson wasn't going to give up without a fight. My uncle didn't want to sell."

Mark sensed a *but* somewhere. "What made your uncle change his mind?"

"No one would tell me. I was frantic, worried that something bad happened. I'd heard about those criminals that attacked businesses who refused to sell to Mr. Ferguson." She wrung her hands. "My uncle is a proud man, and he wouldn't give up anything belonging to him. That bakery is his lifeblood."

Mark was still missing a piece of the puzzle but decided to forge ahead. "We need to talk about the briefcase—what's in it?"

"I'm pretty sure the contracts to sign over my uncle's

bakery. Mr. Ferguson bragged that evening about how he was going to purchase one of the best properties in the Lawrence and Bathurst area. I knew he meant my uncle's business."

He frowned, staring at the housekeeper. Was it possible…?

She gave him a hard look. "I didn't kill Mr. Ferguson, if that's what you're implying. He's not worth going to jail."

He'd still check her fingerprints against the database to be sure. "What *did* you do?"

"Nothing. I couldn't do anything at all. I went home and called my uncle to try to talk him out of it, but he wouldn't listen, wouldn't tell me what Mr. Ferguson offered. He said it was no one's business but his own." She covered her face with a hand and cried quietly. "That man had no right to destroy my uncle's work, or anyone else's."

Mark waited a few minutes to give Gloria a chance to compose herself. "And you didn't know anything else until you saw Mr. Ferguson's body Tuesday morning?"

She shook her head. "I saw the briefcase and believed it had the contract for my uncle to sign. I kicked it under the Jeep and prayed no one found it. I thought with Mr. Ferguson dead, his company might forget about buying my uncle's bakery."

Well, this was an interesting turn of events. Tampering with evidence usually meant covering up a crime, but the housekeeper didn't hide the briefcase because it was the murder weapon. She wanted to avoid selling her uncle's business.

Man, what a tangled net. Ferguson was like a spider, and anything caught in his web was doomed. "Is there anything else you'd like to tell me?" he asked gently.

"I wanted to know about the protester you caught."

She sighed. "My male cousins talked about joining the anti-MBB protests. I hope it's not one of them, but they're adults—they knew what they were getting into." Gloria shook her head. "I'm sorry. I was scared. I didn't know what else to do."

"I'm glad you told me what you know. I have a couple more inquiries. What you've done would normally result in a criminal offense charge, but I'll try to have that rejected. You won't lose your job and you won't have a criminal record."

She smiled through her tears. "Thank you, Detective."

"Oh, and tell your uncle not to worry about anyone destroying his business if he changes his mind and doesn't want to sell." He winked.

Gloria was a smart woman—her look of surprise changed to relief, and she nodded while fighting back tears.

Mark felt better about himself. He hadn't thought she'd done anything as horrifying as murder, and his instincts proved him right.

She was escorted out while he headed to his office and organized his notes yet again. He saw that Captain Fraust had called and buzzed her. "Captain."

"Tell me you have good news."

He updated her on the housekeeper, the MBB security guards and the one protester they had managed to catch. "We have the briefcase, ma'am, and it's stained with blood. I'm waiting for Walsh to provide me with her results."

A short pause, then she said, "Good work, Hawthorne. As soon as you get something, let me know." She hung up.

He had a few minutes, so he called Britt's cell. No answer, and it went to voice mail. "Hey, it's me," he announced. "Sorry I couldn't call you sooner. The case I'm working on is growing intense, but I'm finding answers. I'll call you or drop by later. Talk soon."

Mark could feel a headache coming on. When this was over, he was going to take a vacation. Maybe Britt would join him.

He let that thought roll pleasantly through his mind as he headed down to the forensics lab. Timmins and Solberg hadn't returned, and he was getting antsy.

Myrna was hurrying from one end of the room to the other when he paused in the doorway. She looked stressed, so he waited a few moments until she sat down in front of a large microscope. "Hey, how's it going?"

"Oh, Hawthorne, you're just in time. Have a seat." She gestured at a chair opposite her.

"What have you got for me?"

"Good news and bad news." She jerked her thumb at the briefcase lying on an examination table, along with a small stack of legal papers. "The good news is, the bloodstains belong to Mr. Ferguson. And there's a good-sized dent in the briefcase, too. The murderer must have hit the CEO hard several times. The bad news, no prints."

Mark swore with a few choice words that had Myrna's eyebrows go up. "What was inside?" he asked.

"A contract for a Levi's Bread & Bakery. I know that place—they make the best bagels in Toronto."

He nodded. "Do me a favor. Keep that contract locked someplace where I can't find it—for now."

She gave him a look. "Because?"

"I want the owner to have time to think about whether selling his life's work is what he really wants to do."

"Well…yeah, I could do that and sort of forget where I've put the documents."

"Thanks." It's not something he would normally do, but Mark knew he'd feel horrible if he didn't at least try to reverse a situation that shouldn't have happened in the first place.

"So, let me provide you with better news," Myrna told him. "The coroner found hairs in Mr. Ferguson's clenched fist and sent those to me for analysis."

Just then the database pinged, and Myrna rubbed her hands together. "Let's see what we've got."

Mark came around the wide table and stood behind her as information flowed onto the computer screen—a name, face in three poses and information he hadn't expected.

"This guy has an international warrant?" he exclaimed. He scanned the charges—domestic terrorism, uttering death threats, aggravated assault, possession of illegal weapons. "How the hell are we going to find him?"

"Like we always do—we have one of the best teams, Hawthorne. We'll get it done."

Myrna's confidence was stronger than his. A tendril of doubt trickled into his consciousness, but he slapped it away. "Print everything for me," he told her. "After I update the captain, I'm pulling everyone in on this."

She hit a couple of buttons, then sat back. "I heard over the intercom this morning you needed officers. What happened?"

He gave her a rundown of what had occurred at the funeral. "If everyone hadn't panicked at once, I might have caught the leader."

"Well, you caught someone, so it's a start."

He gathered everything and headed out, then stopped. "Myrna, I want you in on the meeting with the captain. Can you make it?"

"I'll come up now." She grabbed some additional paperwork and followed him.

In the office, Timmins and Solberg provided their findings.

The protester knew nothing about the leader and insisted he had only joined because he wanted to impress his girlfriend, which made Mark throw up his hands in frustration. "What about those three heavies?" he asked Timmins.

The older detective propped his hands on his hips. "They couldn't talk fast enough. Said that Ferguson paid them under the table to rough up anyone who resisted his buyout offers." He shook his head. "That dude was a piece of work. The CEO sounded like a mafia leader, for crap's sake."

"Those guys are bad news. Keep them locked up—I'll have them charged and sent to prison for the B and E at least. Personally, I think there's more to them than they're letting on."

Mark buzzed Fraust, who told him to come up. With Myrna at his side, they entered the captain's office. "Ma'am."

"Have a seat."

They arranged their investigative work on the meeting table.

"I don't have to tell you that after the melee at Ferguson's funeral, the media and populace are demanding to know what we're doing, among other things," Fraust stated.

Fraust's words made him unreasonably nervous. She had backed him up on everything he'd done so far. Still… "I'll provide a rundown of our findings, and Walsh can interrupt if I'm missing anything."

Mark condensed his detailed notes into a fifteen-minute speech, summarizing everything that had occurred, up until his conversation with Myrna today in the lab.

"What are your conclusions?"

He nodded toward Myrna. "Walsh has been in contact with the coroner, as we couldn't find any prints on the briefcase. The footprints found in the flower bed are a size 10 for a construction boot. Unfortunately, they're the wrong size. Jenny wears a size 7, so the footprints don't belong to her. Our next best chance was finding something on Ferguson's body. Foreign hairs were clenched in the CEO's fist and provided us with a solid hit." He slid the photo across to the captain. "The suspect is dangerous."

Fraust picked up the photo, her gaze scanning across the page. "Agreed." She looked at him, eyes sharp. "What do you suggest?"

Mark knew his face held surprise—he had expected the captain to provide ideas, especially now with the knowledge that the case had developed into a high-profile investigation. "Originally, I would have said to get this perp's face on all the news channels, but…" He stopped, knowing now that wouldn't work. "It's not a good idea. As soon as he sees that he's on the news, he'll go underground. We'll never find him."

"Very true." The captain paused, waiting, her gaze intent.

"We could advise all law enforcement officers, but I think…" He was taking a big risk on this theory. "I think the perp is still in our area. I also believe he's the protest leader, but that's only speculation."

"But a solid one. Excellent call on making that decision." Her smile was brief, but he noticed it. "I'll put out an all-points bulletin and give the media a general summary of our progress. Like you said, we can't afford the perp seeing his face on the news. Let's catch the son of a bitch first."

Chapter 15

It had only been a day, yet Britt was surprised and happy at the progress made on Konditori. It was as if someone had lit a fire under their butts.

No, that wasn't it—everyone was determined to resurrect the bakery. Her staff had stayed last night, cleaning up and deciding what to keep or toss. Today, Joyce came in with a contractor and a small team, and Britt stayed out of their way as they measured and discussed ideas.

"I want to run something by you," her friend said as she sat down in the other office chair. She plunked her laptop on the desk. "You've been saying how busy it's been, which is never a complaint in my books, but I think a bit more space would help. Have you thought about relocating to a larger building?"

Britt shook her head. "I can't move. I have a lease for another four years. Honestly, I never expected the growth to happen so fast, but I don't want to overextend myself or the staff, either."

Joyce nodded. "Smart. So this is what I'm thinking. Could we make your office a little smaller? The wall between it and the front room isn't load-bearing, so we could knock it down and shave off…" She glanced around the office, her gaze calculating. "About a foot?"

Britt did the same thing, carefully looking about the room. She only used it when she needed privacy, and if she was honest with herself, she wouldn't mind an update, either. "A foot should be fine. It makes the room a bit narrow, but I don't need the built-in bookcase in the corner. Just one set of fireproof metal drawers with a lock, a sit-stand table and a comfy office chair. The window brings in plenty of light, which was always a plus."

"Trust me, sweetie. I'll make this room look nice. The extra foot will also let me add some additional recessed storage behind the cash register. There'll be more space for people to come inside. And you can still have your little area for tables and chairs, but the furniture will be built in a way that'll take up less space. Even the bookcase you used to have out there? The contractor mentioned we can build that into the wall. No more fears that it might tip over."

Britt gave her friend a tight hug. "What would I do without you?"

"That's why I'm here. I'd like to do some last-minute measurements while you and the others continue cleaning, if I'm not in the way?"

"Never."

Just then, someone knocked, and Kevin poked his head around the door. "Hey, Britt, your friend Mark is here."

"Thanks." She glanced at Joyce, who had an unapologetic grin on her face. "What?"

"Girl, if this isn't a hint, I don't know what is."

"Oh, Mark's been throwing clues around." Britt thought of a movie character for her impersonation. "The force is strong in this one, Mistress Joyce," she said in a booming voice.

Joyce rolled her eyes, then laughed. "How do you feel about it?"

Britt got up from the chair. "Let's just say I'm leaning in his direction."

In the front room, Mark walked the perimeter of the space, his gaze taking in their hard work. "Hello, *vakker*," he said softly as she approached, and kissed her on the lips. "You've made some great progress here."

"We did. The staff has been fantastic. I want to give them a bonus or something to show how happy I am."

"You'll think of something."

She mentioned the new layout, and he asked some questions, showing his interest. This feeling of having him in her corner made Britt think she could conquer the world.

"Do you need any help with tidying?" He rolled up his sleeves and glanced around. "Anything heavy that needs moving?"

She opened her mouth when an amused voice chipped in. "Hey there, Detective Romeo."

Oh God, why did Joyce keep embarrassing her? Mark grinned, as if reading her thoughts, then turned to her friend. "Joyce, how are you? Oh, since you're here, I can give you ladies an update."

Britt knew her mouth hung open in surprise when he had finished. "So all the rumors *were* true. Mr. Ferguson hired those creeps to wreck my bakery."

"I'm just glad you got those assholes off the streets," Joyce grumbled. "They were as bad as their boss, except Ferguson didn't want to get his hands dirty. Scumbag." She stepped closer. "I guess you can't say anything about the CEO's murder investigation, can you?" she whispered dramatically. "Clues, updates?"

"Joyce!" Britt exclaimed, but truthfully, she was curious, too.

Mark winked. "All I can say is we're getting somewhere. My captain held a media conference earlier. It should be on the evening news."

"Thank God for that." Joyce hid a yawn behind her hand. "I'm going to head out. Britt, I'll be here tomorrow morning with the contractor to start the renovations, so it'll be best if you give your staff the day off tomorrow. They should be able to finish the wall in one day, then start installing the display cabinets and shelving."

"Maybe I could hire you to renovate my condo," Mark said with an innocent look.

"As long as you could afford me!" Joyce called out as she left.

Mark helped Kevin with the remaining pieces of the broken bookshelf and took the tables and chairs out back by the garbage bins. "That's done," he said, brushing off his hands. "Anything else?"

"No, thank you. I'm going to close up. Everyone, thank you as always. We'll need to close the store tomorrow so Joyce can work on the wall, but I'll keep all of you up to date via email." She turned to Mark and gave him a big smile. "Let me see if Jacques and Thomas are ready to leave, then I'll get my things."

"I'll be here."

In the kitchen, Jacques was putting on his jacket. "I think another day, *chérie*, and we'll be back in business."

Britt couldn't contain her joy and clapped her hands. "You have been amazing! I can't thank you enough. I admit, I was worried you or the others might have started looking for other jobs."

"Of course not! You treat us very well, Britt. You stood

up against that horrible Ferguson man, and with every-one's love and support, you and I shall be ready to give pastry comas to our loyal customers."

She laughed—she loved Jacques's play on words. "Joyce needs to work her magic tomorrow, so you won't need to come in."

"Do you think we'll be in the way if we do?" Thomas asked unexpectedly. "She doesn't need to come into the kitchen. Nothing has been touched."

"Thomas has a point. We'll need all the time required to be ready for our grand reopening," Jacques added.

She pursed her lips. "I don't see why not. I'm just con-cerned that the dust will get in here. But if Joyce puts a thick piece of plastic over the entrance leading to the front room and tapes all the edges down properly…"

"*Voilà*, that should work. Thomas and I will use the back door, if that is all right."

Britt nodded, her decision made. "I'll talk to her tonight and let you know." She grasped Jacques's arm. "Thank you again."

He placed his hand over hers. "Anything for you, dear boss."

After Jacques and Thomas left, Britt locked up and set the alarm, then returned to where Mark was waiting. "Almost done."

In the office, she grabbed her stuff and made sure ev-erything was secure. She was excited about the plans Joyce had shown her, and she couldn't wait to see how it progressed.

Outside, the early-evening rush hour had already started—the sidewalk was getting crowded. She man-handled the large padlock into place to secure the front and closed it with a loud click.

"What do you want to do, Britt?"

Startled, she looked at him. "I thought you had to get back to work."

"Nah, not right now. I need to clean up some paperwork, but I want to spend some time with my Nordic princess first."

How did Mark always manage to say the right things at the right time? She didn't want to go home yet—she was too excited about reopening the store—but spending time alone was never fun. It had been okay when she started planning Konditori because it kept her busy. But now with Mark in her life, she realized how much she craved having another person to share in her triumphs and challenges. "I feel like celebrating," she told him.

He arched a brow as he moved in close enough to brush against her. "I can think of a few ideas," he said quietly.

Britt couldn't move, couldn't speak. It was as if a bubble had surrounded them and everything else disappeared. She didn't hear people talking or cars honking—it was only Mark. She fought to get air into her lungs.

His hand clasped hers, warm and strong. "Tell me what you'd like to do."

If Mark had started walking, she would have followed him without a second thought. That scared and excited her at the same time. Yet here he was, asking her what she'd like to do, and Britt could feel herself falling for him just a little bit more.

A chorus of screams suddenly caught her attention, and Britt looked around until she spied the top half of a Ferris wheel. She pointed. "Let's go to the carnival."

He looked to where she indicated, then turned back, his expression skeptical.

"What?" she asked.

"Are you sure?"

She gave him a look. "Of course I am! Why are you asking?"

He grinned. "Because I love getting on the wildest, fastest rides they have. You don't have a problem with that, do you?"

She glanced again at the Ferris wheel. It looked like the tallest ride, and she enjoyed riding those. Everything else should be a piece of cake. "Lead on, brave knight," she told him.

Twenty minutes later, they stood in line to get in. The upbeat music and the kids running around in a frenzy lifted her spirits.

"So, what do you want to go on first?" He held up a batch of tickets.

"Let's walk around a bit, then maybe I'll see a ride I'd like to try."

It wasn't packed with people, but children bounced around them like Ping-Pong balls. "I'm scared I'm going to step on one!" she yelled out as another child zipped between them.

Britt paused in front of a ride consisting of huge teacups that sat four people each, and as she watched, they spun in circles. It also stayed on the ground. "How about this one?"

Mark gave her a cautious glance. "Do you get sick easily?"

She looked at him. "No, why?"

He got to the front and handed the employee several tickets. "Guess we'll find out."

There were no seat belts, just a circular bar in the middle.

"Make sure you hold on tight," he warned.

"Mark, it's an oversize teacup spinning on itself."

His grin was evil as he grabbed the bar. "Don't say I didn't warn you."

The ride started out innocently enough, but as it spun faster, she kept sliding around the teacup. Finally hanging on to the bar helped a bit but not enough. "What fresh kind of hell is this?" She had to scream over the suddenly loud eighties music blasting through the speakers around them.

"I said you needed to be sure!" Mark yelled back. "The ride isn't called Mad Teacup for nothing!"

It was a wild ride, all right. While the kids were screaming with glee, she was screaming to be let off. "Oh my God, how much longer?"

"Don't know. Just hang on!"

After what felt like an eternity, the spinning ride finally slowed down. When Britt managed to step out, her vision started spinning like those damn teacups.

Mark grabbed her arm. "Are you okay?"

"I need to sit down." They walked slowly until he grabbed both of her arms and lowered her to a bench.

She covered her face with a hand. "How could a teacup be so menacing?"

He laughed out loud. "I'm a detective, and I view everything with a critical mind. I honestly didn't think those teacups could knock us about like that."

His laughter, so full of life and contagious. She couldn't help but giggle along with him. "Wasn't there a mystery story by a famous author called *Murder in a Teacup*? Did she mean this?"

"Who knows?" He was still laughing as he wiped tears from his face.

Now that Britt knew what to expect, she eyed every ride with suspicion. The kiddie roller coaster looked okay, and it was a snug fit for the two of them. "I think I like this," Mark told her with a wink and sexy smile.

"Until I throw up on you," she retorted.

The highest peak was about twenty feet off the ground, so it didn't gain enough momentum to turn into a heart-dropping dip. But as the ride reached the end of the line, something happened that she'd never have suspected. The damn thing started to go backward.

"Oh, come on!" she yelled out, while Mark busted a gut, laughing beside her.

The ride was more disorienting, since she couldn't see where she was going, and the sudden dips and twists made her body ache in places she didn't know she had.

"You knew about this," she accused him when it was over. She felt like a pretzel, trying to untangle herself from the seat.

"Honestly, I didn't!"

No more rides. Instead, she told Mark they should play it safe with the games and walking through the attractions. One of them caught her attention—a maze of mirrors. "Let's try that one."

Bad choice. She got turned around so badly she had no idea how to get out. Britt tried not to panic as she slowly refocused, managed to get her bearings and finally made it outside.

"Hey." Mark wrapped her in a hug. How he knew she needed one, she didn't know and didn't care. She leaned into his embrace, inhaling his scent. "I guess that wasn't a good idea, either," he said.

"You think? How can this be called fun if all it does is scare people half to death?"

His body shook as he chuckled. "The kids seem to love it."

"The little tyrants have a warped sense of the word *fun*."

They walked through the carnival as the sun set and the bright, colorful lights were turned on. The atmosphere felt electric, and as more people arrived, the air around her came alive as a multitude of voices spoke in different languages. Britt stood in the midst of this diverse populace and loved every moment.

Although maybe not as much as standing beside a man who accepted her for exactly who she was.

Britt paused on that thought. Was she falling in love? This past week had seen some strange incidents, enough to last her a lifetime. Through it all, Mark had remained her constant rock, despite the unexpected and nerve-racking interview at the police station. He hadn't disappeared when her situation got rough—he'd been there to support, advise and protect. And in her world, that was saying a lot.

"I want to stay with you tonight."

Despite the frantic day he knew he would have tomorrow, Mark didn't want to leave. He stood just inside Britt's condo, his arms wrapped around her waist. He kissed her soft lips, losing track of time within her warm embrace.

She caressed his cheek. "Mark, I want that, too."

Something in her tone made him pause. He'd been absorbed in discovering all he could about his Nordic princess, but he was worried that he might have missed something important. Was he moving too fast? Being too demanding? He searched her face, and it was the small movement of her licking her bottom lip that told him she was nervous. "I'm overstepping, aren't I?"

She frowned now. "I'm not sure what you're talking about."

"I think I'm pushing your boundaries." He'd promised himself that he would let her take the lead between them, but the last few days had been so amazing, spending time with her, just chatting, touching, understanding how she ticked. He'd been enveloped in her scent, drowned every time she looked at him with those ocean-colored eyes, and he had wanted more—so much more.

Yet he kept forgetting that Britt might not be as eager.

Oh, he knew she liked being around him. She hadn't hesitated when they'd made love that first time—in fact, it was as if she couldn't get enough, and Mark had plenty of energy to satisfy her. But her slight hesitation now reminded him that she might want to take things slow, and she was right. With their busy jobs, they needed to make sure any relationship would work.

"No, you're not," she said softly. "Meeting you has pulled me into the light, so to speak. I've had my head buried in the sand for too long with work and ignoring my emotions. It's about time I enjoyed myself with people who want to be with *me*, instead of me using my bakery as a crutch.

"Having said that…" She sighed. "I do have a business to fix, and it couldn't happen at a worse time."

His heart did a funny thump in his chest. It sounded like Britt was ready to take the next step. He wanted to shout his joy but kept a tight leash on his excitement. "Oh, so you're saying you don't mind having me around."

Her smile was sweet. "Yeah, I guess I am saying that. Just…not tonight, Romeo."

He groaned. "Are you going to call me that now? I'm not sure I'm going to like it."

"What's wrong with Romeo?"

"He was a kid with family issues." He bit the inside of his cheek. *Ouch—like me.*

"He was also a romantic. Sort of like you."

"Okay, okay. Compliment it is." Speaking of family, he would have just enough time to see Mom before visiting hours were over. "I'll talk to you tomorrow?"

"You'd better."

He kept their kiss going as long as possible before Britt pushed him away, laughing. "You're stalling."

He waggled his eyebrows. "Of course I am."

That didn't work. Britt firmly turned him around and gently pushed him out. "Sorry, Romeo, but this Juliet needs her beauty rest."

"Like my Nordic princess needs to improve what's already perfect."

She smiled. "Smooth move. Not going to work, though, at least not tonight."

With a final kiss and a glance, she closed her front door.

Mark jogged downstairs, adrenaline flowing through him. Things couldn't get any better between them. He would surprise Mom with a quick hello and a chat before heading home.

Evelyn was off duty, but she had told him she'd updated all the nursing staff who worked on Mom's floor. The envelope she had given him a few days ago didn't get any hits on the AFIS database either. If the letter Mom had received wasn't from Dad, then who?

He stopped in front of the nurses station. "Hi there. I know it's late, but I'd like to see Mrs. Hawthorne before she goes to bed."

Mark had never met this nurse before—he'd never come to the hospital this late. She gave him an odd look that sent chills down his spine. "She has a visitor. But it's not Mr. Hawthorne—it's someone who comes at this time to see her for a few minutes."

He felt his blood start to boil. "And no one thought fit to tell me this?"

He ran down the hallway, the nurse calling after him, but he refused to listen. He slowed down to a stealthy walk as he approached the door, then stopped when he heard laughter.

Mom's laughter.

He pushed the door open without knocking and stopped dead in his tracks at what he saw.

Mom was sitting up in bed, chatting with a man who looked vaguely familiar. When he saw Mark, he stood up quickly, his face flushing red. Mom turned around and gasped, actually raising her hand to her throat. "Mark! What on earth are you doing here so late?"

Not her usual greeting. He stepped inside and let the door swing shut. "I was in the area and decided to come up and visit." He kept a hard glare on the stranger. "I hadn't realized you were entertaining other people."

"Oh, Mark, stop scowling. It makes you look like an ogre." She turned to the man. "Don't you remember Stanley?"

Mark couldn't breathe. It felt like he'd been hit with a baseball bat. Stanley Tucker—coach, mentor and the father figure Mark had desperately needed. This man had saved him from spiraling into a morass of hatred, revenge and depression. Stanley hadn't put up with Mark's shit and had coached him with prompts and a firm hand until Mark became the human being his mother deserved.

"Hi, Mark. Wow, your mom's right—you really have grown into a fine man." Stanley came around the bed, his hand extended.

"Mr. Tucker," was all Mark could manage to say.

"There's no need to be formal, young man." His coach gently grasped his hand and shook it. "Damn, it's good to see you."

Past memories flooded Mark's mind, the ones that meant something, recollections that he'd never forget. Someone else other than his mom had cared for his well-being, stamping their imprint on his conscience. The handshake wasn't enough, and Mark enveloped his mentor in a rough bear hug. "It's so good to see you, too," he whispered in a choked breath.

"Well, there goes my little secret," Mom said out loud, with a sniff for added emphasis.

He released Stanley with a couple of slaps on the shoulder. "Why was this a secret?" he asked, confused.

"Because I wanted to surprise you when I was home from the hospital." Her glance at Stanley was tender.

"That wasn't going to work. I asked the nurses to—" Mark stopped, changing his words at the last moment. "I asked them to keep an eye on you."

"You mean spying. You're letting work take over."

Mark changed the subject. "How did you two find each other?"

"I was scrolling through social media a few weeks ago and found your mom's profile. I was actually looking for yours," Stanley added. "But you don't have anything."

"Too busy to have one."

"I get it. Your mom and I chatted, then next thing I knew, she posted a picture of herself in the hospital." Stanley had a worried expression on his face, but Mark sensed these two weren't telling him everything. The dozen roses sitting on the side table was another hint. "I work late, but I've managed to squeeze in visits."

"Thanks for checking up on her." He meant it. Stanley was a great guy, and Mark felt more comfortable knowing there was someone in Mom's corner he could trust. "I'll leave you two lovebirds alone."

"What—Mark Hawthorne, what's wrong with you?" Mom's voice gave it away, even though her words didn't.

"Oh, nothing." He walked over and planted a big smoochy kiss on her cheek. "I'll try to come visit tomorrow. Work has ramped up, and I've got to be around when an arrest is made."

"I've been watching the news," she said, her voice filled with excitement. "Did you find Mr. Ferguson's killer?"

Mark glanced at Stanley, but his former coach held up his hands. "Nothing will leave this room. To be honest, I don't even watch the news."

He grinned. "We've identified a potential suspect. Now it's just getting our hands on him."

"I knew it! I knew you'd crack your investigation." She held out her arms. "Let me give my detective son a big hug and kiss before he goes."

"Mom," he groaned, but he let himself be fussed over while Stanley watched in amusement.

"Didn't I tell you Mark was doing well?" she said.

Stanley nodded. "Better than well." He grabbed Mark's shoulder. "I'm proud of you."

Mark left the hospital in good spirits. Not only did he manage to see Mom, but Stanley had reappeared at the most opportune time. He had suspected his mentor had a crush on Mom after her divorce, but he couldn't prove it. But watching them just now gave him hope that it was true.

It seemed like his life was filled with second chances, opportunities and love again.

* * *

Britt was mentally floating on air, and she couldn't concentrate on anything. Except for a pair of golden-brown eyes that made her feel like she was the only woman in the room. How the heck could she get anything done when Mark talked and looked at her that way? But he'd warned her he would stick around, so she'd have to get used to it.

She made a light dinner and placed that and her work laptop down on the kitchen table. She started to eat as it powered up, then paused while scrolling through some messages. Customers knew Konditori was closed, so she wasn't expecting anything important.

So when she saw the email labeled Please, it's urgent! Britt, can you help?! she hesitated, wondering if it was spam. However, looking at the email in Preview mode, she saw the message was from the very rich client who had sung her bakery's praises to her circle of high-class friends.

Britt, I hope you're well, and I hope you might help me— I'm desperate!

My husband and I are hosting a very important dinner Friday evening for the Defense Minister of Canada. I know, it's an honor for us!

It's only ten guests. I heard your bakery was wrecked during a break and enter—so sorry!—but I wanted to ask if there was any way you could supply some of your delicious treats? If you can't, is there anyone you could recommend? I really hope you can help me!

Thank you,

Angela Weinstein

Mrs. Weinstein was married to a powerful CEO who provided materials to build aircraft. She'd been to the store and asked exclusively for Britt's assistance in choosing the best pastries for her women's club meeting. Ever since that day, Mrs. Weinstein would place an order every week without fail. Even though she knew Britt's business wasn't functional at the moment, she had emailed anyway.

Under other circumstances, Britt would have made the painful decision to say no to the lady's request. However, Britt had to wonder if Mrs. Weinstein was entertaining more than a defense minister. Was it possible one of her guests could also be the prime minister?

"Damn it!" The opportunity was too good to pass up, but it would all hinge on Jacques.

She grabbed her phone. "Jacques, it's Britt."

"*Chérie*, you're calling later than usual. Is there something wrong?"

"Sort of." She hoped he understood her excitement behind this. "What do you think of providing an order for tomorrow evening?"

Silence on the other end. "Jacques?"

"My apologies. Your request stunned me for a moment."

Britt swore under her breath. "I'm sorry, Jacques, but this one is really important. Mrs. Weinstein will be entertaining ten very high-level guests tomorrow." She paused for emphasis. "I think one of them is the prime minister."

"*Merde!* Are you certain?"

"No." She wouldn't lie to him. "But Mrs. Weinstein let it slip that the defense minister will be there."

"That's good enough for me. There are only ten guests, so it will not be difficult to bake some specialties for Madame Weinstein. Thomas and I have finished cleaning and sorting the kitchen, and we've purchased the supplies. As long as your friend Joyce provides adequate protection from the debris, we shall be fine."

She wanted to squeal with delight. "You're amazing, Jacques, you know that? I could kiss you."

He laughed. "I will hold you to that promise, *chérie*. I'll be in the bakery about seven thirty tomorrow morning. I will contact Thomas to come in as well."

"*Merci beaucoup*, Jacques. I'll come in, too, and help keep the contractors' mess to a minimum. See you tomorrow."

Britt didn't know how much better today could be. If Mrs. Weinstein's guests offered even one compliment about Konditori, she would be overrun with customers. She would seriously have to consider a bigger space if that happened, and more staff...

She got up and grabbed today's mail, then turned on the television. As she flicked through the channels, she stopped on the twenty-four-hour news, listening to a female officer describing the progress on Mr. Ferguson's murder. She kept the information vague, and as reporters clamored for more details, she ended the news conference and walked off. She must be Mark's boss.

Britt flicked through more channels until she settled on an action movie, then slowly sifted through the envelopes. A couple of bills, something from her insurance company—probably a letter formalizing the activation of the renovations—a flyer insisting she vote for her MP candidate in her region. The four nominees, offering their best smiles, didn't interest her, but she guessed she'd better make time to find out what promises they were throwing out to voters.

The last piece of mail was a plain white envelope with her name and address. There was no return address on it. She cut the top with her mail opener and pulled out a single sheet of white paper. As she read it, the air around her seemed to turn ice-cold, and her body trembled, her hands shaking so badly the paper fell to her lap. Britt couldn't tear away her frozen gaze from the terrifying sentences typed in cap letters.

YOU ARE MAKING A MISTAKE THAT YOU'LL REGRET. I URGE YOU TO RECONSIDER.

Chapter 16

Britt didn't sleep for half the night—her mind poked and prodded that elusive message until she thought she'd pull her hair out in frustration. She finally managed to fall into a restless slumber, but her alarm clock rang much too soon.

She got in the shower and turned the nozzle to Cold, letting the icy water wash over her, dissolving the cobwebs in her head. She needed to think clearly, which she sure as hell hadn't managed last night.

The only person she could think of who would send such a note was Mr. Ferguson. His verbal intimidation toward her that past Monday morning was definitely reflected in that letter. What an asshole, sending her another threat after he was dead. Seriously?

She finished getting ready, putting on a pair of flared yoga leggings and a short-sleeved T-shirt. It would be hot in the kitchen, so she packed her duffel bag with three reusable two-liter bottles filled with water for herself and the guys.

At the last moment, she stuck the unknown letter in her purse. It was probably a good idea to call Mark and let him know about it. Not that she thought it would matter—the bakery CEO was dead.

"Ah, whatever," she mumbled. She had other important things to concentrate on.

The bus ride to the bakery was uneventful, but as she stared out the window, that letter came back into focus. The sooner she got rid of it, the better.

She thought she may as well text Mark and let him know. Maybe he could meet her at the bakery and take it off her hands.

Less than a minute later, her phone rang—it was Mark. "Britt, when did you get that letter?" he demanded. "What does it say?"

She repeated its contents. "It was in yesterday's mail. I assumed it was Mr. Ferguson being a jerk and threatening me again."

"What do you mean, *again*?"

She sighed. "Sorry, my mind is... I meant when he grabbed me in the alley and I kicked him."

"And he retaliated by sending those criminals to your store!" His voice rose on each word, but he suddenly stopped. "Damn it, I'm sorry, *vakker*. But you knew what Ferguson was like. You could have gotten hurt, and I'd never forgive myself."

She sighed again. Mark was right—she probably should have handled the situation differently, but Britt believed she gave Mr. Ferguson a very good hint on how she felt about his financial offer. "I'm sorry, too."

The bus arrived at her stop. "I'm at the bakery now," she told him. "I need to help with a special order I received last night."

"That's not a good idea. You don't know if that letter came from Ferguson or someone else."

"Who else could it be?" She blew out a breath. "Look,

if you want to grab it and check for fingerprints or whatever, I have it with me."

A pause. "Fine. I'll be there in about twenty." He hung up.

He was angrier than she expected.

She walked around to the back and entered the kitchen, where Jacques was prepping ingredients for tonight's event. "Do you need help with anything?" she asked, then looked around. "Where's Thomas?"

"He's a little late, but he promised he will come in."

"Okay, I'm going to get settled in. Joyce should be here between nine and ten, and I'll make sure the doorway to the front room is taped up tight before she starts the renovations. I'm just waiting for a friend to come by to pick up something first, then I'll help."

By the time she dropped her stuff in the office and got the padlock off the front door, Mark was strolling toward her. "Hi," he said in a short tone.

His stance spoke volumes—he *was* angry. "Mark, there's no need to get huffed up about this," she told him as he walked in.

"Britt, I have to. Do you have proof that letter came from Ferguson?"

She made a face. "Of course I don't."

"Then until I know for sure otherwise, I have to treat that note and envelope as criminal evidence. Do you have them?"

"They're in my office." Britt didn't wait for him, just turned on her heel and headed to the room. She plucked the envelope out of her purse and held it out.

He produced a plastic lunch bag. "Drop it in here for me."

She did as she was told, feeling a bit flustered at his

attitude. He was in work mode, which she now recognized after his treatment of her when she'd been questioned about her bracelet being found in Mr. Ferguson's car. "Was there anything else you needed?"

He tucked the evidence and bag into a jacket pocket. Now he looked at her, blinking. "What's that?"

"Do you need anything else? If not, I have a special order to make for a prestigious client." She left the office, but halfway to the boarded door, Mark grabbed her arm, and she stumbled. "Hey!"

"I'm sorry," he apologized. He released her and ran a hand through his hair. "I don't mean to sound like a bastard, but I'm worried."

"About what? The only person that note could have come from was Mr. Ferguson."

He stared at her, his expression growing more concerned. "Has Ferguson ever sent you a threatening letter before?"

"He's—" Britt stopped, uncertain. She let her mind travel back to when she first met the CEO. "No, he hasn't." She looked at him, the fear she fought and won against last night threatening to overwhelm her. "Mark…"

"There's a first time for everything. I won't know for sure until my forensics colleague analyzes the letter and tells me the prints belong to Ferguson. I'd ask you to stay home until I figured this out, but I know you won't." He moved close and brushed his fingers against her cheek.

"Any other time, I'd do whatever you asked, but tonight… It's really important."

"I get it." He took out his phone. "Where are you going?"

She gave him Mrs. Weinstein's name and address and the reason for the unexpected delivery.

"The defense minister will have plenty of security, but I'll be there as well. Find me when you arrive, and I'll drive you home after you're finished."

"Mark, do you really think…?" She stopped when she saw the stubborn expression on his face. "I don't have a choice, do I?"

"Nope."

She nodded, feeling a bit better about having him around.

"Hey." He brushed a thumb across her lips. "Don't worry. If you go in, get everything set up and then leave, things should be okay." He frowned. "You're not catering, are you?"

"No, Mrs. Weinstein hires help for that. We do it exactly as how you just described it."

"As soon as you're finished, come out to the car, okay?"

"Mark…"

This time, he shut her up with a kiss that left her speechless. "You were saying?" he asked, smiling.

Despite the late arrival of Joyce and the contractors, and the constant noise they created, the last batch of specialty pastries—a secret recipe from Jacques—was almost finished. Britt helped to get the boxes assembled, labels printed off and pasted on each container, then gathered a small stack of business cards to leave on the table where the pastries would be displayed. This was the adrenaline-induced excitement she loved—cooking, preparing, organizing. She loved fitting the pieces together until they created a masterpiece filled with pride, love and, of course, sweet deliciousness.

Jacques and Thomas even managed to bake a couple of cakes, both covered in icing the same colors as

Konditori—they even wrote the store name on each one with blue icing. She looked around in wonder at what her team had created—along with the two cakes, there was an assortment of Nordic and French tarts, Danishes, cinnamon rolls and cream-filled croissants. "Jacques, Thomas, you truly outdid yourselves. Bravo."

Jacques bowed. "*Chérie*, you and Konditori are in a class of your own. I'm proud to be part of your staff."

Thomas nodded. "I really like working here."

"Thank you both. Shall we get going?"

They carefully loaded the pastry-filled boxes onto special built-in shelves in the van. "Thomas, Jacques and I can handle it from here," Britt told him. "Thank you so much again for coming in on short notice. I'll lock up—I think the contractors have already left."

Britt hurried around to the front and went inside to grab her things—the plastic and tape still covered the door to the kitchen. She made sure the boarded-up front door was secure, then walked back down the alley to Jacques. Britt punched in the code for the security alarm and locked the back door. "Ready to roll," she announced as she got into the van.

Mrs. Weinstein's residence, located in the exclusive Uplands, was a twenty-minute drive east. They decided to get on the toll highway because the other routes would be busy with cars coming home from work. As they got off the ramp going south on Bathurst, traffic on this major street was packed.

"We can turn left here onto Flamingo Road," Britt said to Jacques, checking a map on her phone. "Then onto Golfer's Gate to Callaway Court."

Ten minutes later, they halted in front of an imposing set of black iron gates guarded by four security men. The enormous two-story stone mansion within the grounds was ablaze with light. Britt rolled down her window. "Britt Gronlund. I'm with Konditori Bakery," she announced. "Mrs. Weinstein is expecting us."

The guard repeated the information into a radio and was given the go-ahead. "Take your vehicle over there," he said, pointing out the direction. "There's a York Regional officer parked back there, too, a Detective Mark Hawthorne. He informed us that he's here to escort you home afterward."

"Yes, that's right. Thank you."

They were instructed to park next to a side entrance. As Britt got out and looked around, all she saw were luxury cars in front of the five-car garage located beside the home. Others were parked in an empty lot across the street, and surrounded by several security guards.

"Your new boyfriend must be worried about something if he's here," Jacques said.

She turned around, wondering about her baker's choice of words. "I guess he wants to make sure I get home safely."

"*Chérie*, I could drive you home."

"You've been up since six in the morning, Jacques. I'm sure you're exhausted. It just saves you an extra trip."

As she approached Mark's car, he climbed out, smiling. *"Vakker."*

"Hey." She wasn't sure if kissing him in front of security was a good idea.

Mark didn't seem bothered and pressed his lips to hers, firm and insistent. "All ready to go? Anyone else with you?"

The security lights were bright in the parking area, with waitstaff, security and valets jostling around each other to get to their destinations. "My head baker is with me." She turned and pointed out Jacques, standing by the front of the van. "My van is the bright pink one."

He laughed. "Why am I not surprised?"

When she turned back to him, though, Britt noticed Mark's gaze had narrowed as he glanced over her shoulder. "Is something wrong?" she asked.

"Everything's fine." He kissed her again. "I'll be here. Good luck with tonight."

As she and Jacques started bringing in their desserts, uniformed staff surrounded them in a chaotic, but organized manner.

Jacques whistled. "This will be a night to remember, I think."

"Over here!" a young woman called out to them. Her uniform was different from the others, with a name and her position printed on it—Sylvia, Head Caterer. She held a clipboard. "You are?"

"Britt Gronlund, Konditori Bakery." She nodded at Jacques. "And my head baker, Jacques Baudin."

"Ah yes, yours was a last-minute order." She smiled. "Mrs. Weinstein loves your pastries. I'm glad it worked out. This way."

She led them to a small butler's pantry off to one side of the huge kitchen. "The other pantry is being used for the dining ware and service," she told them. "Thank God it's a small number of guests, but it's a very exclusive dinner event. The serving trays are in the cupboards above you—choose whatever you require. You can leave it all in here—the waitstaff will bring everything out when ready. They've just served the hors d'oeuvres, so it'll be about two hours before the desserts are served. You have some time."

"Thank you."

"If you need anything, I'll be in the hallway where you found me." With a bright smile, she was gone.

Britt and Jacques took turns bringing in their food-stuffs until everything was stacked on the wide counters. "I think we should just get our desserts on the serving plates and call it a night," Jacques said quietly.

She nodded. "Good idea. It's not like we'll get close to Mrs. Weinstein to thank her."

They arranged everything accordingly. Britt heard detailed instructions shouted through the back rooms, all timed down to the minute. "You know, I thought about hosting catering events in the future, but if they're going to run it like a military operation, it's going to be a big nope in my books."

Jacques laughed. "For diplomats such as these, there's no choice. They have their schedules, and everything else works around them."

She glanced at him while he arranged the cakes on stands, then covered them with glass domes. "It sounds like you've catered something like this."

"Oui." He fussed over the Danishes. "Back home, my events were all planned. It made things easier."

Britt checked her watch—fifteen minutes to spare. "Looks like we're done. Honestly, I'd like to get out of here before we're descended upon by the waitstaff."

Just as they left the pantry, a contingent of servers hurried in their direction, and they flattened themselves against the wall as the horde went by. "So glad we're not staying," she muttered.

Once outside, Britt inhaled a deep breath of the cool summer air, scented with roses and other flowers. She stretched her arms over her head, looking out into the vast backyard lit with solar lighting and lanterns and bordered by tall hedges and colorful foliage. A stone pathway led from the extensive back porch to a small gate at the opposite end. Britt was curious as to what lay beyond. "Jacques, I'm going to take a walk around the backyard."

He raised a brow. "Do you think that's wise, Britt? What if a security guard finds you out there?"

She laughed. "We're at a party. They must expect guests to come outside and admire the scenery."

"Then let me join you before we leave. I just need to use the bathroom, if you don't mind waiting?"

"Of course not." She wished Mark was here to enjoy such a lovely sight with her.

Mark stood just within the open door leading out to the parking area. His body was on full alert, adrenaline pumping through his veins as he studied his immediate surroundings. The long, wide hallway before him was filled with staff, and as he tried to angle himself to look at the various faces that hurried past him, he realized it was impossible to pick out an individual person.

But something—or rather, someone—had triggered an internal red flag.

When he had been talking to Britt outside earlier, he noticed a man that looked vaguely like Ferguson's murderer—Mark had memorized every detail from the picture Myrna provided—but he wasn't sure. And if he wasn't sure, he couldn't alert security and cause a panic.

A young woman approached him. "Excuse me, are you a guest? The entrance is that way…"

He pulled out his badge. "I'm here to assist security. I'd like to take a quick look around, if you don't mind."

"Yes, of course." She passed by without another word.

Mark walked casually down the hall, listening to the

shouts and clatter of a dining service being prepared. Britt would be in the midst of that, which meant she'd be far away and, more important, safe from anything that might happen.

The end of the hallway revealed an enormous dining room. Everything had been set up, but the room was currently empty. Beyond, he saw several guests in another room, holding champagne glasses as they chatted. That had to be the reception area.

He walked quickly to the other side, his gaze searching. Here, Mark had to be more careful, as his presence would certainly be noticed among the bejeweled women and men in tuxedos. Bodyguards stood at strategic points around the room, their scrutiny taking in everything around them. He stood just behind the grand archway and studied the room, looking for any sign of his adversary. Nothing.

He turned around, intending to backtrack and try another hallway, when he heard several ladies laughing. He wasn't sure why it attracted his attention, but Mark looked over his shoulder...

Damn—it was him.

Before Mark got his wits together, the murderer left the reception via another door. But shit, that was the guy.

He went back the way he came, knowing that discretion was critical. He got outside and hurried to his car, then grabbed his walkie-talkie. "This is Detective Hawthorne!" he said urgently. "Get every available unit to Callaway Court. Ferguson's murderer has been spotted. No sirens and park at the corner of Callaway and Golfers Gate. The house is directly across, with all its lights on. Head for the main gate—I'll meet you there. We don't want to spook him."

He dialed another number on his work phone. "This

is Detective Mark Hawthorne with York Regional Police 4 District," he said. "I had a request for the Emergency Response Team to be on standby to assist with the arrest of an international criminal. He's been located."

He gave them the address, and then called Britt, but there was no answer. It was possible she was still busy with setting up, but…

Mark sent her a quick text instead, telling her to get in his car when she was finished and lock the doors. He knew she would freak out when she read the message, but hopefully she'd just do it and wait until he returned.

Now he had to alert security. If the murderer tried anything during the party…

Jacques remained in the guest bathroom for a few extra minutes to freshen up. The work he and Britt had done left him feeling sweaty and unfit for such esteemed company.

He checked his clothing, making sure he wasn't dabbed with icing or fruit, swiped away a few flecks of pastry and looked at himself in the mirror, thinking it would do. He needed to hurry as Britt was waiting for him in the gardens. He sighed. This detective was a very lucky man to be dating his boss.

When he opened the door, he stared in surprise at the familiar face before him. "What are you doing here, *mon ami*? I thought—"

Thomas slammed into him, knocking them both into the powder room, and locked the door.

Jacques's brain clicked into overdrive. He held his hands up, palms facing forward. "Now, now, there's no need for this…"

"Why do you have a cop following you?" he snarled.

"An officer? He is not following us. He's here to escort Britt home. He's waiting in his car."

"Not anymore. He came into the house and was hanging around in the hallway."

"I—" Jacques thought fast. If he wasn't careful… "There's no way the police can trace anything back to me. I've played my part leading the Ferguson protests, but I did not expect the police to make a surprise appearance at the funeral. I was lucky to get away. How do I know *you* haven't done something stupid?"

"Because I'm not in jail. But if we're not careful, we will be."

Jacques considered the situation. Thomas was agitated for some reason. "Where is the police officer now?"

"I don't know."

"Mon Dieu." Jacques knew he hadn't been spotted at Ferguson's funeral—he had kept himself well camouflaged. As for Thomas… "We must be very careful as we leave," he warned. "We cannot be seen together, and Britt will ask questions if she notices you."

Thomas stared at him. "I'm leaving the city tonight."

Jacques knew his brows went up at that. "What are you talking about? Why would you go?"

Thomas's expression held a chilling quality that made Jacques nervous. "Because I killed him."

Jacques felt his body grow still with dread at the terrifying response. "You killed an officer? What is wrong with you? Why would you do…?"

Thomas slashed his hand in a downward motion. "Not the cop. I wasted Ferguson."

Jacques's mind couldn't keep up with the horror story Thomas was telling him. The young man had twisted all of Jacques's hard work until he felt like he couldn't escape. "Why?" When Thomas didn't answer, he slammed his palm against the wall. "Why?" he demanded.

"Because he deserved it." Thomas spat on the ground.

Jacques swore. Their plan to terrorize Ferguson into backing off from buying neighborhood businesses had gotten messed up. Somehow, young Thomas had turned it into some kind of personal vendetta, and he didn't know why. "Is that it? Because he deserved it? You need to provide a better reason than that."

"You told me what he's done to you—to other small-business owners. His death could be a warning to Mighty Big Bakery to back off."

"Or it might spur them on, to continue his legacy." Jacques shook his head—where had he made his mistake? His own revenge against Ferguson and Jacques's business partner—who had sold him out behind his back—had gone horribly wrong. It wasn't supposed to go this far... not all the way to murder. He'd have to figure out how to extricate himself from this mess. "*Mon ami*, I think we need to back up and reassess our situation."

"Too late for that." Thomas pulled a gun out from behind his back. A silencer was attached to it.

"*Merde.*" Jacques weighed his options—all of them looked bleak. "There's no need for that," he said gently, keeping his hands out in the open. "I'm not going to say anything to anyone. Just leave—leave the city, the country even. Please, don't hurt a friend."

Thomas hesitated, and Jacques saw his chance, grabbing the young man's weapon and smashing it against the wall. It went off with a muffled pop. Suddenly, Thomas dipped low, and Jacques howled in pain, his eyes watering from the excruciating blow to his crotch. His grip loosened, but before he could regain his balance, hot, searing pain burned in his leg and stomach. Jacques slumped to the ground, his vision darkening as Thomas pushed him out of the way to make his escape.

Britt glanced at her watch again—Jacques had been gone for over fifteen minutes. Then she realized he must have found an opportunity to schmooze with the guests. "What a guy," she said out loud. She'd take her stroll through the beautiful garden, then head to Mark's car and go home.

She walked down the few steps into the sunken space and stayed on the main path. The grass was a lush green beneath the lights, and on an impulse, she took off her sneakers and walked through it, the soft blades tickling her toes, the earth cool beneath her feet. It felt amazing.

She reached the other end of the garden. Here, the tall gate led out onto small undulating hills with sandbanks in between—a golf course, and to either side of her, the blackness of a forest.

Odd, the gate didn't have a lock on it. She assumed the course and surrounding area were possibly so secure that a lock wasn't needed. It must be nice to live in this type of luxury.

She heard footsteps from behind. "Holy crap, Jacques, you took your time," Britt called out to him as she turned. "Did you score an opportunity to talk with Mrs.—" She stopped.

Thomas stood a few feet away. "Hey, Britt."

"Um, hey." She glanced at the house. "Why are you here? I thought I mentioned Jacques and I wouldn't need you tonight. We're already finished."

"Oh." He laughed, but it didn't sound right. "Sorry,

I guess I thought…maybe you and Jacques would need help cleaning up."

"No, we're done, thank you. You can go home. You've had a long day." She had no idea how she kept her voice steady—her body was ready to bolt because something didn't feel right in this conversation.

"Would you like a ride home?"

Her stomach was turning into knots of fear. There was no reason for Thomas to be out here—none. And the way he was acting in front of her was not the same young man who worked in her bakery. "No, thanks. Jacques said he'd take me home," she lied.

"Oh." Thomas scratched his head. "I thought your detective boyfriend was driving you back."

Thomas couldn't know that—there was no way. Britt swallowed the large lump in her throat. "He's supposed to, but he hasn't come back from wherever he is. Actually, I think I'll go wait for him at the car." Her laugh was forced. "I don't want to have an officer waiting on me."

She almost screamed when her cell phone pinged with a text. She dug it out of her bag and looked at the screen—Mark. He had called and texted several times, but she had turned the phone off when she and Jacques were in the house.

She glanced at Thomas, who had remained still. Something very spooky surrounded him, like a bad aura, and if she didn't get away, Britt was scared she'd be sucked into it. "It's Jacques," she lied again, hoping it sounded convincing. "He's wondering where I am." She started typing a reply.

HELP. IN BACK GARDEN!

"Don't do that."

Startled, she looked up. Thomas was swaying from side to side, as if listening to a song only he could hear. "Come on, I'll take you home."

"No." She backed up until she bumped into the iron gate, slipping her phone into her pocket. "I told you, I have a ride."

"Not anymore." His voice had gone quiet, menacing.

"Thomas, what the hell do you want?" she demanded in a loud voice. Despite the fear coursing through every limb, she had to ask the question.

"I did something bad, and the police are after me." He took a step forward. "If I kept you as a hostage, your boyfriend would back off. I just want to get out of the country."

That was a big OH, HELL NO in her mind.

Britt didn't think, just reacted. She threw her shoes and bag at him, scoring a direct hit in his face, then raced out the gate, turning left and rushing into the depth of the trees.

She immediately slowed down, wincing as her bare feet stepped on small rocks and stubbed against tree roots. She looked over her shoulder but couldn't see Thomas.

She hunkered down against a tree, her breaths panting out in short gasps. Her instincts had taken over, allowing her to escape a potentially dangerous situation. As she fought to gather her wits, she heard shouting. "York Regional Police! Remain where you are and get your hands in the air!"

Mark's voice. "Oh my God." Britt started crawling in the opposite direction, desperate to stay out of sight until he came for her. Bile rose in her throat, her fear a tangible thing as it wrapped around her ankles to slow her down.

"It's okay. You're okay," she whispered to herself. She used her hands to feel her way around tree trunks and thick bushes. A noise caught her attention, and turning around, the glare of a flashlight wove erractically behind her. Britt heard a shout—was that Mark? She wasn't sure, and decided to keep going.

Britt looked around, hoping to spot something for reference. She knew there was another house beside the Weinsteins' and carefully crawled in the general direction. She needed to gain some distance before attempting to call Mark.

Suddenly, a bright light illuminated the forest in front of her, the trees a stark silhouette of dark angles. Glancing behind her, a portion of the golf course appeared. Several officers ran by, but she didn't see Thomas.

And that flashlight continued to dog her steps. Damn it, was it Thomas? "Shit!" She got to her feet and stumbled through the undergrowth, using what light she could navigate by to get away from the mayhem unfolding behind her.

She desperately wanted to call Mark but was terrified that if she hesitated for too long, Thomas might find her. On that thought, she took her phone out and placed it on Mute—if Mark called, it'd vibrate instead, alerting her but not Thomas.

Several agonizing minutes later, Britt spied a square of light some distance away—a window. Sobbing quietly with relief, she got down on her hands and knees again to save her feet, and crawled as fast as she dared, occasionally bumping into a tree trunk, or swearing under her breath as she pulled her tangled hair out of an errant bush. She stopped, noticing the darkness around her had receded—it looked like all the security lights at the golf course were turned on. The police should be able to catch Thomas.

Unless he had escaped through the forest like she was doing and was following her. With all the illumination, he could easily find her if she didn't get her ass moving.

Britt focused her waning strength on that square of light, which meant a house, and people inside who could keep her safe.

God, she hoped Mark was okay. Chasing Thomas like that when he could be armed with a weapon...

Suddenly, she stopped and crouched down beside a large tree as crashing noises caught her attention. It was difficult to tell how far away it was, but as Britt listened, she realized it was getting closer.

"Britt!"

She heard her name, but with fear coursing through her body, it could be Thomas trying to draw her out of hiding.

She'd have no choice but to make a run for it.

Tucking her hair down the back of her T-shirt, she worked out a path of least resistance and got moving, trying to be careful where she placed her feet. A couple of minutes later, she slapped her hand over her mouth to muffle a cry of pain—she had stepped on something sharp that pierced her foot. Not missing a beat, she scrambled to find what broke her stride—a piece of broken branch. She bit her tongue as she yanked it out quickly, then half hobbled, half hopped the rest of the way.

Her phone vibrated. *Damn it, could this be a worse time?* If it was Mark, he'd have to wait while she made her last dash to safety. It felt like every piece of plant life was trying to ensnare her, but fear gave her the strength to fight through the foliage that blocked her escape.

And then, nothing. Britt stumbled to a stop in a clearing

and looked around, breathing hard. The ground seemed level beneath the faint illumination of the golf course security lights. She took hurried, though careful steps through the knee-high grass. Her foot throbbed in pain, punctuated with sharp stabs that almost had her crying in frustration. She knew it was bleeding, and no doubt infected as well. Sparing a few precious minutes, she stripped off her T-shirt and bound it around her foot, feeling the thick stickiness of blood along her fingers.

Just a little farther—at the edge of the clearing, a thick hedge stood like a sentinel, and there, in the middle, a gate.

"Almost there, almost there," she chanted softly. She used her toes on the injured foot to propel herself forward until her hands brushed against the textured leaves, then moved to her left until cool metal replaced the natural border.

The light from the large picture window was bright, a beacon that called out to her. It stretched far into the backyard, which allowed her to find the gate's latch. She carefully lifted it and looked over her shoulder. No one was behind her, but Thomas would easily see her silhouette from the edge of the forest if he made it this far.

Haunted by the thought, Britt slid inside. She moved to the side so that the hedge hid her from view and looked around. Several feet in front of her, a swimming pool lay covered in a dark tarpaulin. Thank God she hadn't charged straight ahead—she would have fallen in. Around it was a stone patio and beyond, the unbroken darkness of grass—a lot of it. The backyard was huge. She had a lot of space to walk through before getting close enough to yell for help.

She gritted her teeth and started limping, spurred on

by the distant shouts behind her. As soon as she managed to get inside, she'd call Mark and let him know she was safe…

Britt hesitated, listening. Above the shouting, she also heard a dog barking. Was it a police dog? Or something else?

When she looked at the window, she froze in her tracks. The large shadow of a canine danced across the grass, and at the window, she spied a German shepherd. It was going wild, jumping up and down, teeth bared, its baleful stare locked on her.

Damn it. Britt needed to weigh her options. If the homeowner released the dog into the backyard before she made it to the door to explain her situation, she didn't stand a chance. It was possible the police had informed anyone living in the area to keep their doors locked and be on the lookout.

"Shit!" She looked around quickly, then took a closer look at a tall square object just beyond the window's light. As she hobbled toward it, she realized it was a garden shed. Perfect, she could hide in there until Mark got her.

A small light winked on when she opened the door. It was a good size, large enough for her to stand in. On the walls, various garden tools hung neatly in rows. Britt grabbed a long-handled aerator, its numerous spikes a couple of inches long. If Thomas opened that door, he'd get a face full of sharp metal.

Mark stood in the middle of a group of security guards and police officers. "I need your help. The police have been hunting a dangerous criminal the past couple of days, and I saw him in this house." Mark gave them a brief summary of the Ferguson murder case. "We can't have a panic on our hands." He pulled out a picture. "This is the man we're looking for."

Several more security guards had hurried over. "I saw that guy," one of them said. "I don't know how he got in, but I saw him hanging around that pink bakery van."

"We have to find him." Mark's anxiety went up with every second that passed without hearing from Britt. "My men will cover the exits. Go inside and take a look around—"

His phone pinged. When he read the message from Britt, his adrenaline skyrocketed. "The back garden! Move!"

He took off at a full run, his officers and several security guards trailing behind him. In the distance, he saw a flash of white and Britt's terrified expression before she bolted. A man was about to give chase.

"Goddamn it!" He ran faster. "York Regional Police!" he yelled. "Remain where you are and get your hands in the air!"

The murderer he'd been hunting sped away, running straight onto the golf course. If they didn't catch him in time, he'd disappear into the darkness.

"Go after him!" he shouted. "Radio for help to block off the course and get some lights on!" Mark turned to the man beside him. "I heard you guys are one of the best ERT units in Canada," he said to Staff Sergeant Victor Moore.

The commander smiled, but it wasn't a friendly expression. "My boys are already circling around the course, detective. I'll follow your men. Don't worry, we'll find him."

As Moore raced off, Mark noticed something white in the grass that worried him—Britt's sneakers, and nearby, her bag. He veered left, following her course. Somehow, she'd already reached the blackness of the forest beyond.

"Britt!" he yelled. He dug a flashlight out of his pocket and switched it on. Thick stands of tree trunks and undergrowth hindered his progress as he pushed through. How the hell did she manage to get through this stuff?

Just then, the remaining security lights at the golf course turned on, illuminating everything in a bright white glare. It didn't quite reach back here, but it offered Mark a little more light to see by.

Several anxious minutes later, his flashlight picked out a gaping hole. The branches were recently broken, still hanging by pieces of bark. He kept going, turning one way, then the other, trying to see through the bush and wondering if she was hiding somewhere.

Something glistened wet on the ground a few feet ahead, and Mark bit back a cry when he realized it was blood—*shit*. "Britt! Where are you?" he yelled out. No answer.

Swearing, he pulled out his phone and dialed her number, hoping she'd pick up or he could hear it ringing in the undergrowth. Nothing.

He continued following her path, shoving at anything that got in his way. He stopped when his walkie-talkie went off. "Staff Sergeant Moore reporting." The ERT commander possessed a thick British accent. "Perpetrator has been captured. Repeat, perpetrator captured."

He hit the send button. "Good work, all of you. Take him to the precinct. I'll be there shortly. The rest of you, get back to the Weinstein residence and make sure everyone's okay. I'm looking for someone—I'll radio when I'm done."

The golf course security lights barely penetrated this far into the forest. Britt must be terrified, hunkered down somewhere and staying quiet until she thought it was safe.

The trees thinned out into a meadow, but before he continued, his trembling fingers wrapped around long, silky strands of blond hair caught on a bush. He was on the right track, but he was frightened for her, wondering what condition she'd be in.

Mark ran across the meadow, following a faint beaten path through the long grass until he stopped at a thick border of hedge reaching almost ten feet in height. As he panned his flashlight, he spied the half-open gate.

Britt must have gone through here.

He opened the gate wider so that he could slip inside. It was eerily quiet, as if the air held its breath.

He jumped at the sound of a dog barking. He looked towards the mansion and saw a large German shepherd thrashing against the glass doors and baring its teeth. The homeowner was nowhere in sight.

Mark started walking the length of the extensive backyard, being careful not to get too close to the edge of the pool. Under his flashlight's glare, he spied a garden shed.

He stopped and looked around. There was nowhere anyone could hide unless they buried themselves beneath the thick hedge.

As a precaution, Mark hunkered down low and swept the flashlight's beam around—nothing.

He rose and blew out a tense breath. With a bloodied foot, Britt wouldn't get too far. And a very angry guard dog would make her think twice about going to the house for help.

He glanced back at the garden shed and started toward it. If he were in Britt's position, he would pick this place to hide and choose a sharp weapon to defend himself.

However, Mark hesitated with his hand on the door handle. He couldn't hear anything, even when he placed his ear to the cool metal. He chewed the inside of his cheek, thinking.

"Britt, it's Mark. Are you in here?"

Silence.

"*Vakker*, it's okay, you can come out. We've caught Ferguson's murderer."

Still nothing.

If Britt was as scared as he guessed, she wouldn't trust anyone right now. She could attack first without realizing it was him.

He looked at the door, noting the hinges—it would swing outward.

Mark stepped to one side, keeping his flashlight up. "Britt, I'm going to open the garden shed door." Tensing himself for a violent reaction, he yanked the door open.

Suddenly, a garden tool with spikes stabbed the air, followed by a pained scream.

"Britt!" He backed away, dodging as she swung her weapon wildly. "Britt, it's me! *Vakker!*"

She stopped, her green eyes wide and unfocused in the flashlight's beam. "Mark?"

He pointed the flashlight at himself so she could see him clearly.

With a sob that tore at his soul, she dropped the garden tool and reached out for him.

Mark snatched her into his arms, crushing her to him, crooning nonsense words as she cried, loud, wracking sounds that broke his heart. He hid his face in her hair, inhaling the sweet scent that was only hers, then kissed her, hoping she'd forget everything until it was just him in her mind. "Britt, shh, it's okay. I'm here, *vakker*. I'm right here."

He swung her into his arms and cradled her against his chest. She had buried her face into the curve of his

neck, and thank God, her sobbing had quieted down—
he'd almost become a gibbering mess when he heard it.

Mark carried her through the backyard and to the front
of the neighboring house. The dog had continued its frenzied barking while he walked past the home, heading to
the Weinstein house so that Britt could get much-needed
care before being transported to the hospital.

Chapter 17

The sound of rain.

Britt slowly became aware of other noises, although her eyes remained closed—footsteps, low voices. Her hands touched something cool and soft, and when she moved her fingers, she realized they were bedsheets. Was she at home? Had it only been a nightmare?

She cracked open an eyelid and squinted at the bright light slamming into her eyeball. She groaned softly and raised her hand to block it out.

"Vakker."

His deep voice, strong yet tender at the same time. She took a breath and winced at the various aches and pains. Her right foot throbbed, and in a moment, she remembered what had happened—Thomas's uneasy appearance, the escape through the woods, hiding in the garden shed...

Britt slowly opened her eyes and held still as her vision adjusted to the well-lit room, and the first thing she saw was Mark. He leaned over her, his brown-gold eyes filled with concern. "How are you feeling?"

"Sore." She didn't recognize her surroundings. "Where am I?"

"At the hospital. The way your foot looked scared me, and you were pretty scratched up. I wanted to be sure you hadn't picked up an infection."

Damn. She moved her limbs, reassuring herself that nothing had been broken.

"Did you want to sit up? Have some water?"

She nodded, not taking her eyes off him as he raised the bed to an elevated position, then lifted a glass of water with a straw to her mouth. "Not too fast."

She took a few sips, the cool liquid quenching her dry throat.

"Girl, what on earth have you been up to *now*?" Joyce appeared in her line of vision.

"Hey. Um, I'd say nothing, except…" She paused, feeling confused.

"We all know that isn't true. You look like something the cat dragged in."

"I certainly feel like it." Britt was relieved that Joyce was here—right now, her friend offered a sense of balance. Mark, on the other hand… Well, he'd been her anchor in a storm of fear and loneliness. But it didn't feel steady right now… More like it wanted to cast off, and she fought to keep it in place. "Joyce, could I have a few minutes with Mark, please?"

Her friend's eyes widened, almost as if she sensed what Britt was thinking. "Of course. I'll be right outside."

As soon as the door closed, she wrapped her hand around his. "What the hell happened? Why was Thomas there?" Her mind snapped on to another troubling thought. "Where's Jacques? I haven't seen him."

Mark raised her hand to his lips, and she gasped at seeing bandages covering her palm. "You need your rest, but let me try to explain it. It seems that Jacques and Thomas were more than just bakers."

"No." Britt didn't want to believe Jacques had anything to do with Mr. Ferguson's murder.

"Jacques Baudin led the protests against Mighty Big Bakery. Seems he owned his own business for a long time with a business partner. Unfortunately, Ferguson convinced the partner to sell and bought it under Jacques's nose. By the time Jacques found out, he'd lost everything." Mark tilted his head. "He never said anything to you?"

"Nothing." Poor Jacques.

"He took matters into his own hands. Raised quite a crowd of rebels, too. Jacques used scare tactics to slow down construction or force employees to quit."

"Jacques, damn you." She squeezed Mark's hand. "Is he going to jail?"

"I don't know. Thomas shot him at the Weinstein house, but I haven't found out why. Jacques is all right, and I'm hoping he can fill in what happened."

Britt nodded. "What about Thomas? What's his story?"

Mark swore. "He's not talking, but we discovered enough criminal evidence against him that will earn him jail time here or extradition."

"Are you saying I hired criminals?" Britt raised herself from the bed as her voice cracked on the last word. "How did— Thomas had all the paperwork!"

"Documents can be deceiving." He gently grasped her shoulders. "It's okay, lie back down."

She rested back on the bed.

"I'm just glad you're all right, *vakker.*" He leaned down, and she felt his warm lips on her forehead. "I'd never forgive myself if anything happened to you."

She looked at him. Mark's eyes were suspiciously shiny. "This wasn't your fault. Why are you blaming yourself?"

He swiped at his face with his other hand. "I should have caught him before he got to you. If I had been bet-

ter at understanding the clues, maybe I could have prevented…"

"Hey, hey!" She reached over and grabbed his face,
then pulled him down until he was level with her. "You
did your job. You caught the men responsible, and that's
important. Maybe I shouldn't have run off, but you came
after me and brought me back safely. And I adore you
for that."

His eyes widened in surprise, and she bit her lip, realizing what she'd just said. But she knew it was the truth,
and she shook his head gently to emphasize it. "Did you
hear me, Mr. Detective?"

Something changed in his expression, a look that made
her skin tingle with goose bumps. Britt shivered, but heat
flushed her face until she knew it was bright pink.

"Say it again," he told her, his voice rough.

"What? That I shouldn't have run away from you?" she
teased, but the look in his eyes shut her up.

"Try again."

Britt hesitated, feeling suddenly shy. Somehow, her
perception of Mark had recently shifted. A part of her
recognized a kindred spirit, a man who cared for and had
protected her without question during one of the scari-
est moments in her life. She wanted to tell him her feelings, and she had the perfect way to do it. "Ah, Mark,"
she crooned in her best French accent. "Do you know
how much I adore you? *Mon cher*, talk the language of
love to me."

His look had her laughing so hard her stomach hurt.
"It annoys me that I know you're imitating that lovestruck
cartoon skunk." He groaned out loud. "It annoys me even
more that I like it."

She giggled. "I'll have you know I don't talk about my

favorite cartoons with just anyone." She paused. "You're pretty special."

He kissed her for a long moment, his mouth insistent and filled with promise. "And you are my Nordic princess."

"Mark, you're absolutely wonderful! Have I told you that?"

He tried not to roll his eyes as he smiled. "Yes, Mom. Several times, actually."

Britt was in the same hospital as Mom, so after making sure she was comfortable, he'd ridden the elevator to his mom's floor for a surprise visit. He'd stopped short when he'd seen Stanley standing over Mom, combing her hair. "Sorry," Mark apologized, backing up. "I'll come back later."

"Don't be absurd." She patted Stanley's hand. "We were watching the news. Congratulations on catching your killer."

He always appreciated her enthusiasm. "How are you feeling?"

"So much better." She looked at Stanley. "And Stanley's been a sweetheart. He's been looking after the house and watering my plants."

Stanley touched her chin with a finger. "It's the least I can do."

Wow, these two. He and Britt were very close to that level of relationship, and he couldn't wait until she decided to take that next step. "Thanks for helping out, Stanley. I really appreciate it."

He waved a hand. "Anything for—" He stopped, his surprised expression flushing a deep red. "You're welcome."

"I gotta run, but I'll come around tomorrow, okay?"

"Where's my kiss?" she demanded.

"Mom." But he obliged her as always, presenting his cheek to be noisily smooched.

He finally managed to escape and headed back to Britt's room, but she was sound asleep.

"She just drifted off," Joyce said quietly, closing the door behind them. "Poor thing's been through a lot."

He nodded, his mind on work, thinking on finishing up some loose ends.

"Are you in love with her?"

Startled, Mark stared at her. Her dark eyes danced with amusement. "We've only been seeing each other a week."

"Okay then, do you care for her?"

He stopped. "I'm not sure why you're so curious about us."

Joyce halted beside him, her demeanor now serious. "Britt is a dear friend, and I don't want to see her get hurt. Emotionally speaking."

"I'm not going to do that." This felt like an interview.

"I mean, she's a big girl and can handle herself."

"She certainly can." He crossed his arms. "Where are you going with this?"

"I just wanted to be sure if you were the right guy for her."

Mark couldn't figure out where Joyce was going with this, but he was going to put a stop to it. "I know you're her friend, and I'm glad you're in her life. I'm mature enough to understand my feelings and how to act on them, but in the end it's for Britt to decide if she wants a relationship with me."

Joyce suddenly smiled, her teeth bright against her dark skin. "Well said." She grabbed his arm. "Gotta run, I have a bakery to finish. Grand reopening is planned for next week, and Britt should be on her feet by then."

This past week had been a roller coaster of tension involving…everything. Now that he could take a breath, Mark collapsed into his car, his body limp and boneless. Captain Fraust had run with the final points of his investigation at this morning's news conference, sparing him the spotlight and the thousands of questions he knew would bombard him.

He wanted to go home, but he was too wired despite the exhaustion. Joyce's words rang in his head. He assumed she was being protective, and he got that. But her conversation sounded like she had her doubts, which of course didn't make sense. Obviously he cared for Britt; nothing had changed in that department. If anything, his feelings had only grown stronger in the short time they'd known each other.

But he also understood the merit of not rushing into things—he had learned that lesson the hard way in his early twenties. And Britt had displayed that same caution, which he had no problem with. Mark would respect her thoughts and fears, just as he was sure Britt would do the same thing for him. And when it was time for them to talk and take the next step, they would do it together.

Restless, he drove to the precinct and headed for his office. After his computer booted up, he started working, feeling his mind get into the flow of providing proper documentation. About an hour later, he had an organized file folder containing everything he'd collected.

Mark hadn't found the chance to thank Myrna properly for her hard work on this case—it had been nonstop since yesterday. He sent her a text and wished her a good weekend.

Ten seconds later, his cell phone rang. "Hey," she said. "How's it going? Is your girlfriend all right?"

He'd never said anything definite about being in a relationship, but it seemed everyone thought that way. "Yeah, she's fine. I'm in the office cleaning up."

"Seriously? I'm downstairs. I called because I have news for you, so come down and I'll show you."

Curious, he took the stairs and walked down the hallway, his footsteps echoing eerily in the empty space until he knocked on her door and stepped inside. "What's up?"

Her head appeared from behind a screen. "I'm surprised you're here. I'd thought you would take a day off."

"I wanted to finish up." He grasped her shoulder. "Seriously, thanks for all of your help. You've been outstanding."

"We make a great team, Hawthorne. And this was an interesting case." She pressed a few keys. "So, two things. That envelope and threatening letter you gave me to check? Mr. Ferguson's fingerprints were all over it, so it must have come from him."

Mark nodded. "I figured as much, but thanks for confirming it." He watched as information scrolled across Myrna's computer screens. "And the second thing?"

"Cynthia finished working on that other investigation you asked for help with."

What the hell—she was talking about Dad. His body shook with trepidation. "What did she find?" he whispered in a hoarse voice.

Myrna typed something and several photos of fingerprints appeared, along with a picture of Dad's brooding expression. "She's not sure if he was there when your mom fell down the stairs."

"For God's sake." Either way, Dad had breached his bail conditions by entering Mom's home.

"However, with some of her famous ingenuity, Cynthia discovered his workplace." Another moment of typing, and another photo appeared. "He's been working on a farm north of here. He's been arrested for assaulting the farmer and his wife. Cyn made sure to provide every bit of criminal evidence so that he stays behind bars this time." She glanced up at him.

Mark felt light, as if a terrible weight had been lifted off his shoulders. After all this time, he could breathe easier, knowing Mom was safe. Having Stanley in her life again was an added bonus. "Thanks, Myrna. I needed that."

"I thought that would make your weekend better." She shut down the computer.

He had an idea. "I'm starving. Do you want to grab something?"

She smiled wide. "Sure. I've got just the place. You can update me on last night. Man, I wish I had seen the ERT in action."

Britt stood by the front window of Konditori, looking out onto dozens of customers who had been waiting since the crack of dawn.

She turned in a slow circle, taking in the wonder that Joyce had created. The front room was larger, allowing more guests to come inside. The walls were a pale shade of muted gray, a stunning contrast to the vibrant pink on the outside walls. New furniture that allowed more space, a wider display counter and plenty of hidden storage cupboards made the room look brighter and bigger.

"What do you think?" Joyce asked, standing at the office doorway.

She laughed. "You could tap me with a stick and I would fall over, that's how stunned I am. The bakery…"

She paused, searching for words. "It feels like an extension of me."

"That's exactly what I was going for."

Britt watched as her friend unbuttoned and rolled up her sleeves. "What are you doing?"

Joyce gave her a look. "Did you think you could handle this mob with only the staff and you? Betty's going to help Jacques, so I'm helping behind the counter."

Britt shook her head. "Joyce…"

Her friend wagged her finger at her. "No *but*s. I'm happy to help."

The first pastries had already been stocked in the display case. Kevin, Betty, Jasmine and Oliver were all smiles as they approached. "This looks amazing!" Betty exclaimed, wrapping her arms around Britt's waist. "I'm so proud of you."

"I'm proud of everyone. Honestly, without you all, this wouldn't have happened."

"No, *chérie*, all of this is because of your hard work." Jacques, in his usual apron and baker's hat, stood by the kitchen door. Fully healed, he had provided evidence that resulted in a hefty fine but no jail time. He was more than happy to pay that.

"And your delicious concoctions. Which reminds me— we'll need to think of some new recipes."

"But of course. Now, if you will excuse me, there is baking to be done!" He disappeared into the kitchen, with Betty running after him.

Today would be a zoo, but she wouldn't have it any other way. As she watched everyone making last-minute preparations, she wished Mark was here. Maybe work had gotten in the way…

The sudden loud wail of a police siren startled her—it

was close. As she looked out the window, two police vehicles pulled up to the curb and three officers stepped out. But the fourth...

Mark.

She ran to the door to unlock and open it, then stood there, watching as he flashed his badge so that he could get through the crowd. A collective groan emanated from the customers.

"Don't worry, we're here to help. You all look like a hungry bunch," he yelled.

Britt could only stare as he came up to her, a big smile on his face. "I—I assumed you'd be at work."

He wrapped his arms around her waist. "And miss this most important day for you? Oh ye of little faith."

The officers who came with Mark organized the boisterous crowd into a semblance of a lineup.

"Come on, let's get Konditori open for business," Mark shouted.

A collective cheer rose from the crowd, but Britt only had eyes for Mark as he melded his mouth to hers.

Oh, how sweet life was going to be.

* * * * *